RAVES FOR
JAMES PATTERSON

"Patterson knows where our deepest fears are buried... there's no stopping his imagination."

—*New York Times Book Review*

"James Patterson writes his thrillers as if he were building roller coasters." —Associated Press

"No one gets this big without natural storytelling talent— which is what James Patterson has, in spades."

—Lee Child, #1 *New York Times* bestselling author of the Jack Reacher series

"James Patterson knows how to sell thrills and suspense in clear, unwavering prose." —*People*

"Patterson boils a scene down to a single, telling detail, the element that defines a character or moves a plot along. It's what fires off the movie projector in the reader's mind." —Michael Connelly

MURDER
ISLAND

For a complete list of books, visit JamesPatterson.com.

MURDER ISLAND

JAMES PATTERSON

AND **BRIAN SITTS**

Little, Brown and Company

New York Boston London

Copyright © 2024 by James Patterson

In association with Conde Nast and Neil McGinness

Cover design by James T. Egan of Bookfly Design. Cover images © Shutterstock. Cover copyright © 2024 by Hachette Book Group, Inc.

Little, Brown and Company
Hachette Book Group
1290 Avenue of the Americas, New York, NY 10104
littlebrown.com

First Edition: October 2024

Little, Brown and Company is a division of Hachette Book Group, Inc. The Little, Brown name and logo are trademarks of Hachette Book Group, Inc.

The publisher is not responsible for websites (or their content) that are not owned by the publisher.

The Hachette Speakers Bureau provides a wide range of authors for speaking events. To find out more, go to hachettespeakersbureau.com or email HachetteSpeakers@hbgusa.com.

Little, Brown and Company books may be purchased in bulk for business, educational, or promotional use. For information, please contact your local bookseller or the Hachette Book Group Special Markets Department at special.markets@hbgusa.com.

ISBNs: 9781538721896 (trade paperback), 9781538721902 (hardcover library), 9781538770337 (large print), 9781538721926 (ebook)

LCCN: 2024935728

Printed in the United States of America

CW

10 9 8 7 6 5 4 3 2 1

PROLOGUE

The Bahamas, 1902

IN THE THICK of a midnight squall, a piercing scream burst from the cabin of the tiny schooner. It sounded as if a woman were being murdered. The *Orion* was tucked into a shallow cove, but there was no shelter from the blasting rain. Wind rocked the hull, and lightning struck so close it threatened to split the mast.

Belowdecks, a young woman was lying on a thinly padded cot. Her knees were bent up and spread wide. Her hair was lank with sweat, and her lips were pinched tight with pain. A sturdy brown-skinned midwife leaned over the woman's bulging belly.

"Push!" she shouted. And again: *"Push!"*

The expectant father stood against the opposite wall of the cabin, his head brushing the ceiling beams. He was a physician, but he had assisted in only a few births during his training, and that was years ago. Better to let the island woman take charge. She had delivered hundreds.

The boat creaked, and saltwater spit through the seams around the portholes. "Look at me!" the midwife commanded the expectant mother. "One more push! Do it now!"

The father steadied himself and moved across the tiny cabin. He could see the curve of the midwife's back and, above it, his wife's face, sweaty, eyes squeezed shut. And then he heard a small whimper, followed by a lusty cry. The father stepped to the side of the cot. Between his wife's legs, the midwife cradled a bloody pink baby.

"It's a boy!" she proclaimed.

The midwife sliced the umbilical cord with a pair of scissors and laid the squirming bundle between his mother's breasts. The young woman kissed her child on the head, just once, before his father took him.

Holding the slippery infant tightly in both arms, the father walked up the short staircase onto the pitching deck. The pelting rain washed the baby clean. The father steadied himself. Then he marched to the opposite rail— and dropped his son into the roiling water.

The baby disappeared beneath the waves. A few seconds later, he bobbed up again, arms and legs churning in the foam. The father tipped his head back and howled with pride. At one minute old, his son was already a swimmer! He reached down and scooped up the dripping infant, then turned back toward the glow of the staircase.

Suddenly, there was a lull in the howl of the wind.

Another cry burst from the cabin below. The father gripped his son tight and hurried back down the staircase. His wife's head was tipped back in exhaustion. The midwife grinned as she held up another squirming bundle.

A second baby.

The swimmer had an unexpected brother.

CHAPTER 1

Chicago, not long ago

THE AIR IN the tunnel was fetid and stale. I felt like I was suffocating with every step. Just five minutes earlier, I'd been walking with Kira in the fresh autumn air. Now we were both underground, running for our lives.

If we hadn't been together, I would have been chased down already. Kira knew the city tunnel system by heart—every entrance, every exit, every turn. She knew me inside out, too. After all, she was the one who trained me. She pulled me to a stop and listened. Slimy wastewater rose up to our calves. I could hear the trickle of fresh runoff from the streets above. And then—the splash of footsteps behind us.

"They're still coming," I whispered.

"No shit," Kira whispered back. "It's what they do."

We both understood who was chasing us. They were operatives from a Russian school for killers—the same school Kira had escaped as a girl. That made her a prime target.

So far, our maneuvers hadn't shaken our pursuers. We'd just managed to outpace them. Now we were in a section where the overhead work lights were off. The dark made for good cover, but I could barely see the curve of the tunnel ahead.

"There should be a branch about thirty yards up," Kira said. She pulled me along by my sleeve. "C'mon, Doc. *Move!*"

The nickname still jarred me. I still thought of myself as Brandt. But to Kira and the people trying to kill us, I was now Doc.

Doc Savage.

The name alone made me a wanted man.

The splashing behind us was getting louder. We'd seen a pack of ten or twelve up top. Clean-cut. Young. Like a bunch of college students out for a walk. Except for their sick little smiles. It was a trademark they all seemed to share. When they came for us on the street, we had to move fast. We dodged traffic all the way south from Hyde Park. At first, I thought we'd lost them at the tunnel entrance. I didn't think they saw us go down. I was wrong.

And now I was mad.

I grabbed Kira by the arm and turned her around to face me. "Hold on!" I said. "Maybe we should stand and fight. Get this over with once and for all. We can take them. You and me. Right?"

She looked at me like I was demented. "Did you bring guns?" she asked.

I shook my head.

"Me neither," said Kira. More splashing behind us. "But I guarantee *they* did."

A blast went over our heads. In the tight space, it sounded like a cannon.

We took off again.

Kira was right. They had the advantage. There was no telling how many had followed us down into the tunnel, or how many others were still waiting for us above. They were excellent trackers. I knew that. Kira knew it, too—even better than I did.

A flashlight popped on behind us. All I could see was the center beam and a hazy halo. I turned back toward Kira. Her copper-colored curls now showed bright against the curved tunnel wall.

"Get down!" I grunted.

A bullet hit just above her head, sending chunks of brick flying. We got up again. We were half running, half crawling through the muck at the bottom of the tunnel. Then, there it was! The tunnel branch, right where Kira said it would be. A three-way split.

I looked back. Two lights now. Another shot! The water in front of us exploded in a big white geyser. The next shot would be right down the middle. High-caliber ammo. A round like that would blow right through both of us.

Kira got to the junction first. "C'mon, c'mon!" I knew she was trying to keep her voice low, but even her whisper echoed. She stopped and stared back down the tunnel for a second.

Then she reached down and ripped a button off her blouse.

The splashing was getting closer. Flashlight beams waved across the tunnel.

Kira held the button flat in her palm and slapped it hard against the bricks. A thick curtain of vapor surrounded her. She pulled me into the cloud. I pressed my back against the curved wall next to her and held my breath.

I heard footsteps approach, then pause, then splash down another branch. By the time the fog cleared, the footsteps were fading into the distance.

Safe. For the moment.

I let my breath out slowly. Kira shot me a little smart-ass look. Okay, her button-sized smoke bomb did the trick. But I felt I deserved part of the credit.

Hell, my ancestor invented it.

CHAPTER 2

Three hours later…

"THEY GAVE UP, right?" I said it. But I didn't really believe it.

Kira shook her head. "They won't stop. Not until the mission is complete. Defined as you and me dead."

The two of us were hanging on a metal ladder high above the bottom of the tunnel. We'd been there for a long time, waiting for night. Right above us was a metal street grate, anchored in cement. I watched as darkness slowly settled overhead.

Finally, it was time.

Kira swung herself to the side of the ladder like a trapeze artist. "Okay," she said. "It's all on you now."

I edged past her and pressed one hand up against the grate.

"Use your back, like I taught you," she said. "Remember?"

"We never practiced with a flimsy ladder and a deep-set storm drain," I replied. "It's a unique situation."

I pressed up as hard as I could. I felt the ladder rung starting to buckle under my feet. I moved up two steps, redistributed my weight, and pressed my shoulder up against the grate. I took a deep breath and jolted my body upward. Once! Twice! On the third hit, I felt the near side of the grate loosen. Crumbs of black gravel rained down on our heads and dropped into the tunnel below with distant plinks. One more shove and the whole edge popped up.

"My hero," said Kira. "Now *move!*"

I strained and pushed until a one-foot gap opened up between one side of the grate and the roadway. Kira swung back to the center of the ladder just below me and eyeballed the opening. "You first."

I shoved my head through and then pressed my torso up. I felt like a human can opener. The rusted edges of the grate shredded my shirt and carved grooves in my shoulders and back. But *anything* to get out of that hole. A few seconds later, I yanked my legs and feet through. As soon as I was out, Kira followed, worming her hips through the narrow opening.

"Where the hell are we?" I asked. Our run through the tunnel had taken us a long way from my neighborhood.

"About five miles from home," said Kira. "*My* home."

I stared at her. "The loft?"

She nodded. "It's our only chance."

I really hated that idea.

The loft she was talking about took up the whole tenth floor of a converted factory building. The loft was a total secret—and an architectural illusion. According to the city files, the building had only nine floors.

I spent the most agonizing six months of my life in that place. That was before I had any idea who Kira really was or what she wanted with me. The training she put me through was brutal. It nearly destroyed me. She did it to turn me into a replica of my great-grandfather, the legendary Doc Savage himself.

Not my choice. But she had her reasons.

"If we can get there," Kira said, "we can buy some time, get some weapons."

That damned loft was the last place on earth I wanted to go back to, but what choice did we have? I was sure the killers had the address of my apartment. They were probably waiting there right now.

"Lead on," I said.

I thought I knew Chicago pretty well. I'd lived there since grad school. But I didn't know it like Kira did. She knew the city the way a rat would. Every grimy little path. She pulled me through alleys and underpasses I never knew existed. I got totally turned around.

A few minutes later, we stopped. "Wait here," said Kira. I huddled under a rusted bridge while she checked every which way, making sure we weren't being followed.

After another hour of ducking and dodging, things started to look familiar. Then I saw Kira's building straight ahead. Just looking at the place gave me the creeps. But Kira was already heading toward the rear entrance.

I followed her through the metal door behind the loading bay and down a basement hallway. We stepped into the service elevator. She pushed the button for the ninth floor. When we got out, we walked down a corridor to a fire door. Kira pressed a code to bypass the alarm. One more turn and we were on the hidden staircase that led to her loft. Kira took the stairs two at a time. I was right behind her. The door was ten steps up. Solid steel.

The next instant, a huge blast blew it away.

The stairwell went white, then dark. I hit the landing on my back, with Kira on top of me. There was smoke everywhere. I felt blood trickling from my nose. Kira rolled to the side. She looked stunned. We were both covered in plaster dust.

For some reason, I started crawling toward the staircase, even though it was broken off at the top. My ears were ringing so hard I could hardly hear Kira shouting.

"Doc! Stop!"

I started climbing. The steps were twisted and bent. The railing was scorching hot under my hands. When I got to the last rung, all I could see were flames and bare beams and open sky. The entire loft had been leveled. Walls, doors, windows—all destroyed. I climbed back down. Dazed. Aching. Eyes burning. Kira grabbed for my arm as I got to the bottom step.

"Everything's gone," I said.

The city of Chicago never knew Kira's floor existed.

Now it really didn't.

CHAPTER 3

SHIT! WHAT NOW?

We staggered through the back corridor together and headed down the back staircase. Fire alarms were blaring. Residents from the lower floors poured out of the doorways onto every landing. People were shouting, crying, asking what the hell happened. Gas explosion? Terrorists? Earthquake? Nobody knew.

I knew. So did Kira. But we didn't say a word.

We elbowed our way through the crowd and hurried down to the basement level. We pushed through the loading bay doors. My ears were still ringing. Fire trucks were rolling up out front, but the sirens barely registered.

I looked at Kira. I knew we were both thinking the exact same thing. The assassins thought we were already in the loft. And we almost were. If we'd gotten there just ten seconds sooner...

All we had now were the clothes on our backs. We

were covered in dust. Our shoes and pants were still crusted with tunnel slime. We reeked of smoke and sewage. But we were still breathing.

Kira pulled out her cell phone and tapped out a quick text.

"We need to change," she said.

"Clothes?"

"Everything."

I followed her down the alley behind the building and across an empty parking lot. We worked our way past dumpsters and loading docks, staying off the main streets as she led me on another rat's-eye-level tour of the city.

After about twenty minutes, we stopped across from a small commercial block near Douglas Park. I saw two hole-in-the-wall bars, a pizza shop, and a small beauty salon. The other businesses were buzzing, but the salon was dark. A CLOSED sign hung on the inside of the glass door.

Kira led the way across the street. The salon was named Diva. Kira rang the bell twice. A few seconds later, a light came on inside. A lanky Black woman made her way from the back toward the door. Early thirties. About Kira's age. Thick, beaded dreadlocks dangled around her shoulders. She flicked the lock and pulled the door open. When she saw Kira, she rocked back.

"Whoa, honey!" she said. "How many lives you got left?"

CHAPTER 4

WE STEPPED INSIDE. The woman wrapped Kira in a tight hug, then backed off and held her at arm's length. She curled her nose and turned her head to the side. "What the hell, girl! Did you do a swan dive into a cesspool?" Then she looked over Kira's shoulder at me and lowered her voice. "Okay, now," she said. "Who's the hunk?"

Kira turned and did the intros. "Denise, this is Doc. Doc, this is Denise, an old classmate of mine. We got our personal trainer certifications together way back."

"I cheated off this girl the whole time," said Denise. She did a spin and waved her hand around the salon. "Then I decided I was more into the appearance aspect than the muscular aspect, if you understand me."

"This is your place?" I asked. It was a compact setup, with three styling stations, a reception desk, and a small Aveda retail section. The place smelled like lavender and lemons, with a slight undertone of ammonia.

"Three hundred square feet of prime Chicago real estate," proclaimed Denise. "At a rent I can almost afford." The beads at the tips of her locs clicked together as she talked.

"Thanks for opening up," said Kira.

"You said it was an emergency," said Denise. She looked us both up and down. "You did not lie." She pointed to the back of the shop, which was separated from the salon space by a thin wooden partition. "There's a shower back there. Please use it. Both of you." Denise held her hands up, palms out. "I can't work my art on a dirty canvas."

I still didn't know why we were here, but before I could ask, Kira disappeared behind the partition. After a few seconds, I heard a flimsy door opening and then water coming on. I sat down in one of the salon's vinyl waiting chairs, exhausted.

"Don't get too comfortable," said Denise. "If I remember, that girl takes the fastest showers in the Western Hemisphere."

She was right. I was barely settled in the seat when I heard the water turn off in the back room. About ten seconds later, Kira reappeared, wrapped in a towel. Her wet ringlets were dripping down onto her pale shoulders. I could smell her shampoo and body wash from where I sat. I stared at her. Couldn't help it. Before that afternoon, Kira and I had been apart for nearly twelve months.

I'd almost forgotten how beautiful she was.

Kira tipped her head this way and that to jostle the

water out of her ears. "Careful with the hot tap," she said. "It comes on strong."

I stood up and slipped past her into the back. Behind the partition, there was a simple fiberglass stall alongside a massage chair and a pile of cardboard cartons. A stack of fresh towels sat on a wooden stand. As I stripped off my filthy clothes, I could hear Denise and Kira talking out front. Denise wasn't even *trying* to be discreet.

"What's the situation with the male model?" she was asking. "Bodyguard? Bouncer? Boyfriend?"

"It's complicated," Kira said. "Let's just leave it there."

I don't know what I expected her to say—or what I hoped she would say. *Complicated*. To be honest, I probably would have used the same word.

"Okay, Miss Kira," Denise went on. "None of my damn business. Let's get started on you, okay? How radical?"

"Full on," Kira replied. "Just like we practiced."

I turned on both taps, tested the temperature on my palm, and stepped into the stall. I feathered the hot tap to avoid being scalded. The water soaked my hair and poured over my body. I grabbed a bar of soap from the holder and lathered up. When I looked down, I could see trickles of brown sludge curling into the drain.

The steam opened my breathing passages. The hot water eased my muscles but stung the scrapes on my back. I tried to relax. But I couldn't. My mind was racing.

What now?

Kira's loft was gone—along with everything we needed.

Weapons. Tools. Clothes. Our best hope was that the assassins thought that both of us were now in tiny pieces.

Something told me that Kira had a plan from here. She always did. I wondered if there was any chance she would let me in on it.

I lingered under the water for a while. Then I turned off the tap and reached for a towel. I heard Kira's voice from out front, but it sounded different. Thinner. Weaker. What the hell was Denise doing to her? I wrapped the towel around my waist and stepped around the partition into the salon. I was about to ask for a robe, but I didn't get that far.

All I could do was gape.

Denise spun the chair around so that Kira was facing me. But the Kira I knew was gone. The woman in the chair was maybe seventy-five or eighty years old, with gray hair and wrinkles creasing her face and neck.

"What do you think?" Kira asked, in that weird, creaky voice.

"Wow," I said. "How long was I in the shower?"

Kira slid stiffly off the chair, walking with a hunched posture. Very convincing. When she smiled, her teeth had a slightly yellow tint. "Theatrical makeup," she croaked. "It's one of Denise's hidden talents." She sounded a lot like my late grandmother. Looked like her, too.

Denise patted her chair. "Okay, Hercules, you're next."

CHAPTER 5

Union Station, one hour later...

AS WE APPROACHED the train, two uniformed Amtrak porters pulled out a portable ramp and lined it up with the door of the car. "Need help with your husband, ma'am?" one of them asked.

Kira waved them off. "No worries," she said. "He's lighter than he looks."

She tipped me back in the wheelchair and rolled me right up the ramp and into the aisle of the sleeper car. When we got to our compartment, she slid the heavy door open. Then, just in case anybody was looking, she stuck her arms under mine and hoisted me from the wheelchair to the compartment seat—like the aged invalid I was pretending to be. She folded the chair and stashed it to the side, then slid the door closed with a loud thump. She closed the blinds.

I let out a little breath of relief. We made it. By two minutes.

As soon as we settled into our roomette, an automated voice crackled through the PA system. *"The Lake Shore Limited. Stopping at South Bend, Elkhart, Waterloo, Bryan, Toledo, Sandusky, Elyria Cleveland, Erie, Buffalo Depew Station, Rochester, Syracuse, Utica, Schenectady, Albany-Rensselaer…and New York."*

I slumped back on the seat. Jesus. Twenty-one hours from Chicago to Penn Station. An entire night and day. I looked at Kira. "Is there anywhere we're *not* stopping?"

No reaction.

I tried a different tack. "What's in New York?" I'd asked the same thing back in the salon when I saw Denise booking the tickets. I got the same reply.

"Wrong question."

Kira said that a lot. I'd gotten used to it during my training. It meant I wasn't going to get a straight answer. Most often, no answer at all.

The makeup and spirit gum were starting to irritate my face, and the fake whiskers were driving me crazy. "Can we at least wash this crap off now?" I asked.

Kira started folding the beds down—two narrow berths, one above the other, like offset bunks. "Savor your old age," she said. "It's good practice."

Kira climbed onto the top bunk as the train rolled out of the station. I could see her pulling off her clothes under the covers. I settled into the pod below and did the same. Then I stretched out, or tried to. When I put my head on the pillow, my feet almost hit the wall.

I watched the lights of the station blink by as the train started to roll. My folded-up wheelchair rattled against the wall. I realized that I hadn't been on a train trip for years, not since my expedition to Egypt my junior summer. What everybody says about the rhythm of the rails is true. I don't care where you are in the world—a moving train is one big cradle.

I had a lot more questions for Kira, but I felt myself drifting off to sleep.

I tried to fight it.

I lost.

* * *

My eyes blinked open again somewhere in Ohio. It was about four in the morning. The train was rolling through fields and past small towns. For long stretches, the only light came from barns and farmhouses.

My ears had finally recovered. I could hear the creak of the bunk above me every time Kira flipped over. I went to scratch my forehead and felt deep furrows above my eyebrows. I remembered that I was now a very senior citizen, with wrinkles to match. Even my hands were crinkled and spotty. Very thorough, Denise.

What the hell were we doing here, I asked myself. I knew what we were escaping from, but what were we heading into? And why New York? Did Kira have more contacts there? More secrets? Another damn loft?

I stared out into the dark and thought back...

It had been eighteen months since Kira Sunlight walked into my life. Like a wrecking ball. Up to then, I'd been Brandt Savage, PhD, professor of anthropology at the University of Chicago. Tenured and content. Teaching, writing, research, academic conferences—that was my whole life. A little boring and predictable, maybe, but safe and secure.

Then Kira found me.

Against my will, she turned me into a new man. Thanks to her, I'm two inches taller and four times stronger. I'm down to 9 percent body fat, and my hair is as thick as a teenager's. My skin is tough enough to deflect a small-caliber bullet. Also, I now know lots of ways to kill people.

I didn't ask for any of it. I wasn't given a choice in the matter. The whole training process was torture for me. Then, a year ago, Kira dragged me on a mission that nearly got us both killed. After that, I was done. I just walked away—back to my old life. I never expected to see Kira Sunlight again.

And I didn't.

Until yesterday afternoon.

That's when I realized I was in love with her.

CHAPTER 6

"IS THIS STILL necessary?" I asked.

I was scratching at my cheeks. The makeup was driving me crazy.

"Not much longer," said Kira.

I slumped in my wheelchair as she rolled me through the gate of a tiny marina, about fifty miles east of Manhattan. The cab that brought us from the station was just pulling away.

After our twenty-one-hour Amtrak journey, we'd spent another three hours on the Long Island Rail Road, still looking and acting like two doddering seniors.

"Bump," said Kira. My wheels jolted over a curb as she pushed me toward a long wooden pier. It was almost 10 p.m. The marina was deserted. The only light came from a yellowed bulb on a wooden pole. There were a few boats resting in their slips, mostly run-down cabin cruisers. I could see the flashing beam from a lighthouse across a stretch of dark water.

"Why are we here?" I asked. I was low on patience, and hungry. All I'd eaten for the past twenty-four hours were Amtrak snacks. Kira had slept most of the time, or pretended to. Probably to avoid my questions.

She pointed out over the water. "*That's* why."

I looked in the direction of her finger. I saw a boat moored about fifty yards out, close to the mouth of the small harbor. I didn't know much about boats, but I'd been on a few. This one looked like a two-masted schooner, about forty feet long.

"It's a little late in the day for sailing lessons," I said. My hunger pangs were making me snarky.

Kira made a quick gimme motion with her hand. "Your ID."

I reached into my pocket and dug out my wallet, with a driver's license in the name of Daniel Thunden, born eighty years ago this week. Kira pulled out her own ID. Patricia Thunden, five years younger. Excellent fakes. Denise did fine work.

Kira put the IDs in a plastic bag and picked up a fist-sized stone from the side of the pier. She put the stone in the bag, tied the bag shut, then dropped it into the water. The bag disappeared.

Then she pulled out her phone. She reached into my pocket and took mine. We'd turned them off before we got to the salon. Now Kira put both phones in one hand and heaved them into the harbor. A few seconds later, I heard two splashes, one right after the other.

"Up you go," she said, tugging at my arm.

I looked up at her. "I can walk again?"

"Salt air works wonders."

As soon as I stood up, Kira folded the wheelchair and dropped it off the end of the pier. I watched it sink into the murk.

"Ready?" she asked. She sat down, her legs dangling over the water.

"For what?"

She slid her ass off the pier and started swimming toward the schooner.

"Rejuvenation!" she called back.

Was she *nuts*? I looked around for a dinghy. Didn't see one. I gave up and slipped in after her. The water was deep and cold. A shock to my system.

Kira was already power-stroking across the harbor. By the time I caught up, she was hauling herself aboard the sailboat. As I came around the stern, I could see the boat's name. It was painted in classic gilt lettering, like the title on an old book cover.

Albatross.

I grabbed a rail and climbed up over the transom. The whole topside was covered in thick canvas. Kira was working her way around the boat, freeing the ties one by one. She rolled the canvas into a ragged pile and stowed it in front of the aft mast. Then she stood with her arms flung wide. "Beautiful, right?"

When the deck and cabin were uncovered, I realized that the schooner was all wood—maybe teak—with polished brass fittings. And *really* old, 1930s, I guessed. It looked like it belonged in a sailing museum.

I watched Kira step into the cockpit and stick her head under the control console. A few seconds later, I heard the engine fire up. Maybe she found the key to the ignition. More likely, she just hot-wired it.

She looked at me and pointed toward the bow. "Release the mooring line." When she saw my expression, she added, "Don't argue."

This was really happening. We'd traveled halfway across the country to steal somebody's sailboat in the middle of the night. Was this Kira's big plan? No wonder she didn't tell me about it.

I walked forward and unfastened the line from the cleat on the deck. I pulled it through the loop attached to the mooring ball. The *Albatross* was floating free.

"Clear!" I called back, trying to keep my voice down. I was expecting the harbor patrol to show up at any minute.

When I worked my way back to the cockpit, I noticed that Kira's swim had washed most of the makeup off her face and the powder out of her hair. She looked about fifty years younger. She looked like herself. She also looked happy. I stepped up alongside her as she nudged the throttle forward, steering us slowly out into the channel.

I stared at her. "So we're boat thieves now?"

"Of course not," said Kira. "I spotted this beauty at an estate sale five years ago."

I pulled the last few fake whiskers off my face. "Does that mean...?"

"That's right. She's all mine."

CHAPTER 7

Ten days later…

IT WAS SEVENTY-FIVE degrees on deck. We'd been at full sail for most of the time since we left Long Island, making about 115 nautical miles a day. A good pace, according to Kira. But since yesterday, we'd been in a bit of a lull. The sails were limp and the *Albatross* was barely moving.

Kira still wouldn't say where we were going, but I didn't need a sextant to tell me we were headed due south. The sun and the stars showed me that much.

We hadn't been in sight of land for several days, but I had plenty of distractions. Kira was teaching me how to read the wind and trim the sails, and I'd become an expert at hooking bluefish with a spinning rod. Between my daily catch and canned fruits and veggies from the galley, we'd been eating well.

That morning, I was sitting on the foredeck with an

assortment of gadgets spread out in front of me on a thick canvas. I was fascinated.

Kira came forward from the cockpit. "Enjoying your toy collection?"

She was wearing shorts and a halter top, with her hair tied back with a blue bandana. She'd scavenged her new wardrobe from a bag in one of the deck hatches. For me, all she could dig up was a pair of old khaki pants and a white linen shirt, missing a few buttons at the top. She said it suited me.

The day before, I'd found a big hold belowdecks, right under the cabin floor. That's where I'd discovered the artifacts in front of me. Kira told me she'd been storing them onboard for years.

"Where did you get this stuff?" I asked.

"It was all in the loft when I moved in," she said. "And trust me, this is just a small sample."

Eighty years before Kira discovered it, the loft I'd grown to hate had been the Midwest sanctuary of the original Doc Savage. It was his hideout and research lab. While she was living there, Kira had learned all the loft's secrets.

I was looking at a bunch of them.

"Your great-grandfather was a polymath," said Kira. "A genius."

"*Troubled* genius, if you ask me."

Kira sat down on the deck a few feet away. "You mean

his history of violence? Okay. Yes. That was part of him, too."

I knew my ancestor had brains. He was a physician after all, like his father. But I wondered about his dedication to the Hippocratic oath. Because he definitely did a lot of harm. Most of the people Doc Savage killed over the years were evil, no doubt. True villains. But some things I'd read about him made me think that he enjoyed mayhem a little too much. Sought it out. Maybe got addicted to it.

"You know, he was only sixteen when he fought in World War I," I said. "I think it probably numbed him, or twisted him. At that age, how could it not?"

"Or maybe," said Kira, "it showed him that sometimes you need to fight evil with evil."

She watched as I sorted through the items in front of me one by one. A handcrafted pair of goggles. A handwritten dictionary of the Mayan language. A rubber gas mask. A scientific paper on electromagnetism. A manual for brain surgery.

From there, things got a little weird.

I held up a small device that looked like a 1980s Sony Walkman.

"Prototype for a telephone answering machine," said Kira.

"And this...?" I picked up a wristwatch with a miniature screen built in. "Did it actually work?"

Kira nodded. "Apple Watch, eat your heart out."

Next was a sheet of thin metal, with some kind of powdered coating on one side. I had no clue.

"That's a good one," said Kira. "Image-capture plate for a machine that could see through walls. Like I said—genius."

I rummaged through a box with flash bombs the size of acorns, luminescent flares in the shape of shotgun shells, fake molars filled with chemical powder...

And that was just the small stuff. There were a bunch of heavier items down below that I hadn't even bothered to haul up yet.

Kira stood and put her hands on the rail with her back to me, staring out over the azure water. "Still no wind," she said. "Slow day in paradise."

I looked up at the foresail. Barely a ripple.

"How much farther do we have to go?" I asked. I should have known what the answer would be.

"Wrong question."

I gathered all my little antiques together in the middle of the canvas and wrapped the whole thing up like a sack.

Enough nostalgia for one day.

As I stood up, Kira was walking back from the rail. She pulled the bandana off her head. She stepped up close to me. Very close. Then she pulled my shirt open and put her lips against my ear. "Are you done playing?"

She kissed me. Then she pulled me down into the cabin. My head almost banged into the door frame. With the bandana off, Kira's copper-colored curls spilled free around her shoulders. She undid the two remaining buttons on my shirt. I unfastened my belt and fumbled my way out of my pants.

When I looked up again, Kira was already naked.

Always one step ahead.

CHAPTER 8

IT WAS GLORIOUS, as always.

Afterward, we lay together on a thick blanket in the middle of the cabin floor. The berths on either side were barely wide enough for one person to sleep on. Definitely not wide enough for two people to have amazing sex on.

So we'd learned to make do.

Over the past week, we'd been having a lot of sex on the *Albatross*. On the cabin floor. On the foredeck. In the cockpit. Morning. Noon. Night.

It was making my head spin.

I still hadn't gotten used to my new body, let alone being treated like an object of desire—especially by a woman as stunning as Kira Sunlight. Even on the days when I'd hated her, I had been in awe of her. Back then, the thought that I could ever be with her like this seemed impossible.

Sometimes, it still did.

She was lying half on top of me, half asleep. I could feel her breathing. My forearm was hooked across her bare shoulder. Over the past few days, I'd noticed that the sun was turning my skin from its Chicago pallor to a reddish brown. Another step closer to the real Doc. The Man of Bronze.

Kira's skin was still as pale as ivory, except for some pink on her cheeks and forehead. She didn't tan. But she didn't burn. It was like even her melanocytes were under her total control.

I ran my fingers across her back. Then I saw her eyes pop open.

"Do you hear that?" she said.

"Hear what?"

She pushed herself off me and grabbed her clothes.

Then I heard it, too.

The buzz of an outboard engine.

CHAPTER 9

I PICKED MY pants up off the floor and peeked through one of the cabin portholes. Kira was right next to me, pulling on her shorts and top.

About fifty yards out, a Zodiac boat was heading straight for us. Four men aboard.

Kira reached over and grabbed a pair of binoculars.

"Assassins?" I asked. "Don't tell me they followed us all the way out here."

Kira pressed the binoculars up against the porthole. She stared for a few seconds. "Nope," she said. "But almost as bad. Pirates. Local operators. Probably out for cash or drugs."

I grabbed the binoculars and took a look. The intruders were only about thirty yards away now. They were all scraggly and lean. Wide-eyed. They looked wired and dangerous.

Kira headed out onto the deck. What the hell was she doing? I scrambled up after her. She waved her hands crossways over her head. *"No money! No drugs!"* she shouted.

I picked up the cue. *"No money! No drugs!"*

The boat was about twenty yards away now, and closing fast. The engine sounded like an angry hornet.

"No money! No drugs!" Could they even hear us? Did it matter?

I saw the guy at the front of the boat reach down. He came up with a rifle in his hands. He tucked the stock under his armpit and aimed. I grabbed Kira and pulled her down. A blast of bullets hit the hull and rail.

We squirmed across the deck and tumbled down the cabin stairs. I could hear the buzz getting closer.

"Stay low!" I shouted. Kira flattened herself on the floor. Another volley of bullets hit the boat.

I picked up the blanket we just made love on and tossed it aside. I opened the hatch to the large hold underneath. I pulled up a small tank with a hose attached. The end of the hose had a fixture that looked like the barrel of a blunderbuss.

I waved the device at Kira. "You know what this is?" I read about it in one of the stories about my ancestor.

Kira lifted her head and nodded. "Solid choice."

I climbed up the stairs to the deck, carrying the tank in one hand and the hose in the other. The Zodiac was almost on us. The guy in the back cut the engine and pulled up broadside about ten feet off. One of the others leaned out with a grappling hook and reached for the rail.

I set the tank on the deck and pulled the release. *"No money! No drugs!"* I shouted again, waving the nozzle. All four of them looked at me like I was crazy—as if I were trying to scare them off with a vacuum cleaner.

"No money. No drugs," one of them repeated with a heavy accent. Maybe Haitian. And then, with a menacing sneer, "Pretty boat. Pretty lady."

At that point, he had his hand on the rail and one foot on the deck. My adrenaline was pumping. Now or never. I gripped the wide end of the device and pressed the button on the collar.

A blinding sheet of flame shot out of the barrel. It blasted the boarder and upended the Zodiac. The weapon bucked in my hand. It was like holding onto a fire hose— except it was throwing fire. I could feel the hot blowback on my face and arms. I squinted and kept the pressure on. For a few seconds, all I could see were flames and black smoke. When I let go of the button, a final puff belched out of the barrel.

Then, total silence.

It was over that fast.

Kira ran up behind me and looked over the rail. "Holy shit."

All that was left of the rubber Zodiac was a dark, oily

scum on the surface of the water. As for the four men, there was nothing left at all.

My temples were throbbing. I felt sick to my stomach. I dropped the weapon on the deck.

Kira leaned over the rail and shook her head. "Bad day to be a pirate."

CHAPTER 10

I FELT SICK and unsettled for a while. But I got over it. I had to save the boat. I had to protect Kira. I had no choice, right? That's what I told myself.

Sometimes you have to fight evil with evil.

At the moment, I was feeling like a bit of a pirate myself, or at least a real sailor. A storm had opened up, and I was clinging to the top of the foremast. Kira had sent me up to untangle a fouled line on the rigging. Rain was pouring down, and a strong wind was rocking the boat back and forth. It was blowing so hard it took my breath away.

I was fifty feet above the deck. I felt like I was being whipped on the tip of an antenna.

Once I freed the line, I braced myself on a foothold and held on for dear life. Below me, the sea was churning with whitecaps. Something off the bow caught my eye. I squinted through a gap in the flapping sails and looked again.

There! In the distance. A dim line of green.

I was so excited that my foot slipped off the support. For a few seconds, I was dangling by my arms in midair. My heart was pounding. I wrapped my legs around the mast and half shimmied, half slid all the way down.

As soon as my feet hit the deck, I held on to the railing and worked my way back to the cockpit. Kira was at the wheel, trying to hold a steady course against the wind. Her red windbreaker was whipping around her shoulders like a cape. Her hair was matted and dripping.

"I saw an island!" I shouted. "Straight ahead!"

Kira didn't look the least bit surprised. "Good!" she shouted back. "Right where it should be!"

"What is it? Where are we?"

Kira cranked the wheel hard as another swell hit. "We're in the Bahamas," she yelled. "You just sighted Andros Island!" She looked over at me. "Heard of it?"

I grabbed the cockpit console as the boat pitched and rolled. I couldn't believe this is where we'd been headed the whole time.

Yes. I'd heard of Andros Island.

It's where my ancestor Doc Savage was born.

In a small sailboat. In the middle of a storm.

CHAPTER 11

IT WAS LIKE magic.

As soon as land came into view from the cockpit, the sky started to turn blue. Over the next few minutes, the sea settled down and smoothed out, like God had ironed it flat. By the time we were about a hundred yards offshore, the sun broke through. I stood at the prow, getting my first real look at the island. From this angle, it looked pretty bleak. No dock. No shelter. No people.

"Drop anchor!" Kira called out.

I reached down with both hands and released the line, then leaned over the pulpit to make sure the chain was clear of the hull. The water was so clear I could see a puff of sand when the steel flukes hit bottom.

When I turned around, Kira was inflating a small rubber dinghy with a gas canister. The tiny boat flopped and unfurled on deck like a creature coming to life.

"We're going ashore here?" I asked.

Kira stared at me. "Why else would we sail twelve hundred miles?"

I helped her lower the inflated dinghy over the starboard side. She climbed down the ladder and hopped in. I followed right behind her. The dinghy was low-tech. No motor, just a set of wooden paddles. We knelt on either side of the rubber gunwales and started paddling. Kira angled her blade to turn us to the left, cutting across the current.

"Harder!" she yelled.

For a few minutes, we struggled to move parallel to the shoreline, heading east. The line of foliage and sand gave way to black rocks and then a huge bluff rising hundreds of feet straight up from the water. I could see Kira squinting along the base. She leaned forward in the dinghy and pointed.

"There!" she said. "See those four lines?"

Directly in front of us, the rock striations on the face of the bluff formed four vertical shapes, like fingers reaching down toward the water.

"Now!" Kira called out. "Straight in!" She turned us toward shore. It was an easy glide the rest of the way.

We jumped out about ten feet from the beach, then pulled the dinghy ashore. Kira tied a line to the base of a thick bush.

"This way," she said, turning east.

I looked up at the rock face. Even in broad daylight, it looked inky and forbidding. Like a wall of doom.

"Do we need a map?" I asked.

"Got one," Kira said, tapping her temple. "Right here."

We moved along the base of the bluff until we reached a big shard of rock projecting out of the sand. To the left was a small depression in the cliff side. It looked like a closed door. Kira stepped into the depression. Her eyes lit up. I leaned in to see what she was looking at.

About ten feet above ground was a rough opening, about four feet across. A hole in the wall. Probably carved out by millions of years of wind and waves.

Kira started climbing the cliff. She was strong and nimble. She jammed her toes into small crevices and used her hands and arms to pull herself up the rough stone. When her head was even with the opening, she looked back down at me.

"Doc!" she said. "This is it!"

She muscled her way up and started through headfirst. Suddenly, she disappeared—as if she'd been swallowed whole by a rock monster.

CHAPTER 12

"KIRA!"

I scrambled up the cliff, scraping my arms and legs on the rocks as I climbed. I stuck my head and shoulders into the opening and grunted my way through. There was a wide, sloping passage—about a body length—and then a sudden drop. I landed belly-first on a pile of sand.

It was pitch-black.

I heard a match strike and saw a kerosene lantern light up. Kira's curls caught the glow first. A second later, I could make out the rest of her. She was standing in front of a rock wall. Her shadow rose up about twenty feet behind her. I saw a few empty bottles and a couple of oars half buried in the sand.

I stood up and brushed the grit off my chest. "Where the hell are we? Somebody's tomb?"

"It's a sea cave," said Kira. "Prehistoric." She opened the lantern to full flame and lifted it up. The rock walls were wet and seeping, but the floor was mostly dry sand. The air was warm. It smelled like seaweed.

Kira started walking toward the back.

"Hey!" I called out. "What are we here for?"

No reply.

The small chamber narrowed to a stone arch, barely high enough to fit under. Kira went through first. I ducked my head and followed—reluctantly. I was worried about cave-ins. And bats. I really hated bats.

I caught a flicker of movement out of the corner of my eye.

"*Jesus!*" A small black lizard flitted across my bare foot.

Kira grabbed my arm. "I'll be damned," she said. "X marks the spot."

When I looked up, I saw what she was talking about.

From the light of the lantern, I could make out five huge wooden chests against the back wall, all with thick padlocks. Nearby was a stack of tools—sledgehammers, axes, shovels. Two more kerosene lanterns sat on a rickety wooden table.

Nothing in here was from this century.

I found a tin of waterproof matches and lit a second lantern. The chamber was a rough oval, about thirty feet across. The ceiling went as high as a ship's mast. I ran my hand over one of the chests. It looked thick and sturdy, with tarnished brass hardware.

"What is this?" I asked. "Blackbeard's treasure?"

"No," said Kira. "Doc Savage's."

I stared at her for a few seconds. Damnit. Why did my ancestor keep coming back to haunt me?

"Hold on," I said. "Doc Savage was born here. But he didn't live here. Andros was never his home."

"Correct," said Kira. "He only came back once, in his midthirties. Sailed all the way from New York. Same course we just took."

"Why? Why did he come back?"

"Because there were things he wanted to hide. Things he knew weren't safe anywhere else."

"And who was he hiding them from?"

Kira rested her lamp on one of the chests. "From John Sunlight. My great-grandfather."

At the sound of the name, my gut twisted a little. Sometimes I had to remind myself that my ancestor and Kira's had been mortal enemies. The truth was, she and I were descended from two men who were hell-bent on destroying each other. It wasn't a topic I liked to dwell on. I preferred to leave all that poison in the past. But somehow, it kept bubbling up. Like Kira told Denise, it was complicated.

"Grab a hammer," said Kira. She pointed to the lock on the first chest.

I set my lantern down and pulled a sledgehammer from the pile of tools. Kira stepped back.

I planted my feet directly in front of the chest. I lifted the hammer over my head and brought it down hard on the lock. The metal sparked, but the lock held. I took another swing. Direct hit. The shackle broke and flew off the hasp.

"Well, don't stop there," said Kira.

I hoisted the hammer again and moved from chest to chest, smashing the locks off one by one. When I was finished, I dropped the hammer in the sand. Kira and I stepped up to the first chest together.

I lifted the lid. We peeked inside. I heard a small hiss.

Kira dropped to the ground in a heap.

Me next.

CHAPTER 13

I DON'T THINK I totally lost consciousness. But I felt wobbly and out of it. I did my best to shake it off. A few seconds later, Kira started to stir beside me.

"We should have known," she said, rubbing her head.

"Booby trap."

She nodded.

Clearly, the knockout gas had lost some of its punch over the last century. Impressive that it still worked at all.

We got back on our feet. Slowly. I still felt a little woozy. I looked over at Kira.

"Now what?"

We only had one chest open. Four more to go. I was dying to know what was inside each of them, but I wasn't ready to pass out every time. I thought about the gas mask back on the *Albatross*, but I wasn't sure the filter was still any good.

No matter. Kira was working on a more immediate solution.

"Look," she said. "It's probably a contact spray. Only effective up close." She grabbed a shovel. "Hold your breath!" I filled my lungs and clamped my mouth shut. Kira did the same.

She jammed the shovel blade under the lid of the second chest and flipped it open. Then she went right down the row, one chest after the other. Sure enough, every time a lid popped up, I could hear the same little hiss.

At the end of the row, Kira threw the shovel down and pointed back toward the entrance. We ran back through the arch and stuck our heads in front of the hole we came in through. I felt a warm breeze on my face. We both exhaled and took in deep gulps of fresh air.

To be on the safe side, we waited a few minutes to let the gas dissipate. Then we made our way back toward the chamber.

I went in first and took a few tentative sniffs.

"My own personal canary," said Kira.

A few seconds later, I was still standing. "Seems fine."

We crossed to the first chest and took our first real look inside. The chest was about four feet wide and three feet high. I leaned down. Inside were a pile of scientific notebooks and rolled blueprints. It smelled like musty paper. I pulled out a few of the blueprints and placed one on the ground. Kira hung over my shoulder as I unrolled it, revealing a detailed drawing.

"That's ominous," she said.

She was right. The blueprint showed some kind of massive electronic cannon on a rotating turret. The margin had a chart of ballistic ranges. I flipped the plan aside and unrolled the next. This one had designs for a rocket that looked a lot like a German V-2. Another showed a schematic for a laser-firing satellite. Then I started flipping through the notebooks. More of the same. Designs for death and destruction on every page.

"Superweapons," I said. "Large-scale killing machines."

Kira nodded. "All invented by Doc Savage—but never built. This is the stuff John Sunlight was after. He wouldn't have had any qualms about building the weapons and using them. He was that ruthless. That sick."

I put the notebooks down and looked in the next chest. This one looked like it was filled with military gear. A utility vest. A set of rudimentary body armor. Camouflage clothing. A bizarre metal skullcap.

At the bottom of the chest was a leather case. I pulled it out and set it down on the sand. I flicked the latches. I glanced at Kira. We both held our breaths again and turned our faces away.

I lifted the top. No hiss.

I looked inside the case and poked through the contents. A collection of wigs. An assortment of false beards and mustaches. A set of contact lenses in different colors. Adhesive patches with simulated wounds and scars.

"Should we save this stuff for Denise?" I asked.

Kira waved her hand in front of her nose. Then it hit me, too. A funky stench. Probably all that fake hair. I closed the lid.

Clearly, plans for diabolical weapons were not the only things Doc stored here. This was the stuff he used to pretend he was somebody else.

We kept going. Another chest. Then another...

It took us an hour to sort through everything. Uniforms, masks, badges, maps, pistols...

I reached into the bottom of the last chest and felt something hard and flat inside a piece of burlap. I pulled it out and unwrapped it.

My pulse rate shot up.

Inside the fabric was a cutlass with a curved steel blade, about two feet long. It looked hundreds of years old, maybe a thousand.

I turned it back and forth in my hand. "Look at this thing!"

The blade was polished like a mirror. But that wasn't the most impressive part. The pommel and hand guard were encrusted with jewels. Sapphires. Emeralds. Rubies. Diamonds. Even in the dim light, the stones glowed and glittered.

"This is worth a fortune!" I said.

"Maybe that's why he stashed it here," said Kira. "Like cash under the mattress." She reached over just as I flicked the blade up. It caught the soft pad just below her thumb.

"Jesus! Sorry!" I dropped the cutlass and reached for Kira's hand. A small trickle of blood oozed out. She jerked away and pressed her other palm against the cut. "Not your fault," she said. "I got careless."

"I can't believe it held an edge this long."

"Better than a Ginsu knife."

I suddenly felt very tired. It had been a long day. I craved fresh air. I looked toward the entrance. "I think it's time to get out of here."

"Good idea," said Kira.

I grabbed the cutlass.

"Wrap that thing up," she said. "It's dangerous."

CHAPTER 14

ABOUT TWENTY MINUTES later, we were sitting on the narrow beach below the cave entrance. We'd put the cutlass and a bunch of other items together in a musty tarp and brought them out to take back with us. Plenty of room in the hold of the *Albatross*.

But first things first.

I broke off some dry branches and dug a pit for a small fire. I lit the kindling and waited for the wood to catch. When the flames got high enough, I took my ancestor's plans for mass destruction and tossed them into the blaze, starting with the blueprints.

Nobody would ever see them again.

As the paper crackled, black smoke wafted out of the pit. For some reason, it seemed to head in Kira's direction. She didn't say anything—she just stood up and headed down the beach. About twenty yards away, she stopped and stared out over the water.

I poked the fire and wondered what she was thinking. The plans in the flames belonged to my family, but they had just as much to do with hers. Doc Savage had been afraid that his deadly ideas might fall into John Sunlight's hands. He was worried that Sunlight would use them to rule the world, or destroy it. I wondered if Kira felt guilt by association with her ancestor—like I sometimes did with mine.

Once the flames got high enough, I tossed the notebooks into the fire, one after the other. As I tossed the last one in, an envelope dropped out from between the pages. I caught a glimpse of lettering on the outside as it fell into the fire. I grabbed the envelope just as the edges started to scorch.

By now, I knew the original Doc's handwriting when I saw it. Bold block letters. I glanced down the beach at Kira. She was still gazing out to sea.

I looked at the envelope.

"To my progeny," it said, *"if any survive."*

I stuck it in my pocket and watched everything else burn.

CHAPTER 15

ONCE THE BLUEPRINTS and notebooks plans were reduced to ashes, I doused the fire. Kira and I loaded everything we'd taken from the cave onto the dinghy. Probably about thirty pounds of stuff. A few pistols, some memorabilia, and, of course, my precious cutlass, which Kira wanted nothing more to do with.

We shoved off and paddled back to the *Albatross*. Kira was quiet the whole way. I didn't push her.

As soon as we got aboard, we carried our booty down the cabin stairs and stashed it in the hold under the cabin floor. Safe and secure.

Back on deck, I pulled anchor and helped Kira unfurl the sails. The wind was blowing from the north. The sheets filled right away. Kira took the wheel and maneuvered us out of the shallows.

As soon as we were underway, I went back down into the cabin and pulled the envelope from my pocket. I sat down on one of the berths and tore it open. There was a single page inside—thick bond paper with my ancestor's handwriting in black pen.

It was dated June 15, 1939.

To anyone who has inherited the Savage name—

If you are reading this, you've managed to get past all barriers to uncover my most secret plans. By now, you also know about John Sunlight, and how important it was to hide this work from him.

Sunlight and I were two sides of the same coin. I believe that any small turn of fate could have flipped either of us in the other direction. Good to bad. Bad to good. Or maybe we both possessed a measure of each.

For the sake of the world, I pray that the good is stronger in you—and that Sunlight and his evil are gone forever.

Clark Savage, Jr.

That was it. No secret codes. No magic formulas. I wondered what Doc Savage would think if he knew that John Sunlight's great-granddaughter had led me to his hidden cave—and that she was the woman I loved. I doubted that he would have seen that twist coming.

I folded the letter and tucked it into a corner of the hold. Then I went back up on deck. The *Albatross* was heeling with the wind. I could tell from the sun that we were headed farther south, the opposite direction from home. Was Kira tacking? Or maybe heading to port for supplies?

I walked back along the starboard rail to the cockpit. Kira had two hands on the wheel and her eyes on the horizon. We were moving past the western shore of Andros, pointed toward the Caribbean and the northern coast of South America.

"So when are we heading back north?" I asked.

I expected her to say "wrong question." But this time she actually gave me an answer.

It was one word.

"Never."

Not a joke or her usual sass. She was serious.

I let it sink in for a few seconds.

"Wait," I said. "We're running away? I thought we had more battles to fight together, you and me. Savage and Sunlight against the world, remember?"

Kira stared straight ahead as she gripped the wheel. "I've been fighting my whole life," she said, "since I was a little girl. You were my way out—my way of putting the past in the past. Today was the last of it."

Kira pulled me toward her with one arm and kissed me hard. Then she pulled back and looked me in the eye. "I'm done with fighting," she said. "And you're all the home I need."

Something had changed in her. I could see it. Until this moment, I'd been the reluctant hero, resisting every step of the way. I always saw Kira as hard-core, somebody who would never give up.

I actually felt a huge release inside. Maybe we were finally on the same page. Maybe we could both leave the bad stuff behind. Maybe, like my great-grandfather hoped, the good would finally win out.

I still wanted to know where we were going.

But that could wait until tomorrow.

CHAPTER 16

Bagram, Afghanistan

IN A METAL bunker at the edge of an abandoned airfield, a young woman in a figure-shrouding abaya sat in front of a military-grade laptop. Her desk was covered with spreadsheet printouts. Dozens of pages with hundreds of entries. Items, quantities, customers, prices. But at the moment, the image on the laptop had her full attention. And it was making her furious.

The young woman's name was Lial. She had no idea where she was born. She had no memory at all of her life before age five. All she knew about her genealogy was that she had inherited features that could pass for several nationalities, including Afghani.

Lial's black niqab was pulled back to expose her face. Her long black hair was bunched and clipped on top of her head. She leaned toward the screen and played the same grainy security-camera footage over and over again.

It showed the top floor of a building in Chicago exploding into smithereens.

When she rewound and played the detonation sequence in slo-mo, she could see the whitish glows that marked the placement of the charges. Precise and professional. She couldn't have done better herself. The news reports that followed were what bothered her. *Enraged* her. No bodies recovered. Which meant that the two targets were still alive.

A botched mission. Unforgivable.

"He should have sent me," Lial muttered to herself.

The door to the hut opened abruptly. A tall man appeared in the entrance. He wore a brown vest over a dark blue tunic. His head was covered in a turban. A bandolier of ammo draped diagonally from shoulder to hip. He held an automatic rifle in his hands.

Taliban.

"*As-salamu alaikum,*" he said.

"*Wa alaikum assalam,*" Lial replied.

In this part of the country, a woman without a proper head covering might be beaten or even shot. But Lial felt perfectly safe. She knew Ansar. They were colleagues. In fact, they'd attended the same school—on another continent, years ago. They'd been working together at this remote location for months, and they'd barely made a dent in the job.

Lial closed the laptop and replaced her head covering. She walked outside with her partner.

"The Chicago mission," she said. "It failed."

Both spoke flawless Pashto, but English was easier. And good practice. It was the language used by most of their customers.

"They escaped?" said Ansar. "Both of them?"

Lial nodded. "The charges were set correctly, but the monitoring was off. They lost track of the targets."

She walked with Ansar down a long stretch of pavement lined with thick concrete barriers. "Somebody will answer for it," said Ansar. "Anyway, it's not our problem." As they emerged from the end of the walkway, he looked out and spread his arms wide. "*This* is."

They had reached the edge of a pitted runway stained with thousands of black landing marks. Extending into the distance were rows of bulky mine-resistant trucks called MRAPs, along with SUVs, jeeps, and pickup trucks, some in white, others in desert camo. It looked like the world's most bizarre car dealership.

One side of the runway was filled with stacked cases of MREs. The other side was lined with the real moneymakers—metal cases of M4 carbines, antipersonnel mines, and Javelin missiles, gathered from abandoned FOBs all over Afghanistan.

Ansar was right. Lial knew that she needed to focus on the work in front of her. The logistics were daunting. The assignment was to feed the black market with the base's vast supply of equipment and weaponry—everything the Americans had carelessly left behind.

CHAPTER 17

"*LAND HO!*" I felt a little silly shouting it.

But there it was.

We'd been sailing for days since leaving the Bahamas behind. And still no hint from Kira about where we were going. I'm not sure she even knew where we were headed herself. But now there was a dot of land on the horizon.

I hustled back to the cockpit. "Island! Dead ahead."

Kira peered over the wheel and smiled.

"So where *are* we?" I asked.

"Exactly where we want to be," said Kira. "In the absolute middle of nowhere."

The sea was calm and the wind was favorable, blowing us straight toward the dot in the distance. As we got closer, I could see that a dot was pretty much all it was—a tiny speck of land, too small to be on any map. Maybe the tip of some extinct volcano or the last remains of a sinking atoll.

We anchored about thirty yards off the beach and took the dinghy ashore. When I first sighted land, I was worried we'd stumbled onto some pirate hideout. But as soon as we slogged onto the beach, I could tell that there was nobody else there. The island was just two thick arms of sand curled around a tiny lagoon. End to end, the whole thing was about twenty yards long. It looked like an island in a *New Yorker* cartoon.

"I think we've officially reached the end of the world," I said.

"Perfect," said Kira. She stabbed the handle of her paddle into the sand. "Civilization is overrated."

I walked to the high point of the island and turned in a full 360. Other than the *Albatross*, there was nothing in sight but blue water. At some point in the past, a breeze or a bird must have carried some seeds over from somewhere, because the island had a small stand of palms and a few scraggly bushes. There were clusters of green-jacketed coconuts high in the trees and piles of greenish-brown fronds on the ground.

Kira leaned up against one of the trunks and tipped her face up toward the sky. She looked relaxed and at peace. A few seconds later, she snapped into action.

"We need shelter," she said, clapping her hands together.

"Hold on. We're actually staying here?"

"Why not?"

"Because this whole island could be underwater tomorrow."

Kira slapped me on the shoulder. "Then live for the moment!" I hadn't seen her this cheerful in a while—maybe ever.

She ran back to the dinghy and pulled out a supply bag. I didn't even know she'd packed it. She dumped the contents out on the sand. A survival knife, flint, some parachute cord, and a piece of canvas about ten feet square.

"Is this our roof?" I asked, lifting a corner.

"Our floor. Unless you want sand fleas in your shorts."

Kira started cutting off sections of cord. She tied two long ends to a couple of the palm trees, about five feet off the ground, then stretched the other ends out and tied them to the branches on two low bushes.

"Don't just stand there," she said. "Do what I do." She tossed me a bunch of cord. I watched as she made a cross-laced pattern between the two long lengths. Then she started gathering palm fronds from the ground and weaving them through the lattice. I got to work, but I was all thumbs.

"Weren't you ever in the Boy Scouts?" Kira asked.

"Sorry."

"Of course. I forgot. You went to science camp."

In about ten minutes, we had a substantial lean-to with a canvas sleep mat. I realized that Kira had angled the structure so that the opening faced west. We slipped inside and lay down on our backs, propped up on our elbows. The scene outside looked like paradise. The

Albatross bobbed on the waves in the distance, and the sun was a burnt-orange ball on the horizon.

"It doesn't get any better than this," said Kira.

I rolled toward her and kissed her. She kissed me back. I felt her hands on my belt.

She smiled at me. "Or maybe it does."

CHAPTER 18

THE NEXT MORNING, I woke up to the sound of kids laughing.

At first I thought I was dreaming, but when I opened my eyes, I could see shapes through the gaps in the fronds. Small bodies moving. Fingers poking. And then, a set of brown eyes peeking through an opening.

More laughing.

I realized that Kira and I were both bare-ass naked. Maybe that's what was so damned amusing.

I shook her. "Company," I whispered.

Kira sat straight up. She already had the knife in her hand. She looked alert and ready to fight.

I turned toward the opening of the lean-to. Faces were peeking in from both edges. I counted six skinny brown-skinned boys, maybe ten or eleven years old, grinning like crazy and nudging each other as they stared.

Kira grabbed her clothes and covered herself. "Hey!"

she shouted, waving the knife. A couple of the boys covered their eyes and turned away. One of them made wild circling gestures over his scalp. He was making fun of Kira's curly hair.

I pulled on my pants and crawled out of the shelter on my hands and knees. The kids scattered and regrouped about ten yards away, still laughing. They all wore baggy cargo shorts and torn white T-shirts.

When I stood up to my full height, the laughing stopped. A few of the boys started backing away toward the shoreline. That's when I saw a couple of outrigger canoes sitting next to our dinghy.

Kira emerged from the shelter. She glanced at the crude boats, then stuck her knife under her belt.

"Relax, Doc, they're not here to kill us." She waved to the boys. "They just came to fish."

CHAPTER 19

The Arabian Sea

CAPTAIN CAL SAVAGE IV had been furious for days about the miss in Chicago. But now his anger had turned cold and hard. It was time to see justice done.

Savage sat on the bridge of his 220-foot Russian-built yacht, designed to military specs and painted in mottled gray camouflage.

"Let's get this done," he ordered. He perched impatiently in a leather chair in front of a large monitor. Crew members hovered around him, all dressed in identical black tactical uniforms. No stripes or insignia. On this ship, there were only two ranks—captain, and everybody else.

A technician tapped a keypad. The monitor lit up. Savage could see the relief on the tech's face. The link worked. From eight thousand miles away, the image was crystal clear.

It was afternoon on the ship, but just after three that morning on Lake Michigan, which is where the feed was originating. The screen was split into four frames—a wide shot filling most of the space and three close-ups running across the bottom.

The master view showed the aft end of a powerboat idling in the center of the lake, twenty miles east of Sturgeon Bay—exactly at the coordinates that Savage had directed. Three figures sat on the stern, arms and legs bound. They were all connected by thick cables to a ten-foot length of naval anchor chain, thick and heavy. Two men stood over them.

The smaller images showed the faces of the prisoners in close-up. Two men, one woman, all in their midtwenties. Their faces were illuminated by LED lights from GoPro cameras mounted on their chests. All three captives were blinking in the glare. Their jaws were clenched tight. No emotion showing.

The technician looked at Savage, waiting for the order.

Savage leaned in to study the faces. He could sense the raw terror beneath the stoic expressions. Even with all their training, there was no real way to prepare for a moment like this. But they must have known it was coming. These three had been in charge of the mission to eliminate Doc Savage and Kira Sunlight—the only two people in the world that the captain considered a threat.

And the mission had failed.

As soon as the official news broke that no bodies were found in the wreckage, all three operatives would have realized that it was over for them, and that their bodies would never be found, either.

Savage gave a quick nod. The technician relayed the command through his throat mic. "Execute."

One of the operatives on the tug released the anchor chain. It spilled out over the stern, dragging the two men and the woman over the edge and into the dark water. Savage leaned forward, almost coming out of his chair to follow the action.

The underwater cameras were working perfectly, streaming their images. The lights were bright on each of the faces as they spun down through the water. Twenty feet. Now forty. With the weight of the chain, Savage calculated that it would take less than a minute for all three to reach the bottom, the deepest point in the lake, 922 feet down.

He watched the transformation as they plummeted. Eyes wide now. Cheeks puffed out, heads thrashing from side to side. They had all been trained to hold their breath for long periods. That only made it more interesting.

But the pressure was too much. One by one, the mouths gaped open. Eyes rolled back. All three were now bleeding into their lungs, and their hearts were being crushed. They were inhaling water.

In less than four minutes, it was over. The woman had lasted the longest.

Savage sat back in his chair and smiled. A strange, unsettling smile. Since his school days, he had always enjoyed seeing underachievers punished.

And to him, drowning seemed like the worst possible way to go.

CHAPTER 20

I WAS DIVING with all six boys about a hundred yards offshore, and they were putting me to shame. After all my training with Kira, my lung capacity was probably twice what it used to be. So how could these froggy little kids be swimming rings around me?

They'd been coming back to our little speck of an island every day to fish. They only spoke a few words of English, and even Kira couldn't decipher their native dialect. So we communicated with hand gestures and facial expressions. It worked fine. There wasn't a lot to talk about.

The boys were always grinning and laughing—full of life. Not a care in the world. And they were expert fishermen. They hung nets from their outriggers, pulling up big hauls of grunts and snapper. Every afternoon, they grilled us a feast on the island, then took the rest of the catch home—somewhere over the horizon.

Today, the boys and I were spearfishing in deep water, about thirty feet down. Kira had stayed back to start the fire and crack open some coconuts.

All six kids were zipping around with netted sacks and long wooden sticks with spikes at the end. No snorkels or swim fins. Just natural ability. Occasionally, I'd see one of them shoot up to the surface to grab some air. But I'd swear a few of them had gills. Their sacks were starting to fill with speared catch. The boys all had dead aim. I never saw one of them miss a target.

This far out, the coral on the bottom was mixed with white sand and craggy rocks. I watched a fat moray eel squirm into a crevice as one of the boys swam past.

Lung-wise, I was just about at my limit. I pointed to the surface and got ready to push myself off the bottom. Just then, I saw one of the kids flinch. He started back-pedaling with both feet, his eyes fixed straight ahead. He made a quick hand gesture to his buddies. They all swam toward me. A few of them dropped their sacks of speared fish on the way, trailing thin streams of red through the water.

I stared out into the shadows where the first boy had pointed.

That's when I saw it. A gray shadow, getting more defined with every second. Smooth. Bullet-shaped. Heading toward us.

Shark.

I fought the instinct to rush for the surface. By now, I

felt like my insides were pounding through my skin. The boys banded around me. White bubbles streamed from their noses.

The shark moved its head from side to side in tight rhythmic sweeps.

It circled us—close enough that I could see the remora fish on its fin. We turned as a unit to track its path, our backs pressed together.

The shark's head dipped. Then, with one huge thrust of its tail, it sped straight for us.

I knew we only had one chance.

I held up my own spear—all metal. I waved it an arc across the shark's path. Ten yards away. Now five! The jaws gaped open and the pupils rolled back. Suddenly, the huge fish stopped like it had rammed into an invisible wall. Its whole body shook in a violent spasm. Then it made a flipping turn and swam off into the gloom. A few seconds later, it was gone.

I signaled for the kids to surface. I followed a few yards behind, keeping my eyes toward the bottom the whole way. I could feel my lungs burning and my head pounding. I knew I only had a few seconds of air left.

When my head popped up above water, the boys started jabbering and running their hands across my magic spear.

"Force field generator," I told them, gulping for air. "Invented by my ancestor."

As usual, they didn't understand a single word I said.

CHAPTER 21

LIKE HIS GREAT-GRANDFATHER and namesake, Captain Cal Savage IV was slender and pale. In spite of his light complexion, he enjoyed taking the morning sun on the top deck. The crew knew not to disturb him during his quiet time.

Today, he was doing his best to put the Chicago failure out of his mind. A momentary setback, he kept telling himself, and the guilty had been punished. Far more important was the big picture—and how much he'd already accomplished.

It had been twenty-five years since he graduated from the secret school his ancestor cofounded. As a student, he'd been well trained in espionage, evasion, and assassination. Since then, he'd used his skills to accumulate a fortune from a variety of dark-side ventures—blood diamonds, smuggled fentanyl, bootlegged uranium. The bulk of his wealth was secured in masked accounts in

Belize and Singapore. The onboard safe held a few million dollars in petty cash.

Over the years, he had assembled a tight crew, an elite band of young fellow graduates—expert navigators, skilled engineers, master chefs. And every one a trained killer.

The name of the ship was the *Prizrak*, Russian for *ghost*. It was Savage's home and his base of operations. He had no passport. His name was not registered with any government or authority. For all practical purposes, he did not even exist, and neither did his ship. Which was exactly how he liked it.

Savage took special pride in the fact that he had not touched land in more than ten years. Helicopters ferried fuel, equipment, and supplies to the ship as she moved from sea to sea, never docking.

From his bridge, Savage directed a worldwide network of clandestine operatives, most of them fellow alumni. On his orders, they fomented chaos across the globe. Ethnic cleansing, civil wars, regime changes. Over the past few years alone, Savage had fanned conflicts in Myanmar, Darfur, Syria, Afghanistan, and a dozen other trouble spots. Trouble was his trade, and he was good at it.

But of course, it was all a means to an end. Eventually, when the world order was irretrievably broken down, Savage would step ashore to take over, with his own style of command and justice.

Until then, he would move silently across the seas— like a ghost.

"Captain, he's here."

Savage blinked and opened his eyes. A crew member hovered above him, casting a shadow over his face.

The 10 a.m. meeting. A bother, but necessary.

A Somali warlord needed to be brought into line.

CHAPTER 22

TEN MINUTES LATER, Captain Savage was silently fuming. His guest would simply not budge.

The warlord was called Taifa. If he had a last name, it was long forgotten. He was in his sixties, with hard features and rheumy eyes. His throat was marked by a deep scar, evidence of one of the many attempts on his life.

The negotiations had reached an impasse over a critical point—Taifa's insistence that his oldest son, Cumar, take over a powerful regional militia. Cumar, a thuggish thirtysomething, stood behind his father, flanked by two huge bodyguards with automatic rifles.

Savage was out of patience. "No," he said firmly. "My man will lead the militia, not yours."

He nodded toward the back of the room, where a half dozen crew members stood ready. A young man stepped out of the group and walked to the center of the cabin. He stopped directly in front of Taifa. He was not quite six feet tall, and skinny as a straw. Maybe twenty years old. He looked like a schoolboy.

Savage clapped his hands on the young man's narrow shoulders. "This is Abai. Abai has my trust. He will lead the militia."

Taifa and his son both wrinkled their faces, holding back laughter. The two bodyguards stepped forward, grinning. They poked Abai in the ribs with their gun barrels. "*Digaag caato ah!*" they repeated in a mocking singsong. "*Skinny chicken!*"

Savage just watched.

Abai held his ground, expressionless, as the metal barrels prodded him. He lowered his head slowly, as if in embarrassment. Suddenly, he whipped both hands up and ripped the rifles out of the bodyguards' hands, barrels first. He flipped the guns around his wrists like batons and came up with them pointed at the guards' foreheads.

Taifa's jaw dropped. Savage could tell that he was stunned. The warlord let out a long sigh.

"Impressive," he said. "But still no. Cumar must lead." It was tradition, he explained. A matter of family honor. As the oldest of three brothers, Cumar was born to inherit the top position. There could be no question in the matter. None.

Now it was Savage's turn to sigh. The discussion was going nowhere. It was time to clear the room. He gestured to Cumar and Abai. "Both of you—*out!* Let the grown men talk."

Cumar glanced at his father. Taifa nodded. The warlord's son followed Abai out the door and down the main deck toward the stern of the ship.

Savage leaned in close to Taifa's face. "Listen to me. Your son is weak. The troops don't trust him. He is a coward in battle. All he cares about are drugs and whores."

Taifa said nothing, but Savage could tell he was seething. The warlord stood up and nodded to his two guards. The body language was clear. The meeting was over.

So be it, thought Savage.

A crew member opened the cabin door. Taifa walked out, followed by his gunmen. Savage followed, his mouth clenched. He joined the warlord on deck. Taifa leaned over the railing, looking down at the powerboat that had carried him and his team from shore.

Empty.

"Cumar!" he shouted, looking left and right.

Savage stood back. "Taifa," he said, "the decision has been made. From on high."

The warlord looked up. His expression froze. He dropped to his knees on the deck.

Cumar was hanging forty feet above him, swinging by his neck from a guyline. Abai stood on a platform nearby, arms folded.

Taifa's bodyguards raised their guns. At that moment, a dozen of the *Prizrak*'s crew appeared from behind the rail overhead, rifles pointed down, looking on with unsettling smiles.

Savage stepped up to Taifa and pulled him to his feet. His tone was now conciliatory—even kind. "You have two other sons. They are healthy and well. And they will stay that way—under Abai. Understood?"

Through tight lips, the warlord mumbled, "Understood."

"Good," said Savage.

Before too long, he thought to himself, the whole world would understand.

CHAPTER 23

THE FIRE WAS crackling on the beach. A row of snapper fillets roasted over the flames. Kira had carved the meat from a few fresh coconuts for a side dish.

All six boys were sitting cross-legged on one side of the fire, chatting away in the language I couldn't understand. I assumed they were still talking about our near-death experience on the reef that afternoon.

One of the boys was using a thin stick to poke the fish as it cooked. I sat with Kira on the other side of the fire, observing his technique. I leaned in close to her. "Have you figured out their names yet?"

Clearly, she'd been working on it.

She pointed to the boy with the stick. "That's Nian. I think he's the oldest." She nodded toward the next two boys in line. "That's Bial and Kimo. I think they're brothers. Next to Kimo is Tima, and then Bin. The small one is Dai."

"He's a great diver," I said. "And wicked with a spear." Most of the fish on the grill came from Dai's pouch.

Kira and I had decided early on not to give the boys our real names. We were worried about who else they might tell, even out here in the middle of nowhere. When they were around, we just called each other Tarzan and Jane.

"Hey!" I called out. We'd learned this was the best way to get their attention. I held up a canvas bag that I'd brought from the *Albatross*. Since the boys had been so intrigued with the force field generator, I figured I'd entertain them with some of my ancestors' other treasures.

I pulled the bag open. The boys crawled over like kids on Christmas morning.

The first item I pulled out was a man's shirt made from heavy cloth. It was stained around the collar and it had a few holes in front. I took one sleeve and rubbed it hard against the other cuff. Once. Twice. On the third contact, a spark flew out. The shirt ignited with a bright flame. The fibers had been coated with thermite.

I heard gasps from the boys, then clapping.

Next, I pulled out my prize cutlass. I turned it from side to side so that the gems and steel caught the reflection of the flames. The boys looked dazzled. They leaned in. Dai reached out to touch the blade. I jerked it back.

"Sharp!" said Kira, pointing to the pink ridge at the base of her thumb.

Next up was a cylinder that looked like an oversized

medicine capsule. It was about four inches long and made of tin, with a thin rubber seal around the middle. I handed it to Tima.

He took the cylinder, held it up to the light, then whacked it hard against his knee. The rubber seal broke. Suddenly the air filled with a pungent odor—like a combination of skunk musk and burning sulfur. It was horrendous. The boys covered their faces and backed away on all fours, like spindly crabs.

"Stink bomb!" I yelled, holding my breath. I picked up the cracked capsule and heaved it as far as I could into the water.

"Sting boom!" said Tima, talking with his nose pinched. At the sound, the other boys started laughing hysterically. They all pinched their noses and chanted, *"Sting boom Tarzan! Sting boom Tarzan!"*

I reached for the next gadget in my collection, but Kira grabbed my hand. "Doc. Save it. That's enough for one night." She made a spoon-to-mouth motion with her hands and called out to everybody, "Time to eat!"

Nian pulled the fish out of the fire. Kira passed out the coconut chunks. We used palm leaves for plates, our fingers for forks. We sipped last night's rainwater from small tin cups. I thought it was one of the best meals I'd ever had.

The boys wolfed down their food in huge bites, barely pausing to chew. For a few minutes, the only sounds on the island were lapping waves and smacking lips.

As soon as they were finished, the boys wiped their hands on their shorts and headed for their boats. I stood up and looked in the direction they always paddled at the end of the day. The horizon looked cloudy and ominous. The boys were usually gone by this time. Kira was right. My demonstration had gone on a little too long.

"Hey!" she shouted. The boys stopped. Kira waved them back and knelt down on the beach. She pressed her palms together and leaned her cheek against her hands. "Sleep here tonight," she said. "Go home tomorrow."

Nian seemed to grasp the concept first. He huddled with the others. They tugged their boats farther up the beach so the tide wouldn't take them.

I walked to the palm grove and started gathering fresh fronds. I carried them down to the beach and helped the boys make sleep mats. They all raced to the grove and came back with armfuls of fronds, trying to outdo one another with the most elaborate bedding.

As night fell, I used the bailing bucket from the dinghy to extinguish the fire. I grabbed a windbreaker for Kira. We both sat watching for a few minutes while the boys settled themselves on the beach, jabbering to one another the whole time.

"You're good with kids," said Kira. "A natural teacher."

"I wish," I said. "Most of the time, they've been teaching me."

I thought about my job back at the university. The world of lesson plans and lecture notes seemed very far away, along with everything else in my normal existence. But the sky was an odd reminder.

When I tipped my head back, I recognized constellations I'd taught years ago as an associate professor. Canis Major, Canopus, Hydra. Every damn seat was filled for those lectures. Nothing to do with me. Astronomy was a well-known gut course.

I gathered my cutlass and all the gadgets I hadn't gotten to and put the bag under the shelter of the lean-to. Kira crawled in and added some fresh fronds to our bedding.

I took off my shirt and folded it under my head as a pillow. Kira settled in next to me and pulled the windbreaker over her bare shoulders. Her eyelids started to flutter. I could see that she was already drifting off to sleep.

Not me. My mind was still whirring with excitement.

I leaned over and tapped her arm. "Did I tell you about the shark?"

"You did," she mumbled. "Five times."

CHAPTER 24

WHEN I OPENED my eyes, I saw the first rays of sun poking through the back of the lean-to. I listened for voices, but all I heard was the rolling surf. Strange. Maybe the boys had already gone out to fish, or maybe they'd headed home—wherever home was. I imagined a bunch of angry parents waiting for them on a beach somewhere over the horizon. Maybe they'd be grounded, I thought.

I rolled over. No Kira. Probably off doing her sunrise yoga. She'd tried to get me interested once or twice, but I'd rather sleep than stretch.

I crawled out of the hut and stared across the sand. Two things hit me wrong. The outrigger canoes were floating offshore, empty. And the dinghy was lying halfway up the beach, deflated.

Then I saw the shapes in the surf.

My heart started pounding. For a second, my vision

almost went black. I felt a surge of adrenaline as I ran toward the water.

I got to the smallest boy first. "Dai!" He was face down, half buried in wet sand. The water all around him was pale red. I grabbed his bony shoulder and turned him over. Blood oozed from a deep slash across his throat.

The bile rose in my belly. I felt like vomiting. I held it down and turned toward the other shapes in the water. Five more boys. I ran from one to the next. Same limp bodies. Same bloody gashes.

I looked back up the beach. Near the firepit, my cutlass was stuck into the sand. The blade was glistening red.

"*Kira!*" I shouted at the top of my lungs. I waded out into the surf, looking for another body in the water. Praying I wouldn't find one. Water splashed up to my chest. Then I spotted the *Albatross*. She was mostly underwater, keel up. Sunk.

I was crazed now. "*Kira!*" I shouted again. "*Where are you?*" Nothing.

I waded back to shore and turned around. Suddenly, the horizon was filled with boats—huge outrigger canoes, with four or five brown-skinned men in each, paddling powerfully toward the island.

I knelt down in the sand. All the breath went out of me. I knew in an instant why the men were here.

They were looking for their children.

And they were about to find them.

Dead.

CHAPTER 25

KIRA'S MOUTH WAS dry and her whole body ached. She felt like she was inside a throbbing metal shell. She squeezed her eyes tight, then tried to open them again. Her eyelids felt weighted and crusty.

All she could remember was falling asleep next to Doc in the lean-to. It felt like a long time ago. Her eyes finally opened. She looked down. She was in a narrow seat with strands of plastic-coated cable wrapped around her body. Her arms were pinned to her sides. She felt herself being tipped sideways and heard the whine of an engine above her.

Her brain started to clear. She blinked and pieced together her surroundings, like assembling a puzzle.

She was in a helicopter, tied to a seat in the rear. The cockpit door was closed. She craned her neck to glimpse out a small window in the side of the cabin. The chopper was about a thousand feet up. Nothing but open water below.

The aircraft banked hard and started to descend. Kira stamped her feet on the rubber-lined deck and shouted, *"Doc!"*

No answer.

She twisted her head around as far as she could.

No Doc. No boys. She was alone.

As the chopper leveled out, a shape came into view through the window, about a quarter-mile off. It was a huge yacht, sleek and streamlined. Kira squinted. Yachts were usually painted white, to reflect the sun. This one was covered in naval camouflage, almost invisible against the water. Like a ghost.

As the chopper approached, a big X lit up on the stern. A landing platform.

Kira took in quick breaths through her nostrils, forcing oxygen to her brain. She needed to clear her head and get some answers, then make a plan. Whoever took her could have just killed her on the beach, and they didn't. Which meant they wanted something from her.

Or maybe, Kira thought, they just preferred to kill her here.

CHAPTER 26

CAPTAIN CAL SAVAGE IV watched from the bridge as the chopper touched down. Lial stood beside him, stone-faced. By now, Savage could read her moods clearly. He had trained her himself. She was still irritated about not getting the assignment in Chicago—and newly irked about not getting the assignment on the island. But Savage stood by his decisions. An operative like Lial was too valuable to risk in a fight. He needed her for more nuanced work. Mind, not muscle.

On the platform below, the cockpit door opened. Four black-clad men jumped out onto the deck. From what Savage had seen from their body-cam feeds, the mission had gone flawlessly—all six targets slain silently in the night, with Doc Savage left to take the blame. The captain could not have been more pleased.

"You know what this means?" he asked.

"I do," said Lial curtly.

Savage told her anyway. "It means the end to the Doc Savage saga once and for all. Once news of this crime spreads, the world will remember the Doc Savage name only for its dark side. Mindless cruelty. Sociopathic violence. As it should be."

Lial responded with a tight smile. "You're right. What could be worse than a child killer?"

"And look," said Savage, pointing toward the chopper. "There's the bonus."

The rear door of the helicopter slid open. Two of the men grabbed their prisoner and pulled her down onto the deck, feetfirst.

Savage glanced at Lial. He could see her eyes widen as she tried to control her excitement.

"She's taller than I thought she'd be," Lial said.

One of the men cut the cables around Kira's legs and torso, then pushed her forward along the deck. Even after her ordeal, she looked fit and strong, thought Savage. Plenty of fight left in her. Which was exactly what he needed.

"You're looking at the best operative our alma mater ever produced," said Savage. He rested one hand lightly on Lial's shoulder. "No offense."

She shrugged his hand away. "None taken."

Savage could tell that Lial was more impressed than envious. And with good reason.

It's not every day that you meet a legend.

CHAPTER 27

MY HEAD HURT. My whole body throbbed. Dozens of people were screaming at me in a language I didn't understand. Men and women. The last thing I remembered was being clubbed on the head and loaded into a canoe. No idea how far I traveled, or how long I was out. I knew two things. The island I was on was a lot bigger than the one I left. And I was in serious trouble.

They had me in a wooden chair in the middle of a room with chains wrapped around my torso. A year ago, when I was at my peak strength, I might have been able to snap one of the links. Not today. I wouldn't have gotten far, anyway. Some of the men in the crowd had spears. Some had guns.

We were in a big tin hut with three walls. The onlookers formed a horseshoe around the sides. The fourth wall of the hut was mostly open, looking out toward the water. Sweat was pouring out of my body. It must've been over a hundred degrees under that tin roof. I could smell myself and everybody else in the room. A dank, wet, human stench. The screaming got louder. I heard feet stamping and spear shafts pounding on the floor. These people wanted to kill me. And I couldn't blame them.

They thought I'd murdered their boys.

My cutlass was lying on a wooden table in the middle of the room. The blood had dried to a rusty brown. I kept shaking my head, but I knew everything pointed to me. I'd been the only living person left on the island. And compared to the boys, I was a giant. They would have had no chance against me. None.

I recognized the men from the outriggers. Big, bare-chested guys, with elaborate tattoos across their biceps and pecs. The women in the room wore long patterned skirts with T-shirts or tube tops. Some of them were sobbing. Maybe mothers of the boys, or sisters. A few of them had tried to claw at me, but the men held them back.

The whole room went silent.

Five men entered in a line from the open side. They sat down at a long table at the front. Senior citizens. Wrinkled brown faces. Hunched shoulders. White hair, or none at all. They wore baggy trousers and short-sleeved white shirts, with thick beaded necklaces. I had no hope that any of them would speak English. Then the guy in the middle pointed at me and called out a single word.

"*Killer!*"

It might have been the only English word he knew.

My muscles tensed so hard that my chair jerked back a few inches. "*No!* Not a killer!" I yelled. The crowd started shouting again—louder, angrier. One of the elders raised a hand to quiet the room. I squirmed against the chains. I wanted to use my hands, as if gestures would help. I lowered my voice. I tried to sound calm, reasonable, innocent.

"The boys," I said. "We swam together. Fished together. Ate together." How could I explain that I'd saved them all from a goddamn shark? "I didn't kill them! I don't know who did!"

Out of the corner of my eye, I saw a young woman twist free from the men around her. She bolted toward me. Her eyes were wild. When she was two feet away, she curled her lips and spit in my face. I could feel the warm wetness dripping down my cheek. Then she slapped me, so hard it stung. Two men grabbed her and pulled her back to the wall.

I heard the sound of a motor in the distance, coming from the ocean side. I looked out. A small speedboat was heading toward a wooden dock, kicking up a V-shaped wake. One man aboard behind the wheel. Tall. Tanned. White.

When he got close to shore, he shut off the engine and tossed a line to a girl on the dock. Then he grabbed on to a wooden ladder and climbed out of the boat.

Everybody in the hut quieted down as he walked up the beach toward us.

He was in his thirties, wearing a white tropical suit. I felt a small flutter of hope. A detective? A lawyer?

Whoever he was, he suddenly looked like my best chance of staying alive.

When he reached the open side of the shed, the elders stood up. Everybody else in the room gave a nod of respect. Good sign, I thought. The man stepped in and took a long look at the bloody cutlass on the table. Then he walked over and stopped right in front of me. He folded his hands over his belt.

"Hello," he said. "My name is Aaron Vail."

"You speak English! Thank God! Who are you? Who sent you?"

"Never mind who sent me. I'm a local island magistrate. I deal with the indigenous populations, distributing aid, resolving disputes, making sure justice is done."

"You know these people? Tell them I'm innocent! Get me out of these chains!"

He looked around the hut, then back at me. "You mean so you can look for the real killer? Like O.J.?"

He spoke slowly and precisely, like he had all the time in the world. I was getting a strange feeling in my gut. Then he smiled. A sick, unsettling smile. The same smile I'd seen from the assassins in Chicago. That's the moment I knew that *everybody* on the island wanted me dead.

Including him.

Vail turned to the elders and spoke a few quick phrases

in their language. The elders nodded slowly and muttered to one another.

I twisted against the chains. "What did you say? What did you tell them?"

Vail turned back toward me and leaned in close. "I warned them to keep you properly restrained." He pulled a handkerchief from his pocket and wiped the spittle off my face. "I informed them that you have a history of escapes, Doctor Savage."

CHAPTER 28

KIRA WAS TIED to a pipe that ran up the inside wall of the yacht's glass-enclosed bridge. Her brain was sharper now, and she was taking everything in. The small dark-haired woman had tied the knots while the pale man with the captain's braids on his jacket stood by and watched.

"Tie her tight," he said. "She's drugged, but she's still dangerous."

"Who are you?" Kira asked. "Where's Doc?" She could feel the slight slur in her words.

The captain ignored her. Instead, he tapped his young assistant on the back. "Lial," he said. "Time to go."

"Wait! Not yet!" the young woman said, looking straight at Kira. "Let me do the interrogation." Her eyes were dark and cold.

"No," the captain replied. "Your ride is waiting."

It was clear that the young woman didn't want to leave, but it didn't seem like she had a choice. Kira looked out through the window toward the stern of the ship. The rotors on the chopper that had brought her were still spinning, and two men were waiting near the cockpit door.

The young woman stepped back. She stared at the captain for a few seconds, then looked back at Kira. Then she grabbed a backpack and walked out the door. Kira could hear her footsteps as she descended a metal stairway to the deck.

As soon as she left, the pale man stepped forward to test the ropes around Kira's torso. She could feel his knuckles against her ribs as he tugged.

"Don't worry. She did a professional job," said Kira. "Lial. That was her name, right? Algerian?"

"Good guess, Ms. Sunlight." He stepped back.

"I observed that she never used *your* name."

The man leaned against the console and folded his arms. Slight as he was, he had a definite air of command. Kira could tell that he was accustomed to making decisions and giving orders.

"My name is Cal Savage," he said. "Cal Savage the Fourth."

What? Who?

Kira's mind reeled. She tried not to show any reaction, but she couldn't control the pounding of her heart. Until this moment, she had thought the only Savage alive in the world was the one she'd left behind on the island.

"It's a shame we never met at school," the captain said. "I was several years ahead of you."

Kira's brain was swimming now, but she kept her voice calm and firm. "With a name like Savage," she said, "you'd think I'd have heard of you."

The captain shook his head. "I was never a star pupil like you. Just a legacy admission."

Kira blinked and did some mental calculations. Strange as it was, the story was starting to add up—and it went way, way back. "If you're Cal Savage the Fourth," she said, "then your ancestor was..."

"Yes. Cal Savage the First. The original Doc Savage's twin. The brother who got absolutely no attention from anybody. The one the world forgot all about."

"He was there. In Russia," said Kira. "He cofounded the school." The origin of the academy for killers was a tightly held secret. But Kira had learned the truth before she escaped, years ago.

"Correct," said the captain. "He was in on the beginning, in partnership with your great-grandfather, John Sunlight. Savage and Sunlight. Two neglected geniuses against the world."

"*Sick* geniuses," said Kira. "People are dying every day because of what they taught."

"True, Ms. Sunlight," said Savage reflectively. "But

somehow, not you. I have to admit that I admire your longevity. Even though I've tried to kill you myself. Many times."

"Where's Doc?" Kira asked again.

"Forget him," said Savage. "He can't save you this time."

"Is he dead?"

Savage smiled. "Wrong question."

CHAPTER 29

NILS AND LUCAS Olsson were having the night of their lives. Qatar was a long way from Solberg, the tiny Swedish hamlet where the two brothers grew up. After a couple of years together in the army and another with a UN peacekeeping force in Sudan, their international connections had finally paid off.

Still in their twenties, they were newly minted moguls in the underground weapons business, and they had just filled a huge order for Stinger missiles from an offshoot of Hamas. It meant more money than either of them had ever imagined, and they were spending a small chunk of their advance tonight.

Dinner had been broiled lobster and Kobe steaks, complemented with a very expensive Veuve Clicquot. Their brains were swimming by the time they got to the club, and now they were indulging in yet another luxury—the attentions of four very beautiful young women, wearing very few clothes. The glow in the private upstairs lounge came from dozens of scented candles. Electronic music pulsed from concealed speakers. The chairs were covered in full-grain leather, the pillows in pure satin. Nils and Lucas had paid in cash for the privilege of being the only customers here.

Worth every riyal.

The men sat side by side in lush recliners as the girls took turns dancing for them, kissing them, stroking them, straddling them. From time to time, the siblings turned their heads to grin at each other, as if to say "Can you believe this?"

The curtain to the small alcove parted. Another young woman walked in, even prettier than the others. She carried a silver tray with two thick crystal tumblers. "Your cocktails," she said in perfect Swedish. "With our compliments." She bent forward, displaying an elaborate butterfly brooch clipped to her sheer blouse.

"Do you speak English?" Nils asked. One of the other girls had her tongue in his ear. He pushed her aside.

"Of course," said the hostess, switching effortlessly.

"Good," said Lucas. "None of these girls do. And we need to practice."

"For business," added Nils. The girl on his lap was grinding her hips slowly against his crotch.

"Excellent language to know," the hostess said. "For business." She gave him a charming smile. "But you both need to work on your accents if you want to be taken seriously."

"Is that so?" said Nils. "Maybe you'll be our..." He fumbled for the right word. "Instructor?"

Both men took their drinks from the tray, then clinked the glasses and toasted "To English!" They tipped their heads back and gulped, ice cubes rattling against their teeth.

The hostess glanced at the other four women and made an almost imperceptible flick with her hand. They immediately disengaged and disappeared behind a thick curtain at the rear of the room.

"Lovely," said the hostess, taking a seat on an ottoman across from the two men. "Now it's just us. Let's start our first lesson."

"What's your name?" asked Nils.

The hostess did not answer right away. Instead, she tapped a finger against her lips, as if counting seconds.

Nils twitched once as blood began to spill from his nose and mouth. A second later, the same thing happened to his brother. They didn't flail or cry out. They couldn't. Their motor muscles were already paralyzed. But their minds remained totally alert, and their hearing had become even more acute.

The hostess leaned in. "My name is Lial," she said. "I don't mind telling you that, because there's nothing you can do with the information. I also need to tell you that it was a huge mistake to undercut my price on the Stingers. Very bad business." She leaned back. "I think you realize that now."

Both men just stared at her, frozen in terror. There was nothing else they could do.

"You don't have to say it," said Lial. She reached forward to pat their rigid hands. "It won't happen again."

Then she crossed her legs, folded her arms, and watched the brothers die.

CHAPTER 30

KIRA WAS WATCHING, too. She couldn't help herself. She was now cuffed and tied to a captain's chair near the *Prizrak*'s massive control panel. In the seat next to hers, Cal Savage leaned in toward the monitor.

"Perfect. *Perfect!*" He was admiring the POV from Lial's brooch camera. Kira could see how impressed he was with her skills.

"The poison," he said. "Her formula."

The image rose and fell slightly every second or two. Kira realized that it was from Lial's breathing. In less than a minute, blood started to cake on the chins and shirts of the two brothers. Their eyes were frozen open. Kira saw Lial's right hand reach out. The pad of her middle finger rested on Nils's neck, just below the angle of his jaw. Then Lucas. The camera's angle tilted and swirled as Lial stood and turned toward the exit. There was a moment of black. Then her face filled the frame.

"Done," she said softly into the lens.

The screen turned to static.

Savage turned toward Kira. "Your turn, Ms. Sunlight."

Kira tensed her muscles, looking for an opening. Any chance to make a move. But she was trapped. Was this where it was going to end? She realized that she didn't even know which of the seven seas she was floating on.

But fear was one thing she would not show. *Ever.*

"Do you get off on making snuff films?" she asked. "Is that your thing?"

Savage gave her a twisted smile. "I had hoped to see *you* die, if that's what you're asking. I definitely would have watched that." Savage turned back toward the monitor. "But now I have a much better idea."

Kira's mind flicked through the possibilities. None of them pleasant.

Savage picked up a video controller and selected another input. "I'm about to give you an assignment, Ms. Sunlight. Your chance to live a little longer."

The screen lit up with jerky handheld footage. The time code in the corner was from six days earlier. The scene was midday, bright sunlight. The camera moved along a path through thick tropical foliage. It stopped at a clearing, where a shallow pit had been dug out of the orange-tinted soil.

In the pit were bodies. Maybe a dozen men. Swarms of insects buzzed across the lens as the camera moved closer—close enough to show horrific gunshot wounds. Limbs were nearly torn off, bones exposed. Heads were shattered, some missing jaws or eye sockets or entire craniums. Brains and gore mottled the men's khaki uniforms. Kira inched forward in her chair, scanning quickly for Doc's face. Please, God, no...But the dead men were all young and Black.

"What happened here?" said Kira. "Why am I looking at this?"

Savage seemed to be observing the footage with clinical detachment, sometimes freezing a frame to study an image before moving on.

"This footage was taken near one of my financial interests," he said. "A copper mine. Remote location. A week ago, the mine fell into the wrong hands." He tapped the screen. "These men were my employees. My overseers and guards. Obviously, they were poorly armed, or inadequately motivated."

"Copper?" said Kira. "Copper for what? Your own line of cookware?" She was sure that she knew the real answer. She just wanted to hear it from him.

"Don't play the naïf, Ms. Sunlight. You know as well as I do that a by-product of copper is cobalt, and cobalt is the rock that now runs the world. Extremely profitable. This mine is an investment I can't personally attend to. But it's one I don't intend to surrender."

"So send Lial," said Kira. "Retribution seems to be in her wheelhouse."

"I have other plans for Lial. Other needs. This job is yours."

For a moment, Kira flashed to what would have happened if she'd been classmates with Cal Savage at school. She realized that she would have found an opportunity to drown him.

Kira glared at him. "Work for *you*? I'd rather drink one of Lial's cocktails."

"That would be a shame," said Savage. He had the tone of a man with an ace up his sleeve. "Look what happened the last time you were incapacitated."

He clicked to another image with his controller. This time Kira recognized the scene right away, and it made her heart race. It was the tiny island—the place where, for a short time, life had been perfect.

It was night-vision footage, a ghostly grayish-green. But the picture was clear and sharp. The image showed a pan of the island. The coconut grove. The lean-to. Then the camera pointed toward the water and zoomed in. Kira twisted in her chair. She saw bodies rolling in the surf. She counted six. *The boys!*

She rocked back and forth, trying to loosen the bolts that held the chair to the deck. "*Doc!*" she shouted. She could feel her face burning with rage. "*Is he dead? Did they kill him, too?*"

Savage gave her his sick little smile. "On the contrary," he said. "The evidence will show that Doc Savage wielded the murder weapon. And island culture, I'm afraid, does not look kindly on killers."

"Doc would never hurt those kids!" Kira shouted. "*Never!*"

"I'm happy to see that your sympathy is with children," said Savage. "My copper mine is filled with them. I need you to go there. Discourage the men who are milking my asset. Make them regret their actions." He stared at her. "Or shall I just order up that drink?"

Kira stopped struggling. She relaxed her jaw and calmed her mind. In an instant, she made the kind of cold calculation that had helped her survive her brutal education and the lonely years after her escape.

She realized now that there was only one way off this floating prison. Only one way to find out if the man she loved was dead or alive. Sometimes the worst choice is the only choice. Her eyes turned steely and her voice evened out.

"Give me the coordinates."

CHAPTER 31

I SHOOK MY head to dislodge the bugs crawling on my forehead. I arched my back and jerked my arms and legs as hard as I could—again and again.

No use. I was practically delirious. I hadn't eaten in three days. They gave me just enough water to keep me alive until my trial. Which was due to start in a few hours. *Sham* trial. I knew everybody's mind was already made up.

I was staked out on the dirt floor of a filthy shed, chained to metal posts sunk deep in cement. It was some kind of village workshop. No power tools. Just rusted saws and antique hammers hanging from nails on the walls.

I took a deep breath. My mind cleared for a second.

I knew what I needed.

I turned my head and started wiggling my fingers through the dirt. Right hand. Then left. Scraping. Poking.

Digging. There! Just a few inches from my right finger-tips. A bent, rusted nail. If I could grab it, maybe I could work the cuff lock on that hand. I clenched my teeth and willed my arm to stretch beyond its limits. I could feel my muscles and tendons burning. One more inch...

My fingers brushed the head of the nail. I felt it flip out of reach.

Damnit!

I heard shouts and footsteps outside. Getting closer. I curled my fingers back and looked toward the door. It was corrugated metal, locked from the outside. The voices got louder. More agitated. I heard somebody kicking the door with full strength. The sound reverberated through the shed. The door shook and rattled. The metal bent in at the bottom.

A second later, daylight burst in. Two huge men were ripping the door off its hinges. A half dozen more rushed in and clambered over me, their sweaty chests pressing against me as they tried to unfasten my hands and legs. I saw one guy pull a hammer from the wall. I felt the shock against my wrist as he pounded the cuff. On the third try, the metal broke open. Another man hammered at the cuff on my right ankle. He missed and hit my shin. I gritted my teeth and swallowed a scream.

I started shouting *"No!"* I figured that was one word they could understand. But a few seconds later, all four cuffs were off and I was being carried out of the shed by the mob.

I knew in that instant it was over for me. There wasn't going to be any trial. Just a summary execution. I twisted and kicked. I managed to yank one arm loose and get one of the men in a headlock. I felt a steel rod slam across my midsection. The man squirmed out of my grip and punched me in the neck.

They were carrying me up a small hill behind the shed. My head was tipped backward now. One guy had his hands on my scalp, using my hair as a handle. Then they slammed me down on the ground, face-first. They were chanting a single word I didn't understand. I looked up. Ten yards away, at the peak of the rise, was an eighteenth-century cannon.

I felt weak, sick, helpless.

Now I knew what was coming. It was an execution the British used to inflict on pirates and escaped slaves. I was about to be blown to bits.

By cannon fire.

I looked back toward the water, about fifty yards away. If I could get there, I could dive deep, maybe get away. I gathered my strength and bolted, knocking down two men in my way.

I felt a crack on my skull and dropped to my knees.

My eyes went blurry. When I could focus again, I felt cold metal against my back. The cannon barrel. I was tied to the front of it.

I heard a female voice and jerked my head around. It was the woman from the first day, the one who spit at me in the shed. She pulled a lighter from her pocket and stepped up behind the cannon. I saw a two-foot fuse dangling from the touchhole.

She lit it.

The men started chanting the single word again. Maybe *cannon*? Maybe *murderer*? Maybe *justice*?

At least it would be over in a second. I heard the hiss and crackle of the fuse. I could smell the smoke. I closed my eyes and thought about Kira.

One last time.

Suddenly, the chanting stopped. I turned my head and saw Aaron Vail pushing his way through the crowd in his crisp white suit. I looked behind me. The spark was two inches from the hole. Vail licked two fingers and snuffed it out. The crowd stayed mostly quiet, but there were a few angry shouts.

My knees went wobbly, but the ropes were still holding me up. I knew Vail was no friend, but maybe he could buy me some time. Minutes, even. Enough to bargain, maybe. Not that I had anything to offer.

Suddenly, Vail was in my face. He reached behind me to pat the lip of the cannon. "Dramatic exit," he said. "But much too quick."

He turned to the crowd and shouted a few phrases in their language. He sounded like a fire-and-brimstone preacher. The crowd erupted again, happy now. I felt the ropes loosen around my body. Men grabbed my arms and legs.

I whipped my head toward Vail. "What's happening? What did you say?"

He stepped back and straightened the lapels on his suit jacket. "I told them a child killer deserves a more protracted death." He smiled that sick little smile. "They totally agree."

CHAPTER 32

I WAS BEING carried like a carcass out of the hut down toward the dock. I looked back and saw Vail grab the cutlass off the table. Was he about to behead me on the beach? Or slash my throat and let me bleed out like the boys?

No, I thought, too quick. Too merciful. I had a feeling Vail had other plans.

When we got to the beach, the men slammed me down onto the sand, face-first, knocking the air out of my lungs.

I felt a coil of rope land on my legs.

Vail shouted something from the dock. Then I heard his speedboat start up.

I kicked as hard as I could. It took four men to hold my legs together. I felt them wrapping a narrow cord around my ankles. I looked up. The other end ran to the back of the speedboat.

I saw Vail step into the cockpit. He revved the engines.

The men cleared away. I felt a jolt through my body as

I was dragged off the beach and into the shallow water. I heard the pitch of the engines rise, and then I was bouncing over the surf on my back. About twenty yards from shore, I got raked over a ridge of sharp coral. It felt like the skin on my back was being torn off. The sting of the saltwater added to the agony. I gritted my teeth against the pain.

Now we were in deep water, moving faster. I tried to hold my head up, but it kept tipping back. Water shot up into my nostrils. I was choking. Drowning. The boat picked up more speed. The ropes cut into my ankles. My knee joints felt like they were about to separate. I waited until my head was underwater to scream. I saw a swirl of white bubbles around my face and then I got pulled to the surface again. The boat made a turn, pulling me in a wide sweep behind it, like bait in the water.

I was dying a slow death by speedboat, and there was nobody to help me.

Then I remembered what Kira always said.

"You have only yourself."

I took a deep gulp of air and gathered my strength—everything I had left. I crunched myself forward against the force of the water. It was like trying to do a sit-up against a hurricane. I bent forward and grabbed the rope with one hand, then the other, and pulled myself around until I was headfirst. My back was on fire from coral burns. As I bounced on my belly, I could see the back of Vail's head about fifteen yards ahead. Inch by inch, I muscled myself forward—closer and closer to the back of the boat.

"Don't look back, you prick!" I muttered to myself. I knew if Vail turned around, he'd find a way to break my hold. Or maybe he'd just shoot me.

When I was ten feet from the stern, I found a small center of calm between the wake plumes. I pulled myself quickly the rest of the way. I could feel the churn from the twin props a few feet down. One wrong move and I'd be chopped into chum.

I grabbed the lip of the stern and let the rope go slack, letting it catch around the propeller shafts. The rope snapped. The engines stalled.

I ducked down again, my cheek pressed against the hull. I heard Vail swearing. The boat rocked as he walked back from the cockpit. I slid to the side. He leaned over and spotted the fouled propellers. My feet were still tied, but I managed to thrust myself up with a dolphin kick, just high enough to wrap my hands around Vail's neck. I pulled his head down hard on the metal stern rail. He dropped into the water, blood oozing from his scalp. He was out. Maybe dead. I didn't care.

I ducked under and cleared the propellers, then untied my ankles. I climbed aboard. The cutlass was lying on the deck. The dried blood had washed off in a pool of saltwater and the blade was gleaming again.

I picked up the weapon. Vail's limp body was floating behind the boat. I was thinking that I could pull him aboard, see if he was still alive. Or I could reach down and administer the coup de grâce.

I looked back toward land. We had rounded a point, out of sight of the tin hut and the rest of the settlement. The bulk of the island was covered in thick green foliage. Not another human anywhere in sight.

Vail was floating away, out of reach. I decided to let the sea take him.

I moved to the front of the boat, turned the engine on, and headed toward the horizon. I poured on the power and felt the prow lift. I was free for the moment, but so what?

I had no idea where I was.

I'd lost Kira.

And I was wanted for murder.

CHAPTER 33

Tanganyika Province, Democratic Republic of the Congo

THE SOUND WAS loud. Metallic. Unnatural.

A young woman named Vanda woke up, startled. She lifted her head from her pillow roll and reached for her baby boy, just four months old.

Her tiny village, just a mile from the western shore of Lake Tanganyika, had been carved out of dense foliage, and the jungle constantly threatened to close in again. The villagers constantly hacked at the encroaching vines and bushes with machetes, keeping a clean perimeter around the small collection of huts and gardens.

Vanda stepped outside. Her baby now rested on her back, secured with a long wrap of colorful cloth. The sound was loud and steady. Not like any storm or animal Vanda had ever heard. It came from deep in the trees on the far side of the village.

It was early morning, and the men were already out

on a hunt. Vanda looked out and saw trees waving as if moved by a stiff wind. But the air was still.

The roars got louder and louder.

Vanda's baby started crying. She bent her knees and jostled from side to side to settle him down. Other women were emerging from their huts now, drawn by the sound. Vanda saw skinny boys running toward it, long sticks in their hands, as if ready to do battle. Mothers called them back, but the noise smothered their shouts.

As Vanda watched, the trees nearest the clearing started to tremble and bend. Suddenly, a line of huge yellow machines emerged from the jungle, with massive curved blades forming a solid wall of metal. The trees fell in front of them, landing with hard thuds on the ground.

The boys swarmed the machines, beating on them with their sticks. Mothers screamed and ran after them, waving their hands and leaning their bodies against the giant blades. But the machines kept coming, pushing them back, like ants.

Vanda tightened the wrap around her waist. She grabbed a small sack from her hut and hurried toward the other side of the clearing. She ducked into the underbrush, eyes wide, heart pounding.

The machines pushed through the tree line with growling engines. Vanda thought they would stop there, but they didn't. They plowed through the huts and gardens one by one, belching smoke from their metal pipes.

Vanda looked on, trembling, as her entire village—her

entire world—was leveled, leaving nothing but bare, orange-tinted earth.

Her baby started crying again. She jostled him back to silence and headed off into the jungle. As she ran, she started crying. In her entire eighteen years, she had never once left the place where she'd been born.

But now that place was gone.

And she had nowhere to go.

CHAPTER 34

Ten miles away, later that day

MERCENARY CAPTAIN RUPERT Gurney pulled a large steel locker from under his cot. He dialed the combination on the lock and opened the heavy lid. The locker was packed nearly full with stacks of United States currency, neatly wrapped. From a canvas sack, he added that day's delivery, adding a few thousand dollars more to the pile—enough to cover salaries for his men and a tidy skim for himself.

He counted the new money carefully, checking for broken seals, making sure that the couriers had not taken more than their assigned cut. He understood that lugging cash through the Congo was a dangerous business, and the runners definitely deserved their commission—but not a dollar more.

Satisfied with the take, Gurney secured the locker and slid it back under the cot. He nodded to the guard on his way out of the large tent and stepped out into the blazing sun. He immediately began to sweat through his dark-green uniform. Black patches spread under his arms and across his broad chest. He wiped beads of perspiration from his forehead.

Gurney hated the jungle. Hated everything about it. The heat. The bugs. The lizards. The rain. The dank, unrelenting stench. But the money was too good to turn down. And he'd run out of more comfortable options.

He walked across a broad clearing, past a row of smaller tents and a tin-roofed hut that served as the unit's bar. Above the hum of portable generators, he could already hear supervisors shouting through bullhorns in the distance.

"Faster! No stopping! No resting!"

As he got closer, Gurney could hear that the loudest shouts were coming from Hemple, his second-in-command. Hemple was British, like Gurney himself. Both had been classmates of Prince William at Eton. Hemple was a total psychopath, like most men in the unit, but a good fighter. And, as it turned out, an excellent production manager.

Gurney walked to the edge of the clearing. Hemple stood with his legs apart, cigarette dangling from his lips, AR-15 braced on his hip.

"Morning, sir!" he shouted, offering a sloppy and superfluous salute.

Gurney didn't even bother to return the gesture. He stepped onto a wooden platform and stared down into a bustling abyss. He was fifty feet above a rough-edged pit about half the size of a football field. The hole had been created by earthmovers. The massive scrape marks were still visible in the soil, but the big machines were long gone.

Now the pit was swarming with humans. Hundreds of them. Men, women, and children. All recruited from nearby villages. They worked with shovels and picks and smaller tools, digging and probing in rock walls and small offshoot tunnels. Their clothes and faces were coated with so much dust and grime that they blended in with the earth.

The prize they were digging for was not gold or diamonds.

It was copper.

Gurney had no idea who had owned the mine before. Not his concern. Capturing it on his sponsor's behalf had been child's play—a surprise attack in the middle of the night, with minimal ammunition expended. The previous overseers were rotting in a much smaller hole nearby. Now the humans in the pit worked for him.

A gunshot cracked.

Gurney looked across the pit, where ten of his men ringed the rim. One of them had just fired a warning shot behind the heels of a slacking worker. The terrified man lifted the handles of his wheelbarrow and moved quickly toward one of the tunnels.

Nearby, Hemple finished guzzling a liter-sized bottle of

water, then tossed the empty into the pit. He laughed as a half-dozen scrawny kids dived for the bottle and fought over the last few drops.

"Hey, boss!" A voice from behind.

Gurney turned. Two of his men were holding a young Black woman by the arms. She carried an infant on her back.

"Look what just walked out of the bush," said one of the men.

"Catch of the day," said the other.

Gurney stepped down from the platform and looked the woman over. She was clearly terrified. Probably still a teenager. She was coated in sweat, and so was her baby, mewing softly as he clung to his mother's neck.

Gurney grabbed a water bottle from a case near the platform. He uncapped it and held it out to the woman. She shook loose from the men and grabbed it with both hands. She took a long, deep gulp, almost draining it, then slid her baby off her back and poured the remaining ounces through his lips. The overflow bubbled out of his tiny mouth and down his cheeks.

"Clean?" Gurney asked. It was unit protocol to check all indigenous intruders for hidden weapons and suicide vests.

His men nodded.

Gurney took a step closer to the woman. She looked up and stood her ground.

"Can you work?" he asked. The woman just stared at

him. He tried Swahili. *"Unaweza kufanya kazi?"* This time she gave him a single nod.

Gurney pulled the empty water bottle from her and reached into a wooden tool bin near the platform. He handed her a metal spade, then pointed toward the winding dirt ramp that led down into the pit.

The woman stared for a few moments at the filthy chaos below. Then she swung her baby back onto her shoulders with her free arm and headed down the ramp. The orange dust began to coat her feet and bare legs.

"Jina lako nani?" Gurney called after her.

The woman turned back. "Vanda."

"Vanda," Gurney repeated. He turned to the two men who'd found her. "Put her on the payroll."

Gurney's assignment was to make the mine as productive and profitable as possible, and he knew the natives wouldn't work for nothing. Just close to it.

He took one last look at Vanda as she reached the bottom of the pit. She was young and strong.

Definitely worth fifty cents a day.

CHAPTER 35

PERCHED IN A mesh sling high in the jungle canopy, Kira Sunlight watched it all through her powerful spotting scope. She was in head-to-toe camo, blending in perfectly with the dappled foliage. Her brightly colored curls were tucked under a mottled-green hood. Her cheeks and forehead were daubed with green and yellow face paint.

She watched as the woman and her baby disappeared beneath the rim of the mine, then she swung the scope back to Gurney. He was tall and muscular, with a long nose and an imperious look. Kira could read the body language of the two men in front of him. Their postures telegraphed submission, maybe fear. Maybe they knew what she knew.

Rupert Gurney, she had learned, was a very dangerous and unpredictable man. Kicked out of the British Special Forces for dealing drugs. Convicted of kidnapping, grand larceny, and assault in the years after. Escaped from

England's supermax Belmarsh prison and turned up six months later as a freelancer in Yemen, teaming up with a militia later accused of grisly war crimes.

And now he was in charge here, running a stolen copper mine for persons unknown. Wherever there was nasty work to be done, Gurney was apparently the man to do it. As long as the price was right.

Kira made another of her cold calculations. Cal Savage was evil. She had no doubt about that. Evil ran in his blood. But on paper, Rupert Gurney seemed almost as bad. Besides, Kira had always been adept at compartmentalizing. Her plan was to complete this mission, suck up to Cal, get him to lead her to Doc—assuming he hadn't already been executed. For now, she put that grim possibility in another compartment.

Kira dialed the scope in tight on Gurney's head and put the crosshairs on his temple. One hundred yards. Easy shot.

If she'd brought a gun.

Savage had offered her an SSG, or any weapon she wanted. But Kira told him she wanted to travel light, and she preferred her own methods. Assassination was easy. Bang. Over in a second. But if Savage really wanted to discourage future interlopers, there were more effective techniques. Kira knew them all. She had learned them as a teenager.

She slipped the spotting scope into a pouch and tucked the hood tight around her neck. She grabbed the climbing rope and rappelled down to a lower branch, one wide enough to nap on.

She settled against the smooth curve of the trunk and settled in to wait for dark.

That's when she did her best work.

CHAPTER 36

THE TWO MEN stood by the antique cannon on the hill overlooking the beach. They did not fit in. They were both white, for one thing, and neither spoke the local language. They'd arrived on a small motorboat that morning. The island was small and remote, but sometimes boaters discovered it by accident and hung around for a day or two to enjoy the scenery. The residents were content to ignore them, as long as they didn't cause any trouble. With their Hawaiian shirts and cargo shorts, these two looked like just two more misguided tourists.

As the men watched, a large fishing boat pulled up to the wooden dock. A mass of villagers swept down the beach as the boat tied off. Curious, the two men walked down the slope, too, adjusting their baseball caps to ward off the glaring sun.

As they reached the beach, the three-man boat crew

was working a huge rusty winch amidships. Slowly, a large shape rose from a hatch, held aloft by a thick rope.

A great white. Twenty-footer, at least.

The arm of the winch swung over and deposited the stiff shark onto the dock. There was a huge metal hook through its upper jaw and a harpoon gash in its right flank. From where the two men stood on the beach, they got a potent waft of dead-fish stink, so strong it made them both gag.

Men and teenage boys swarmed around the shark's body as it settled on the dock, tugging on its fins and poking at its rows of daggerlike teeth. One of the village men elbowed the kids aside and whipped out a ten-inch knife. He jabbed it into the underside of the fish just below the gill slits and ran the blade all the way down to the pelvic fin. The pale belly skin parted and the innards spilled out in a froth of pinkish water.

Howls and shouts rose from the crowd. The young boys pushed in closer. The men grabbed them by the shoulders and pulled them back.

Everybody was staring at the freshly released stomach contents.

Two discernable objects had survived the shark's digestion process—a Caucasian male arm from the elbow down, and a wad of clothing that looked like it had once been part of a white suit.

The men in Hawaiian shirts looked at each other.

"Holy shit," said one.

"I think we just found Vail," said the other. He reached into his fanny pack and pulled out a satellite phone.

CHAPTER 37

THE SUN WAS high and hot over the Indian Ocean. The *Prizrak* was moving south at a leisurely ten knots. No particular destination. Cal Savage's standing orders were to keep moving, avoid shipping lanes, and always stick to international waters. He left the rest to his able navigators.

Savage was lying in a lounge chair on the balcony outside his private cabin, bare-chested, slathered in white sunscreen. He picked at an assortment of grapes and dates from a silver tray and sipped from a tall tumbler of iced tea.

"Captain!" A crew member was shouting up from the main deck. Savage slipped off his sunglasses and peered down through the railing. The young man was holding up a sat phone.

Savage waved the kid up the metal stairway to his perch. He reached out and grabbed the device, then spoke curtly into the mouthpiece. "What?" The young man backed himself against the railing, hands clasped behind him.

Savage held the phone tight to his ear. He stood up abruptly as he took in the report from his spies.

Aaron Vail was dead. Shark attack.

"Okay," the captain said evenly. "Then where the hell is Doc Savage?"

Missing, came the reply. No obvious remains. Location unknown.

"Sonofabitch!"

Savage grabbed the food tray and whipped it off the balcony, barely missing the young man's head. Loose grapes and dates plopped into the ocean below. The tray hit a swell and sank out of sight.

The call disconnected.

Savage clenched his teeth. He gripped the sat phone so tight his knuckles seemed to bulge. Then he drew his arm back and heaved it into the water, too.

The young man grabbed the railing behind his back, clearly worried that he would be next. If there's one thing the crew had learned while serving on the *Prizrak*, it was that the captain did not react well to bad news.

CHAPTER 38

Azov, Russia, twelve years earlier

CAL SAVAGE IV, far from being a captain, was near the end of his rope. He was sitting in a bleak, cluttered office overlooking a bustling shipyard. The sound of rivet guns reverberated from below. Sparks flared from welding torches.

Across the table from Savage sat Alek Ivanov—a large man with an outsized reputation. Banker. Bootlegger. Oligarch. He and Savage were the only two people in the room. The shipyard's manager had obligingly found a task in the warehouse.

Outside the office window loomed the superstructure of a 220-foot yacht, still in dry dock, surrounded by scaffolding—a six-hundred-ton work in progress.

The yacht was Ivanov's. His dream. His design. Paid for in advance.

Cal Savage had been working out of a safe house nearly, and he frequently wandered past the shipyard at night.

He had admired the magnificent ship from the day its keel was laid, and his admiration had grown with each step in its construction—from shaping the hull to the delivery of the teak planks for the decks. Something about the ship called to him, and he dreamed of having it for himself, even if he'd never piloted anything bigger than a sailboat. And even if the yacht was already spoken for by one of the most powerful men in the country.

For Savage, money was no object. Through various illegal enterprises, he had already accumulated a substantial fortune. He had made offers over the years through intermediaries, raising his ante every time. But Ivanov was unreceptive. He was building the yacht for his children. That's what Savage kept hearing. The oligarch wanted something substantial and beautiful to leave behind. A legacy.

When Ivanov had finally agreed to a face-to-face meeting, Savage polished his Russian and worked hard on his inflections. He wanted to be sure every word was clear. He realized that today was his last, best chance.

Savage knew that Ivanov had already done a background check on him and discovered that nobody in the Russian state hierarchy or secret police had ever heard of him. To the authorities, he was a total cipher. A nobody.

So be it.

He would have to rely on personal persuasion.

Ivanov puffed away vigorously on a worn meerschaum pipe. The small office was clouded with smoke, so dense that Cal found himself rubbing his eyes. Maybe a deliberate distraction on Ivanov's part, or an intimidation tactic. Or maybe just an annoying habit.

Since Savage knew that Ivanov had warm feelings for his children, that seemed like a perfect place to start the conversation.

"This tremendous ship," said Savage, in his well-rehearsed Russian. "You're building it for your son and daughter?"

"Correct," said Ivanov. "As I've said."

"How old?"

Ivanov pulled the pipe stem from his mouth. "Oleg is seventeen. Irina is sixteen." Savage detected the hint of a thaw in the oligarch's expression. When he spoke his children's names, even his voice turned warmer.

Ivanov stared at Savage for a few seconds, resumed his puffing, then reached into his pocket and pulled out his Android phone. He leaned across the table and clicked to a photo of two teenagers, heads together, at some kind of lavish gala.

"Handsome boy," said Savage. "Pretty girl."

"They're in Zermatt," said Ivanov, putting his phone away. "Ski holiday."

Savage took a deep breath. He pulled an iPad from his briefcase. His turn for show-and-tell. It was now or never.

"Correction," he said. "They *were*." He was careful to use the Russian past tense.

Ivanov took a heavy draw on his pipe and scowled.

"No. They *are*," he said curtly. The warmth was gone from his voice. "They don't return until the weekend."

Savage clicked on the iPad's photo gallery. There were several pictures in the series to choose from. He picked the one he thought would be most effective, then angled the device so that both he and Ivanov could see it.

Ivanov's pipe dropped onto the table, ashes flying. His face was suddenly flushed. He grabbed for the iPad. "No!" he shouted.

Savage pulled the screen out of the oligarch's reach, then stroked the photo as if admiring a fine painting.

The image showed Ivanov's teenage children in a non-descript cellar. The lighting was dim. The kids were bound back-to-back, faces toward camera. Oleg had a bruise on his chin and one eye was blackened. Irina's right cheek was red and swollen and her pert nose was bloodied. The look in her eyes was a mix of shock and terror. Same for her brother.

"*Where are they?*" demanded Ivanov, rising out of his seat.

"Wrong question," said Savage, leaning forward. "They can be back on the slopes by noon." He clicked the iPad off. "Or not."

Ivanov's lips had turned pale and fishy. He was breathing hard. His pupils were dilated to huge black pools.

Savage pulled a slip of paper from his pocket and slid it across the table. There was a number on it. One hundred thousand rubles over his last bid.

"My final offer," he said. "That—and your children's lives."

Ivanov was gasping so hard that Savage thought he might be having a heart attack. The oligarch grabbed the paper and crushed it in his huge hand.

"Yes!" he wheezed. "She's yours!"

Savage stood up and gave Ivanov a twisted little smile. He walked to the window and looked out at the ship. *His* ship.

She was yet to be christened. But he already had a name in mind.

CHAPTER 39

I HAD NO idea where I was. I just knew I had to keep going.

I'd run through a full tank of diesel and a can of reserve. Now I was completely out of gas. For the last two days, I'd been rowing the boat like a damn canoe. My muscles ached from fighting the wind and the current. My knees were scraped raw. I hadn't seen land since I left Vail and the island behind. But I knew I couldn't go back, only forward.

I was trying to head south. I figured I was out past the Bahamas. I knew Brazil was down there somewhere, but the boat had zero navigation gear. It was built for short hops. There wasn't even a compass on board. I was stuck with reading the sky. The anchor line wasn't long enough to reach bottom out here. So when I fell asleep, the boat just drifted aimlessly. I had to recalibrate my position and direction every morning, hoping I'd be sighted by a freighter or a cruise ship. This boat was not meant for the high seas.

I wiped the sweat out of my eyes. The sun was torture. The coral scrapes on my back burned like fire. Probably infected. I felt feverish and delirious. There was no shelter from the elements, and not a scrap of food on board. No fishing tackle, either. I'd checked every hatch and hideaway.

I'd found a few bottles of water, but I'd finished the last of it a day ago. I was probably losing at least a liter every hour in sweat. Not a good equation. If I didn't get some nutrition and fluids soon, I'd die out here. I started to have wild thoughts—like whether the admin office at the university had reported me missing.

Not that it mattered. Nobody would be looking for me out here.

And I thought about Kira. I was praying she was still alive, somewhere. But I didn't hold out much hope for that, either. Whoever slaughtered the boys probably killed her, too. For some reason, they only wanted one person left to take the fall.

Me.

I heard a thud from the back of the boat. I jerked my head around.

A large bird had just landed on the stern.

My muscles tensed and my brain went into overdrive. I blinked hard. It took a second to realize that I wasn't hallucinating.

It looked like some kind of tern or gull, and it was about ten feet away from where I was kneeling. I slowly pulled my plastic paddle out of the water and got ready to swing it. I knew I'd only have one shot. The bird's head was swiveling and ducking, like it was nervous about something. Maybe it knew what was coming.

I gripped the end of the paddle with both hands and turned slowly until I was facing backward. I raised the paddle like a baseball bat and tightened my grip. When I cocked my shoulders, my festering back felt like it was ripping open.

"Don't move," I whispered, my eyes locked on the bird. "Don't you dare move…"

I lunged forward and swung the paddle as hard as I could.

Shit!

Missed by an inch.

The momentum threw me off balance. I landed hard on my side. Pain shot through my whole body. The bird fluttered its wings and pushed off the back of the boat. I made one last desperate grab, but I was way off. The damn thing was already in the air, mocking me.

I collapsed face-first on the deck. I didn't have much left. Maybe nothing. My mouth was dry. My vision was blurred. I heard buzzing in my ears.

I turned my head to the side and pounded my head with my fist, trying to get rid of the sound. When I stopped, the buzzing was still there.

I pushed myself up from the deck. Agony.

The buzzing wasn't in my head.

It was coming from a distance.

I turned around and crawled back to the cockpit. I peeked over the cowling. Two bright orange dots were heading straight for me. I pulled a small pair of binoculars from the console and looked out. Two inflatables. Two men each. Ragged and lean.

Goddamnit!

More pirates.

CHAPTER 40

I HAD TO move fast.

This time I was in no shape for a fight, and I had no magical weapons. If the pirates saw me, I was dead. Simple as that.

I grabbed my cutlass from under a seat cushion and slipped over the side of the boat. At the last second, I ripped a section of rubber tubing from one of the engines. Then I slid the cutlass through my belt and let go of the boat rail.

I hyperventilated to pump extra oxygen into my lungs, but the pain from my back made me seize up. I gulped in what air I could and slid under. I prayed to God the pirates would be happy with the fancy speedboat and not be too curious about the owner.

I saw the white swirls from the propellers from underwater as the two inflatables stopped on opposite sides of the speedboat. Both engines were idling. I could hear the muffled sound of men's voices above. Excited. Impatient.

I was treading water about ten feet under, fifteen feet from the nearest Zodiac. The water was murky enough to give me cover, but my lungs were already about to burst. I started to black out. I pulled the hose from my pocket and stuck it in my mouth. Then I rose slowly— so slowly—toward the surface and let the tip of the hose poke up into the air. I blew once to clear it, then inhaled. I gagged on the diesel residue, but I clamped my mouth tight and took another breath. I dropped my arms to my sides and sank back down again.

I needed a plan.

I knew that if the pirates took off with my boat, I had no chance. For a second, I thought about making a big splash and just letting them shoot me. A quick, merciful headshot—then peace. Let somebody else take on the evil in the world.

Then I thought about Kira again. What would *she* do?

I reached down and pulled out my cutlass.

I clenched my hose between my teeth and swam underwater toward the nearest inflatable. When I was directly under the right pontoon, I jammed the cutlass tip into the hard rubber and cut a long slice through it. I heard a shout. The hull of the speedboat rocked as the pirates abandoned the sinking inflatable.

Angry voices from above. Then, a length of rope

dropped into the water. I saw hands lashing the wounded inflatable to the speedboat. I swam back and cut the inflatable's fuel line.

My lungs were burning, but adrenaline kept me moving. I swam under the speedboat until I reached the inflatable on the other side. All four pirates were aboard the speedboat now. I could hear two of them at the stern, probably checking the engines.

I swam to the front of the good Zodiac and sliced the prow line tying it to the speedboat, then I moved around to the other side, staying out of sight. The inflatable started to drift off. I drifted with it, kicking my feet underwater to speed it along. When I had opened a gap of about ten yards, I pulled myself aboard and flopped onto the deck below the gunwale.

I held my breath.

I heard voices. But no shouts. And no shots.

The engine was still idling. I lay flat on my back and worked by touch. The control grip felt like a recycled bicycle handle. I yanked it. The boat surged forward. I grabbed the bottom curve of the steering wheel and cranked it in the opposite direction of the speedboat—toward open water.

Now I heard shouts. Loud and angry. I was twenty yards away. Then forty. I straightened out and picked up speed. Fifty yards. More shouts. Then whip-crack gunshots. I stayed low. Seventy-five yards!

At about a hundred yards out, I lifted my head above the side and saw the pirates furiously trying to start the speedboat.

"Good luck with that, maties!" I shouted.

I pointed the boat toward the horizon, and cranked the throttle.

I was gone.

CHAPTER 41

Democratic Republic of the Congo, 2 a.m.

KIRA WIPED THE sweat from her forehead.

She was nestled in the brush about twenty yards from the mercenary unit's command center—a cluster of large military tents and a row of plastic outhouses.

A flag hung on the back wall of an open-sided hut the men used as a bar. It had black and red stripes with a yellow star in the center. Kira had been staring at it for hours, but couldn't ID it. Maybe the unit's official banner?

From where she was nestled, Kira could see the glow of distant campfires from the squalid tent city where the workers slept—*barely* slept—between shifts.

Kira heard footsteps approaching. Two sets. She leaned back into the shadows and took slow, even breaths.

She'd been waiting all night for this.

Two men were stumbling from the bar toward their quarters on the far side of the compound. Krupen and Horvat. Kira had learned their names by reading lips.

They were always posted side by side on the rim of the mine pit, taking frequent potshots at the workers from above—and laughing about it.

Everything about them was predictable.

Every night, they drank themselves into a stupor at the bar. And every night, they took the same path back to their tent. Like rats.

For three nights straight, Kira had watched. And listened.

Krupen was German. Horvat was Croatian. They communicated with each other in a crude pidgin English, with a lot of wild gesturing involved.

Kira peeked through the foliage as Horvat grunted and pointed to his crotch. He unzipped, then took a few steps off the path and into the brush. Kira heard a mild sigh as a hard stream of piss hit the leaves.

Krupen kept heading down the path.

Fine with Kira. She didn't care which one went first.

Kira heard another zip. Horvat reemerged and stepped back onto the path.

A loud snap sounded from the darkness, then a guttural gasp.

Horvat froze. He pulled out his .45 and moved toward the sound. Kira eased herself out of her hiding spot and crawled in the same direction.

Horvat called out. "Krupen?"

Silence.

Kira crouched behind a tree to watch as Horvat rounded a curve in the trail.

He rocked back as he saw his drinking buddy suspended in the air from a bent branch, his neck snapped and reddened from a wire wrapped tight below his jawline.

Horvat could see what it was. A spring trap. The kind used to snare animals. But man-sized.

He spun around, pointing his pistol into the dark jungle. He inched over and tapped Krupen's leg. Then he bent over and vomited his entire night's beer consumption into the bushes.

Horvat staggered back toward the lights of the compound. Along the way he fired a succession of three shots into the air. Then another three. Sounding the alarm.

Kira headed in the opposite direction, back into the deep jungle.

By the time they cut Krupen down, she would be sleeping like a baby.

CHAPTER 42

I WAS IN big trouble.

The inflatable was pitching like crazy and rain was coming down like bullets. The wind was spinning the boat and water crashed over the sides.

I'd already thrown up my seaweed supper. Now I was just hanging on for dear life.

I was out of fuel again. Not that it mattered. There was no way I could push through this storm. I just had to ride it out and hope that I was still in one piece when it ended.

Lightning split the sky in long jagged lines. For a few seconds at a time, I could see twenty-foot waves rising and falling around me. Otherwise, it was pitch-black.

The salt spray hit my coral wounds like a sandblaster, opening up the blisters again through my shirt. I crawled forward and grabbed a filthy tarp. I bunched it into a shallow pouch and let the rainwater fill it. I put the edge to my lips and took a long deep sip. The wind ripped the tarp out of my hands. Another wave hit. The right side of the boat tipped almost vertical. I grabbed for some knotted netting and felt myself falling.

Bang!

I hit the engine housing hard and blacked out.

CHAPTER 43

Democratic Republic of the Congo, 7 p.m.

KIRA SUCKED THE last drop of juice from a ripe mango and tossed the skin on the ground. A light supper. It was all her belly could handle in the heat. Time for a nap.

She climbed back up into the crook of one of her favorite trees and stuffed her backpack behind her head for a pillow. She was in deep cover, about a half mile from the mine and the human sounds that went with it. The air was filled with a chorus of cicadas and the bubbly rush from a nearby stream—her daily bath and fresh water supply.

As darkness closed in, she could hear monkeys screech and predators growl. Kira ticked off the binomial of each one in her head. It was a habit from her training. Always know what you're up against.

Pan troglodytes...Panthera pardus...Cercopithecus pogonias...

The mental exercise was also her way of not thinking about Doc, and how much she was missing him. After she'd ripped him away from his humdrum university life, they'd spent six months together. She'd trained him. Molded him. She helped him see what he was capable of, and showed him the evil that was taking over the world. She and Doc had risked their lives together, nearly died together—more than once.

At the beginning, the professor wouldn't have survived without her. By the end, she needed him just as much. Maybe more. Kira wasn't crazy about that feeling. She'd always hated being dependent on anybody but herself.

But she loved Doc. She couldn't help it. If that was a weakness, she'd decided that she was willing to live with it. And she wouldn't give up on finding him.

Ever.

Kira tipped her head back and looked up through the crazy pattern of branches and vines in the canopy above her. She felt a slight tickle on her neck.

She froze.

Now only her eyes moved, darting sideways. The tickle intensified. Her heart was pounding. A slender green snake slithered over her shoulder.

Dispholidus typus. A boomslang.

It was one of the deadliest snakes in Africa.

Kira held perfectly still. The snake started to curl across her chest, tongue flicking. Kira tensed her muscles, then whipped her left hand over and grabbed it behind the head. The snake coiled furiously around her forearm. Its jaws gaped wide, exposing a pink mouth and pin-like fangs.

Kira unwrapped the snake carefully from her arm and dangled it at arm's length, ready to drop it to the ground. But then she had second thoughts.

She pulled a nylon bag from a side pouch of her backpack and stuffed the squirming little killer inside.

Her new pet.

"Welcome to the jungle," she whispered.

CHAPTER 44

WAS I DEAD?

Not quite. I could still move and breathe.

It was still pitch-black. My head was covered by a soaking wet blanket. I ached from head to toe. The rain had slowed, but the boat was being blown by a strong wind. A loud throbbing sound was blasting down from above.

I pulled the blanket aside and got blinded by a huge light from about thirty feet up. It was all I could see. Then a shape came down through the glare.

A basket stretcher!

Was I hallucinating?

The padded edge of the basket whacked me in the head and I heard a man's voice through a loudspeaker.

"Climb into the basket! Center yourself and hold on to the sides! Do not let go!"

I grabbed the basket with both hands and rolled into

it. The steel ribs and straps cut into my back, but at this point I didn't care.

It was a helicopter! I was being rescued!

I felt a sudden tug from above as I was lifted off the inflatable—or what was left of it. When I looked down, I could see that the engine cowling had been torn off and one pontoon was underwater. At this point, it was barely a life raft. More like a deflated pool toy.

The chopper engine was pulsing above me. The higher I went, the louder it got, until my ears were pounding. The downdraft from the prop swung the basket back and forth until a pair of gloved hands grabbed the cable to steady it.

A few seconds later, I was inside the door and somebody was sliding me onto a rubber cushion. The basket went away. The chopper door slid shut. The nose of the chopper dipped and we surged forward.

We were flying. Fast.

I felt a plastic straw between my lips. *Omigod, yes!* I sucked in something cool and sweet, gulp after gulp, until somebody pulled the straw away. I felt my shirt being ripped open. I heard Velcro ripping and felt a strap being wrapped around my bicep. The inside of the chopper was dim, but I could see four or five helmeted heads hovering over me with small lights pointed down.

I felt somebody holding my hand and then the sting of a needle on the back of my wrist.

"Who are you?" I asked. "Where the hell am I?"

"Off the grid, that's where," said one of the helmets. "You're lucky we found you." Western European accent. I couldn't quite place it.

For a second, I felt a swell of panic. I stared up at the faces. Were any of them smiling—like the killers in Chicago? Like Aaron Vail? Had I been rescued, or had I been captured again? I looked for patches on the uniforms. Flags or military badges. But all I saw was the glare from the headlamps.

I lifted my head and grabbed at somebody's arm. "Who the hell *are* you? Who *sent* you?"

I felt a slight burn at the site of the needlestick. My head was being pushed back onto the cushion.

"Good night, Doctor."

And that was that.

CHAPTER 45

Democratic Republic of the Congo, 1 p.m.

AT MIDDAY, CONDITIONS in the mine were stifling.

One hundred and ten degrees. Eighty-five percent humidity.

Still, parents labored side by side with their children, scraping away at the dirt, prying stone after stone out of the earth, their eyes trained to separate the reddish, brownish treasure from the rest of the deposits that had built up over the last four billion years or so.

Vanda, the mother from the bulldozed village, still had only her spade to work with. Her right hand was now calloused and blistered from digging. Her whole body ached from kneeling and bending, hour after hour, day after day. As she worked, her baby hung on her back, a constant extra fifteen pounds of weight.

Vanda stabbed her blade under a fist-sized stone and worked it free with cracked fingernails. She held it up, spit on it once, and wiped the dirt off the wet corner with her thumb.

A woman next to her in a filthy green blouse reached over and tapped the stone with her own blade. "*Taka-taka*," she said. Garbage.

Vanda tossed the stone into a reject pile and looked for another.

A woman on the other side gasped and tugged at Vanda's arm. Vanda elbowed the woman away. She had claimed her spot for the day. Nobody was taking it from her.

The woman stood up and started shouting.

Vanda kept on digging, head down. Then she saw the bare feet of other workers moving in close. She looked up and realized that all work in her area had stopped. A circle of workers was closing around her, everybody pointing toward...

The baby!

Vanda grabbed for her son and pulled him down off her back. He was limp. Hot to the touch. Eyes open. Not moving.

Vanda laid him down in the dirt and shook him by the shoulders. "*Maji!*" she screamed. *Water!*

Somebody handed her a half-empty bottle. She washed the dust from her baby's face and dribbled water between his stiff lips. She patted his belly. Squeezed his legs. Rested her cheek against his bare chest.

Then she screamed—so loud it echoed off the stone walls.

The woman in green pulled at Vanda's shoulders. Vanda shook her off and clung even tighter to her son.

Her dead son.

A loud crack rang out. A ping of dirt kicked up three inches from Vanda's head. The workers flinched, then looked up.

Hemple was looking down at them from the rim of the pit. His rifle was pointed in their direction. He wiggled the barrel. "Back to work!" he shouted.

It was one of the English sentences they all understood.

The woman in green was joined by four other women, all tall and silent. They formed a wall around Vanda as she wept.

"*Njia hii,*" the woman in green said softly. This way.

Vanda stood up slowly, holding her baby in her arms. She followed the women to a small hollow in the side of the pit. A young man was scraping at the walls with a pickaxe. The woman in green grabbed him by his belt and pulled him out of the way.

Vanda slipped into the tiny carve out and sat down, pressing her back against the dirt, sheltered from the glare. She wrapped her baby in the folds of her dress, leaving only his face exposed.

She closed his eyes gently with two fingers and rocked him, singing softly in Swahili.

Standing just outside the tiny cave like a human curtain, the four other women swayed their hips and sang with her.

Behind their backs, under the blazing sun, work went on.

CHAPTER 46

STRANGE. NO WINDOWS.

For some reason, that was my first impression. Then, when I tried to move, I realized that I was chained to a metal cot. I could hear the slow beeping of medical equipment. When I looked up, I saw that I was surrounded by all kinds of high-tech machines. Heart monitor. EKG. Portable X-ray. I looked down and saw an IV line taped to the inside of my right elbow.

I blinked a few times and tried to clear the fog. My brain was waking up, but slowly. Whatever they gave me on the chopper had knocked me out in a snap. I had no idea how long I'd been unconscious, or how long I'd been here.

Wherever this was.

They had me in some kind of gown, but the place didn't feel or smell like a hospital. It felt like a bunker. On the wall across from me was a banner that looked like a national flag, but I didn't recognize it. A black and red stripe on each side, with a yellow star in the middle.

I heard a door open behind me. I craned my neck around. A man walked in. Late thirties or early forties. Generic military camo fatigues. He had a trimmed beard with a sprinkle of gray. He also had a deformed right hand. He wasn't trying to hide it.

"Good morning, Doctor Savage," he said. "My name is Leo." Perfect English, French accent. But not from France.

"Thanks for the pickup," I said. When I lifted my arms, the chains rattled. "But am I under arrest here?" I worried that I was in another cell—a modern one this time.

Leo ignored my question. He walked to the foot of the bed and picked up an iPad from a rack. He shook his head as if he couldn't believe what he was reading. "Incredible recovery," he said. Then he put the device down and looked straight at me.

"Doctor Savage," he said. "I've been looking for men like you all over the world."

Men. Plural. I wasn't the only one.

"I made myself hard to locate," I said.

"Yes. It took some effort to find you," said Leo. "Let's hope you were worth it."

He walked over and turned off the monitors, silencing the beeps one by one. With his good hand, he lifted the surgical tape and pulled the IV needle out of my arm. Then he unlocked the chains. He opened a narrow closet and grabbed a cotton robe. He tossed it over my lap.

"Let's go, Doctor," he said.

I swung my feet off the cot. I sat there for a few seconds, letting my balance come back. Then I eased my butt off the mattress and planted my bare feet on the tile floor, making sure I could support my own weight.

So far, so good. Nothing broken. I slipped on the robe. My back still stung, but not as much.

"We applied bacitracin and bandaged your cuts. You had some nasty scrapes back there. Coral?"

"Bodysurfing," I said. "I'm getting way too old for that sport." I was being a wiseass for a reason. I didn't want to reveal any more than I had to.

Leo held the door open. We walked out into a white-walled tunnel. Nobody else around. I looked for cameras. Didn't see any. That didn't mean they weren't there.

At the end of the hall, an elevator door slid open. We stepped into the car. The door closed. We were standing side by side as we started going up. Leo stared straight ahead.

Leo was tall, but I had a few inches on him. I wasn't in peak condition, but I was pretty confident that I could take him down. But I wanted more information. This time, I wasn't about to make a move until I knew for sure exactly where I was. I'd been lost at sea for days. Now that I was finally back on dry land, I needed to get my bearings.

I looked over at Leo's fatigues. Loose creases, sturdy seams. No name tag. No arm patches. No chest insignia.

"Is this a military base?" I asked.

"No," he said curtly. "It's my personal residence."

It was a short ride, maybe two or three floors at most.

The elevator opened into a huge hall with an arched wood ceiling and granite floors. The timbers overhead looked hundreds of years old. The wall stones were hand cut. The windows were leaded glass.

Leo led the way out. I looked around.

No mere bunker.

We were in a goddamn castle.

CHAPTER 47

"ARE WE IN a time warp, Leo?"

"That's one way to put it," he said.

On the wall next to a row of medieval tapestries, I saw the same mysterious flag I'd seen in the infirmary. Outside the arched windows, I could see trees—tall, leafy, deciduous. Northern Hemisphere. Temperate latitude. Leo could see my mind turning.

"I can save you the triangulation, Doctor Savage. We're in Belgium."

Belgium? That was a long way from the tropics—and an impossible distance for a helicopter. We must have refueled somewhere. On a ship? In midair?

"You were unconscious for forty-eight hours," said Leo.

"How did they find me—your crew? I had no beacon. No radio. They just happened to be doing a midocean flyover in the middle of a forty-knot gale?"

"Word travels in my circles," he said. "I heard you were

missing. I mobilized my resources. And here you are. Like I said, I'm a collector."

"Of incompetent sailors?"

"Of men with specific abilities."

Leo led me into a side room where there was a table heaped high with food. Sliced meat, cheese, fruit, bread. He must have seen my eyes go wide.

"Go ahead," he said. "I promise it's not laced."

I grabbed a few slices of ham and washed them down with a bottle of water. I took a fistful of bread, and then a handful of strawberries. Leo was watching me like I was a zoo specimen.

"What do you know about me?" I asked between mouthfuls. "Other than my name?"

"I know that you're highly educated and well trained." He took a single blueberry with his deformed hand and popped it into his mouth. "I also know you stand accused of multiple murders."

I felt a twist in my gut.

"Relax," said Leo. "It happens to the best of us."

"I had nothing to do with it," I said. "It was a setup, by people who've wanted me dead for a long time."

Leo waved his good hand dismissively. "Innocent, guilty," he said. "I assure you, I could not care less."

I was desperate to ask him about Kira. But I didn't want to tip him off. Not until I figured out whose side he was on. Maybe he'd never heard of her. Maybe it was better that way.

"Are you a bounty hunter?" I asked. "Am I some kind of prize?"

"If that were the case, I would already have cashed in," he said. "I have a pretty good idea of what you'd fetch." He offered a tight smile. "Especially if I threw in the murder weapon."

I tried not to react, but he saw me flinch. "Don't worry. Your blade is in a locker, safe and sound."

"For safekeeping? Or for evidence?" I still didn't trust him. I kept waiting for somebody from Interpol to walk in with extradition papers.

Leo waved me over to a sitting area near a fireplace. High-backed wooden chairs. Velvet cushions. He settled in and rested both hands on the carved armrests.

"Have a seat, Doctor Savage," he said. "I know your story. Let me tell you mine."

CHAPTER 48

I SAT DOWN and leaned back, trying to look neutral. But inside, I was dying for information. *Any* information. At this point, I'd take whatever I could get. Like Kira told me, always know what you're up against.

"You come from a fabled family, Doctor Savage," said Leo. "We have that in common."

"My family was all about science," I said. That wasn't entirely true. There was a lot of adventure and violence in there, too. I looked around the room. "If this castle belongs to you, you must come from money. Lots of it."

Leo nodded. "Money. And power." He took a breath, then launched right in. "Doctor Savage, I'm the descendant of the illegitimate son of King Leopold the Second of Belgium. The child was born to the king's teenage French mistress in 1907. He was born with a deformed hand."

"Philippe," I said. "The bastard son's name was Philippe."

I'd heard this story in one of my graduate European history classes.

"Correct," said Leo. "Philippe, Count of Ravenstein—a minor title his father conferred on him." Leo gave me another tight smile. "See? I *knew* you were well educated."

*Over*educated, probably. But at least I knew some historical trivia. "Philippe died young," I said. "Age six or seven."

Leo nodded. "So everybody thought. The truth is, his mother got weary of people mocking his deformity, so she faked his death and hid him away in a castle." Leo gestured toward the walls. "*This* castle."

It was getting harder and harder to look objective. This story was getting wilder by the minute.

"Philippe grew up here, totally in secret," said Leo. "Eventually, he took a mistress of his own. He had a son. And a grandson. And a great-grandson." Leo tapped his chest. "Me." He held up his gnarled right hand. "All with the same unfortunate genome."

"So . . . you're royalty."

"*Tainted* royalty," he said. "The most interesting kind."

I felt uncomfortable staring at his hand. So I glanced across the room at the flag. "Your family crest?"

"It's aspirational," said Leo. "The standard of my future regime." He stood up and started pacing across the stone floor. "As a student of history, you know that my ancestor King Leopold once owned a huge chunk of the African continent. A million square miles, give or take."

No mystery about that. King Leopold's massive African colony was on every world map for most of the twentieth century.

"The Congo," I said. "The Belgian Congo. What about it?" The Congo was now a so-called democratic republic, splintered by ethnic conflicts. It was one of the most fractious and dangerous places on earth.

"My family gave it up more than sixty years ago," said Leo. He turned to face me. "I want it back. Every steaming acre. And you're going to help me get it."

Leo sounded intelligent. But now I wondered if he was all there.

"Retake the *Congo*?" I said. "You'd need an army for that."

"Correct," he said. "I've started on one."

"Just out of curiosity," I asked. "Why would I want to be part of that kind of illegal insanity?"

"First," said Leo, "because I saved your life. Second, because I can keep you from being executed for homicide. And third…because I pay very, very well."

CHAPTER 49

Democratic Republic of the Congo, 11 p.m.

FOR TONIGHT'S MISSION, Kira had picked a hiding spot closer to the compound, across from a specific tent—the one occupied by Hemple.

Kira had been trained to be dispassionate, but she'd developed a special contempt for this particular mercenary. Hatred, even. Through her scope, she'd observed his daily cruelty to the mine workers, pushing them, shouting at them, *shooting* at them. For the pure pleasure of it.

Kira had known more than a few sadists in her life. Some of them had been her teachers. They had always aroused a deep fury in her. That's what she was feeling right now.

From her position in a thicket of raffia palms, Kira could see Hemple's burly silhouette inside the tent, backlit by a lamp. She pulled a small straight plastic tube from her pocket and placed a smooth pebble in her mouth. She took aim with the tiny blowgun and shot at a metal pail outside the tent.

The pebble struck with a loud *ping*.

No reaction.

Kira wet another pebble with her tongue. Another shot. Another direct hit. This time, she saw Hemple grab his rifle and head for the tent opening. He whipped the flap open, then recoiled as if hit by an invisible punch. He staggered backward.

Through her scope, Kira saw two red dots appear on Hemple's forehead. A long green snake, tied by its tail to the top of the tent post, was now squirming and twitching, its venom spent. The boomslang.

Kira watched Hemple drop to the ground, feet thrashing, hands clawed. She put away her scope and slipped back into the jungle. Based on her estimate of his weight and the potency of the neurotoxin, Kira figured Hemple had about three agonizing hours to live.

She smiled with bitter satisfaction.

Couldn't happen to a nicer guy.

CHAPTER 50

IT WAS MORNING, but barely. The sky was just turning from black to purple. I was bouncing in the passenger seat of a beat-up Land Rover with my right ankle chained to a metal bar running across the footwell. We were splashing through streams and weaving through stands of tall oaks and evergreens. Leo was at the wheel. Clearly, he knew the route.

"Where are we headed?" I asked. "Company picnic?"

"You've had enough rest," said Leo curtly. "Time for evaluation."

I thought again about killing him, but it still felt premature.

This was my first time outdoors since I got plucked off my sinking boat. I'd spent most of my time locked in a cell equipped with a universal and free weights.

My meals were delivered through a slot in the wall. It was top-notch fare, heavy on protein—chicken, salmon, venison. Every day, I worked out for hours on the gym equipment. I could feel my muscle mass returning.

I also had a lot of time to think. I spent most thinking about escaping. I knew it wouldn't be easy. I expected that Leo would be pretty solid on security.

And then, there was the money. Leo hadn't been lying about that. Every night, at exactly 10 p.m., somebody slid a wrapper through my slot containing a pile of hundred-dollar bills—ten grand in crisp American currency, neatly wrapped. I stacked it in the corner like building blocks. My little nest egg.

But for what?

Even if I could find my way out, where would I go? Back to Chicago, where a pack of assassins was probably waiting? No way. For all I knew, they'd bombed my apartment, too. I was probably homeless. Sure felt that way.

But that was nothing compared to how desperately I missed Kira. I had to believe she was alive; it was the only thing that kept me going. But I had no clue about where to start looking for her.

"Hold on," said Leo. I braced myself as we headed down a steep ravine. For a few seconds, we were almost vertical. We bounced over an outcropping of rocks. I thought we were about to tip over. Leo held the steering wheel with his left hand. His right hand—the gnarly one—rested on the shift lever.

We hit bottom, scraping the undercarriage, then started climbing up the other side. As soon as we were back on level ground, we cut through a stand of trees into a small clearing, about the size of a tennis court. It was covered in stubby grass, and the center was worn down like a playing field.

Leo cut the engine and reached over to unlock my leg.

"Get out," he said. "We're here."

He led the way to the center of the clearing and stood there with his arms folded. I looked around. Thanks to Kira's conditioning, my hearing and eyesight were almost superhuman. But all I could hear was wind, and all I could see were trees.

Then, suddenly, I sensed movement. Not just on one side.

On *every* side.

Five men emerged from the tree line all around me. Three white guys. One Black guy. One Polynesian guy. They were all bare-chested—and built.

I thought I was big.

They were all a lot bigger.

CHAPTER 51

I TURNED IN a slow circle, muscles tensed, adrenaline pumping. Was this some kind of initiation rite? Maybe Leo wanted to see how I handled myself when I was jumped by a gang of giants.

The five guys moved closer in a ring around me. Then—at the same time—they just stopped. Almost like robots.

"Weapons ready!" shouted Leo. He was a twig compared to the rest of us, but he had a definite command presence.

Weapons? What weapons?

I saw the other guys look toward their boots. That's when I realized there was a camouflaged sack in the grass in front of each of them. I looked down. There was a bag in front of me, too.

The other five guys reached down and jerked their bags open. Each one pulled out a different weapon, like a goodie from a prize bag. I saw a spear. A cleaver. A heavy chain. A broadaxe. A spiked cudgel. Medieval stuff, crude but deadly.

I bent down and opened the sack at my feet.

I froze for a second.

Inside was my jeweled cutlass, polished and gleaming. I stood up, gripping it tight in my right hand.

There was a quick laugh from behind me. I swung around.

The Black guy was chuckling, holding his chain in his fist. He jerked his chin toward me. "Who's this? Aladdin?"

The others started chuckling, too.

"Enough!" Leo called out. Everybody shut right up. He raised his right hand, then dropped it. *"Engage!"*

That's when the mayhem started.

I expected everybody to come for me. Instead, four of the guys turned on one another. One of the white guys had a crew cut and scars all over his torso. He had the spear. He thrust it at the Polynesian guy, who looked like The Rock, only more massive.

The Rock shouted and parried the spear with his axe. The two other white guys went at it with a cleaver and a cudgel. One had a droopy walrus mustache, the other had his long blond hair pulled tight into a ponytail. They were doing their best to slice and batter each other into submission.

I spun around to see the Black guy rushing at me,

swinging the chain over his head like a lasso. He let out an earsplitting yell and whipped the loose end toward my neck. I ducked and felt the wind as the chain whizzed over my shoulders.

The Rock and Crew Cut were now locked together, shoving each other with the wooden shafts of their weapons. They looked like two rutting bulls. Ponytail knocked Walrus down with a cudgel blow between the shoulder blades. Then he started in my direction, spinning his club like a cheerleader's baton. Out of the corner of my eye, I saw the Black guy with his chain, ready to take another swing at me.

I was now in full battle mode. My vision narrowed. My muscles pulsed. I could feel my face flushing and my blood pumping.

Ponytail swung at me with his cudgel. I whipped my blade down—hard. It sliced through the narrow end of the cudgel like it wasn't even there. The heavy part of the club went flying. Before he could even react, I planted a kick in his solar plexus, taking him down to the ground. He face-planted in the dirt, ponytail flopping.

I heard a rattle behind me. Spun around. Saw the chain whipping through the air in a blur. I did a shoulder roll underneath it and slammed the hilt of my cutlass against the Black guy's temple. He dropped to his knees, stunned and shuddering. With one flick of my wrist, I could have beheaded him. I'm not sure what stopped me.

The Rock comes at me next, holding his axe over his head. I swung my blade to drive him back, slicing the air just an inch from his belly. He dodged and charged me again, swinging the blunt end of his weapon at my head. I sidestepped him at the last second and gave him a hard kick just above his right knee. He howled in pain and dropped his axe.

Now it was just me and Crew Cut, the guy with the spear. He took his time, moving in slow circles, closer and closer. He gripped the shaft of the spear overhand. At any second, he could thrust it, or throw it. Compared to my blade, he definitely had the length advantage. He jabbed the point of the spear at me, pushing me toward the edge of the clearing.

My back hit the trunk of a tree.

Crew Cut bent his knees and lunged. At the last instant, I bent my body like a batter evading an inside pitch. The blade hit the pine trunk and sunk in. I whipped my cutlass down and sliced the spear shaft in half. Then I cut it in half again. Crew Cut lost his balance and fell backward. I was on him before he landed, my knee in his belly, my blade resting on the skin over his jugular. The edge was so sharp that just pressing it drew blood.

"Hold it!" Leo yelled.

I looked up.

The other four were gathering around, leaving what was left of their weapons on the ground. A couple guys were spitting blood, and The Rock was wincing in pain. He could barely stand.

I rolled to the side and let Crew Cut get up. He wiped the side of his neck with his fingers. They came away bloody. He grinned and held his hand out to me.

Apparently, I'd made the team.

CHAPTER 52

Democratic Republic of the Congo, 10 a.m.

CAPTAIN RUPERT GURNEY stood with a bullhorn at the top of the mine pit. A dozen of his men were gathered around him. It was the bulk of the unit. The men looked edgy and hollow-eyed. Not much sleep the past few nights.

The rest of his team were down in the pit with the workers.

The day after Hemple's body had been found, two more men were crushed by a deadfall on their way back from the latrine. The next morning, another man was found at the bottom of a pit not far from the compound, impaled on a wooden stake.

Word about the killings had spread to the mine workers, and most of them were terrified, especially the children. They called the killer *shetani*. Swahili for devil.

Now Gurney was out of patience. The gossip in the pit was starting to affect production, which affected profit.

And he was tired of losing men in the middle of the night. It had been a small unit to start with. Now he was actually shorthanded. And he wasn't about to risk losing more men in jungle searches.

Gurney put the bullhorn to his mouth and pressed the Talk button.

"You all know about the devil in the jungle." He spoke in his crisp British accent, knowing that the assorted English speakers among the workers would translate for the others. His men circulated through the workers, rifles ready. "We're tired of letting him run loose," Gurney continued. "Tired of seeing fine men die at his hands." He paused for a moment to let the translators catch up. "So I've decided that he will be caught, and killed—by *you*."

As the word spread through the pit, the soldiers worked their way through the crowd, pulling out the hardiest-looking males. A few of the men pushed back, but after a few pokes with a rifle barrel, they stopped resisting. Soon ten of them were being marched up the ramp toward the rim of the mine.

Gurney held up the bullhorn again as the rest of the workers stared up at him. Some of the wives and children were wailing. "Tonight, these men will hunt the killer— the *shetani*. If they fail, tomorrow, ten more will go. Then ten more. Until the devil is dead at my feet."

The ten men had reached the top of the mine, rifles at their backs. They were doing their best not to look terrified in front of their families.

"Are we giving them guns, boss?" asked one of the soldiers.

"Just knives and spears," said Gurney. "What they're used to."

He walked up and down the row of ten men, as if he were reviewing the troops. "First squad goes out tonight. And if we lose a few, no worries." He clapped the tallest worker on the shoulder. "Plenty more where they came from."

CHAPTER 53

ALL SIX OF us—the five giants and me—were inching through the forest in a staggered line. We were in head-to-toe camo. When we moved, we looked like blowing leaves. When we stood still, we were simply invisible.

Our exercises so far had been arduous, but basic. Long hikes with full packs. Hand-to-hand combat. Night recon.

For some reason, today felt different.

I was on the right wing of the formation. My only weapon was a hunting bow—a compound carbon model with string silencers. Apart from a toy I had as a kid, it was the first bow I'd ever held. For some reason, archery wasn't in Kira's curriculum. She was more about guns and knives. But I watched my teammates and picked up the basics in about two minutes. I realized that I now possessed an intuitive grasp of killing tools. My first practice shot was a bull's-eye.

Every time we were out in the field by ourselves, I had no doubt that Leo was watching us from somewhere. I assumed he had the whole forest wired. Or maybe he was somewhere nearby in camouflage himself.

I took three or four small steps at a time, with the outer edge of my feet touching first. Low impact, minimal sound. The five guys to my left probably weighed at least 280 pounds apiece, but they moved as softly as foxes through the leaves. Well-trained stalkers, all of them.

We held our bows ready, arrows notched, prepared to shoot at any moment. But we had no idea what was out here. It was a seek-and-destroy exercise, with no designated target.

I scanned the trees ahead, looking for movement or unnatural patterns. I listened for cracking twigs or shuffling brush.

Then something made me stop in my tracks.

I looked up and saw two startled sparrows fly off a sycamore branch.

Suddenly the air cracked with gunfire. The bark of the tree at my elbow was blasted into splinters. Live ammo! I saw the others hit the ground. Another volley kicked up leaves and black dirt right in front of them.

I jumped behind the bulk of a fallen tree as bullets zinged overhead. I crawled to the uprooted end and peeked around. Another blast blew the moss off the bark two inches from my face.

These weren't warning shots. Somebody was trying to kill us.

I rolled back to the cover of the log and took a breath. I'd seen all I needed to see. Smoke from a rifle barrel, about forty yards ahead and twenty feet up. The shooter was hidden in a tree stand.

I glanced to my left. My training partners had all taken cover in depressions or behind stumps. They blended in with the forest floor.

Another blast swept our position. A large branch dropped behind me, sliced off by automatic rounds.

Enough.

This was no game.

And I didn't come this far to die in the woods.

I stayed low behind the trunk and drew my bowstring. I made my mental calculations of distance and height. I glanced up into the leaves for wind direction. The rest happened in an instant. I rolled into a kneeling position and aimed. The smoke was just clearing from the last volley.

I sent the arrow.

A half second later, I saw a figure drop from the stand and jerk to a stop, dangling by one ankle. A rifle clattered against branches as it fell.

Then all I heard were birds.

I reached into my quiver and notched another shaft. I saw my teammates break from cover and start advancing.

I wondered who the hell I'd just killed. But did it really matter?

It was him or me.

CHAPTER 54

DINNER AT THE castle that night felt like a medieval bacchanal. After the shoot-out in the forest, a fleet of jeeps had appeared. Masked guards with tasers and pistols escorted us back to the castle. When we arrived in the great hall, the table was filled with platters of grilled steaks, bowls of fried potatoes, and pitchers of cold beer.

The guards disappeared. Leo was nowhere to be seen. But I had no doubt he could see us.

I was eager to find out more about my squadmates. They were the strong, silent type, and our cells were all in different parts of the bunker. So far, I'd only picked out last names. Thanks to my fancy cutlass, I was still "Aladdin" to everybody. After the second round of beers, I started asking questions.

After the third round, I started getting some answers.

Crew Cut's name was Blodgett. Turned out he was a former professional wrestler from Iowa. First name Neil. The guy with the walrus mustache was Jack Fenwick, a triathlete from Scotland. He had a brogue so thick I could barely decipher it.

The guy with the blond ponytail was Johnny Harper. He'd worked as a bouncer in Hamburg and a bodyguard in Iran. T.J. Tagaloa, The Rock's doppelgänger, was an Ironman competitor from Hawaii. Brooks Marley, the Black guy, was retired from Delta Force. He put the word *retired* in air quotes. We left it at that.

Blodgett pointed his fork at me. "What about you, Aladdin?"

"My name is Brandt," I said. "I'm a professor of anthropology."

Marley snorted. I could tell he thought I was a total bullshitter. I could only imagine how they'd react if I told them I was also known as Doc Savage.

The other guys were digging into the feast, but I didn't have much of an appetite. The thought of blood-rare steak wasn't sitting well.

"Who was the shooter in the woods?" I asked.

"Disposable," said Blodgett, his mouth full of meat.

"Meaning what?" I said.

Fenwick put down a stein of beer, leaving foam dripping from his mustache. "Disposable. Some loser who washed out of training, or maybe tried to escape. Leo keeps a few around for cannon fodder."

"Could happen to any of us," said Harper. "So stay sharp."

If Leo was building an army, I hadn't seen much evidence of it. For the whole time I'd been here, these five guys were my only comrades. Maybe he was keeping his forces separated. Maybe he had cells of operatives in different locations around the world. Or maybe the six of us were just the vanguard—the few, the proud, the huge.

"What are we doing here—really?" I asked. I was still wondering if Leo was delusional or deranged.

"We're getting ready to take back a third of a continent," Harper said.

"And get rich doing it," added Tagaloa.

At least we'd all been told the same story.

I looked up at the wall and took another hard look at the flag hanging there. Now it made sense. Black and red for Belgium. A yellow star for the Congo. Leo was serious. He was out to win back his family's long-lost colony. He thought he deserved to be a king. It ran in his tainted blood.

"I heard he already sent a squad to take over a copper mine near Lake Tanganyika," said Marley. "Skeleton force."

"Maybe they need more muscle," said Harper.

Fenwick licked the meat grease from his fingers. "What I need," he said, "is somebody nubile and willing!" He was slurring his words as he pushed away from the table. But everybody knew what he meant. He meant sex. The others grunted in agreement.

From what I'd seen, there were no women anywhere in the castle—or anywhere on the property, for that matter. Abstinence was apparently part of Leo's program. At least, abstinence from women.

"Look! I've spotted one!" Fenwick.

He staggered over to the wall and stared up at a life-sized painting of a female nude—a pale, well-rounded woman standing in a garden, with tendrils of her long red hair curled around her breasts. The artwork was old—maybe sixteenth century. And possibly priceless.

Fenwick grabbed the gilded frame with two hands and yanked the painting off the wall. Then he pressed his crotch against the figure of the woman and started humping it wildly.

"Better than nothing!" he shouted with a crazy grin. "What about you, Brandt? Got a honey stashed somewhere?" He kept thrusting his hips against the woman's painted privates.

I flashed on Kira's face. Her voice. Her body.

Something snapped.

"Knock it off!" I shouted.

Before I knew it, my fist was cocked and aimed at Fenwick's jaw. Just as I threw my punch, I felt Marley grab my arm from behind.

Fenwick backed away, hands up, leaving the abused nude leaning against the wall. "Sorry, laddie. Did I tweak a nerve?"

I twisted free and went for him again. Marley and Tagaloa both grabbed me and held me back.

A door burst open. Six masked guards stepped into the room, rifles raised.

Party over.

CHAPTER 55

ONE OF THE guards led me to my cell like a naughty schoolboy. No words. Just a few annoying prods with his rifle. After he slammed my door and locked it, I walked over to my pile of cash and started counting, just to be sure it was all still there. One hundred thousand dollars. Ten grand for every day I'd awakened at the castle.

Leo was right. It was a pretty strong incentive to hang around.

But not strong enough. Not for me. Not anymore. I had no intention of being turned into a killing machine for some crazed royal.

I sat down on my cot and yanked off the thin cotton sheet. I started a tear with my teeth and ripped a long strip down the whole length. Then I looked for the sturdiest object I could find. The weight rack. Welded steel, bolted to the cement floor.

My way out.

I tied one end of the sheet strip to the upper rail of the rack, then looped the other end around my neck. I leaned against the bottom of the rack until I was sure I had enough tension. Then I slid down and let gravity do its work. I felt my arteries pulsing. I saw sparks in the periphery of my vision.

I figured it wouldn't take too long.

It didn't.

Within a few seconds, I heard the bang of the door opening again. Two masked guards rushed in. One sliced the sheet with a knife as the other pulled me to my feet. They expected me to be dizzy and weak.

But I recovered fast.

I knocked out the first one with a chop to the neck. When the other one turned on me, I clocked him in the jaw. His head hit the weight rack on the way down. I grabbed flex cuffs from his belt and tied them both to the leg post. I grabbed one of their pistols and a ten-pound weight and headed out into the corridor. There, recessed into the wall, was a steel locker. It had the same number as my cell.

I gave the lock a solid whack with the weight. The door flew open.

Inside on a narrow metal shelf were my clothes—shirt, shoes, pants, socks, underwear—all clean and neatly folded in a fabric bag. There was only one other item. The cutlass. I grabbed it and stuck it through the belt of my fatigues. Then I ducked back into my cell and stuffed the money into the bag with my clothes.

I glanced at the two guards. Breathing, but still out. I locked the door after me and headed for the elevator. I expected to see more men waiting when it opened, but the car was empty. Leo ran a lean operation. Maybe the two guards were the only ones on duty in my wing.

I pressed the only button. The car started moving up. It opened on the ground floor of the castle, the same place I'd exited with Leo.

I looked around. No guards here, either. And no alarms blaring.

It looked like security wasn't as tight as I had thought.

I moved through the room with my back against the wall. I found a side door that faced the courtyard. It was locked from the inside. I threw the latch and pulled it open. I held my pistol in front of me in shooting stance, but all I saw were manicured trees and flower bushes. I tucked my bag under my arm and took off.

I didn't have a mental map of the whole property, just the routes for our training exercises. The forest was west, so I headed in that direction.

We'd always taken roads that led out from the back of the castle. I'd never seen the landscaping in front.

I felt like I was running through the grounds at Versailles.

Everywhere I looked, there were sculpted bushes and stone fountains and rolling lawns. I ducked behind a tall bush to change from my fatigues into my own clothes. I moved along a tall hedge that ran the length of a garden, then broke into a run across an open field. At the far end was a stone wall, about ten feet tall. When I got closer, I spotted some ridges and hollows in the stonework.

Totally climbable.

I tossed the money bag over the wall. Then I reached out to test a handhold about seven feet up.

Bam!

Something knocked me to my knees.

I grabbed my gut and looked around.

Nobody there.

I stood up, still shaky. I raised my foot toward the wall and touched a small ledge with the toe of my shoe. *Bam!* Another huge shock knocked me on my ass. It felt like it was radiating from inside my body! I yanked the sleeves of my shirt up and angled my right forearm to catch the moonlight.

Then I saw it—a tiny scar, hidden in the coral scrapes and other bruises.

I reached for the wall again. Got knocked down again. This time, it felt like my brain was about to explode.

I sat on the grass and pulled out the cutlass.

I put the tip of the blade on the edge of the scar and pushed. I grimaced and grunted as blood started to ooze out. I dug deeper. And then I got another shock—even stronger. I dropped to the ground again. Almost blacked out.

I grabbed the blade again. Blood was dripping down over my wrist. I knew what I had to do. Against every instinct, I poked the blade into the wound again. No shock this time. Just nerve-wrenching pain. I twisted the blade tip and there it was—a tiny metal chip. The equivalent of an electronic dog collar.

No need for guard towers or electric fencing. Leo's barriers were built in.

I pulled out the chip and placed it on a stone. Then I smashed it with the hilt of the cutlass. At that point, I had so much adrenaline shooting through me that I probably could have vaulted over the wall.

But I didn't. I climbed it.

In a few seconds, I was on the other side and running hard toward the woods. I looked back over my shoulder. Nobody coming. At least nobody that I could see. Pulling out the chip must have set off an alarm, right? Or had I just performed a surgery that Leo had never anticipated?

Was I really free?

Or was I disposable?

CHAPTER 56

Democratic Republic of the Congo, 1 a.m.

FOR THE FIFTH night in a row, Kira hid in the jungle canopy while a fresh set of terrified mine workers moved through the thick foliage below. They carried flaming torches, as if they were looking for a monster.

In an odd way, Kira felt validated. A monster was what she had become.

As the men started to move close to where she was hiding, she pulled a thin plastic packet from her pocket and wrapped her legs tight around a sturdy branch. She drew her arm back, then whipped the packet toward a tree trunk about twenty feet down. The packet splattered on the rough bark, leaving thick red juice dripping down. Like blood. The man closest to the tree jumped back in horror and started shouting to the others.

An hour earlier, Kira had watched these same men being pushed into the jungle at gunpoint, like the other teams before them. She had no intention of hurting them, but she didn't mind scaring them out of their skulls. She knew the fear would spread back to Gurney and his minions. And fear had a way of eroding everything—order, discipline, loyalty. It made people careless and weak. It took the fight out of them.

After the searchers passed beneath her, Kira grabbed a rope and rappelled down from her perch. She deliberately stopped ten feet from the ground and dropped the rest of the way, landing hard on a pile of sticks and leaves. Immediately, she heard more shouts from the searchers. The torches turned around and started moving in her direction.

The chase was on. Again.

Kira waited a few seconds before heading through the foliage along a narrow animal trail. Her heart was pounding. Her night vision was crisp. She felt alive and confident, totally in her element.

At school, Kira had been at the top of her class in concealment and evasion. By the time she was sixteen, she had practiced hundreds of getaways, on foot, in cars, on motorcycles, across all types of terrain, against some of the most skilled and deadly trackers in the world—her instructors.

Compared to those terrifying lessons, this was child's play.

Kira pushed branches aside and paced herself, never getting too far ahead of the pack. She wanted to keep it interesting—give the men at least some hope of actually bringing down the *shetani*.

Kira actually felt a deep sympathy for her pursuers. She knew that just one generation back, men like these would have been formidable hunters, capable of tracking prey through the jungle for days at a time. Now they hunted for rocks in a sweltering pit. They were brave and strong, but hardly a threat. She anticipated their every move.

Kira took a winding route, keeping the men clear of her deadly traps. If they got too close to her position, she paused to let out a loud screech that froze them for a few seconds, letting her gain a few more steps.

As she rounded another bend in the trail, Kira stopped short. It had rained hard the night before. The trail was now blocked by a huge wallow of mud. And mud would leave tracks. That would make things a little too easy.

Kira grabbed a vine at the base of an afrormosia tree and pulled herself up into the branches. She braced herself against the trunk and watched the torches weaving through the jungle toward her. She let the men close in again, then grabbed the vine to swing across the giant mud pit to another tree.

In her rush, she didn't pause to test the vine's strength. Rookie mistake.

At the high point of her swing, twenty feet up, the vine snapped with a sound like a pistol shot. The ground came up in a blur. Kira landed hard on her belly. It knocked the breath out of her, and she felt a sharp stabbing pain in her side. She bit her lip to stifle a groan. For a few seconds, it hurt too much to move.

Kira heard shouts. She rolled over and looked up. The torches were converging. She could see the light reflecting off the wet leaves near her head. The men must have heard the sound of her fall. They were headed right for her, just yards away. And she was practically in the open.

Kira flexed her limbs and wrists. No breaks. She ran her fingers down her side and winced as she touched a spot on her upper torso. Seventh rib, right side. Probably cracked.

She looked up. The torches were almost on top of her.

She shrugged off the pain and stumbled into the underbrush. As she looked back, she tripped over a fat surface root. A flash of torchlight hit her—just for a second, before she disappeared again.

She heard a shout from the man in the lead. *"Shaba!"*

Kira knew the word. She ran her fingers over her head. Damnit! Her camo cap was gone, knocked off in the fall. The man must have seen her hair.

Her curly, reddish-brown hair.

Shaba was a common word for her pursuers. It was Swahili for copper.

Kira realized that she now had a new name.

CHAPTER 57

The Arabian Sea, midnight

IN HIS TEAK-PANELED quarters one level below the *Prizrak*'s bridge, Cal Savage sat at a sleek communications console, monitoring reports and video feeds from operatives in hot spots around the world.

No word yet on the missing Doc Savage, but his entire network was on high alert. Everybody knew that the fugitive was a priority target, with a huge bonus for his capture—and a miserable death for anybody who let him escape again.

It was only a matter of time, the captain told himself. A man like Doc Savage would stand out anywhere.

With the annoying exception of his missing relative, Captain Savage's plans were proceeding briskly. His militias were gaining ground in Sudan. His former crew member Abai was straightening matters out in Somalia. Other operatives were at work in Burkina Faso, Nay Pyi

Taw, and other remote locales, fanning conflicts still too obscure to earn a breaking-news banner on CNN.

In bits and pieces, the world was coming apart. And soon the spoils would fall into his hands.

"Cal! *Enough!*"

Savage swiveled around in his high-backed chair. Lial was lying on her side in bed on the other side of the cabin, her head propped on one hand, her dark eyes flashing.

Beautiful and impatient. As always.

Savage shut down his monitors and stood up. Lial slid over to make room as he undressed. Naked except for his briefs, he slipped under the covers next to her, then grabbed a laptop from the nightstand.

Lial slid one leg slowly over Savage's thigh, but his focus stayed on the screen. "Just checking one more thing…"

Lial put her hand on the laptop lid. "Let it wait."

Savage nudged her away. "Hold on…"

He was scanning a report from a depot in Tanzania where he sometimes sourced his fuel. Scowling, Lial rested her chin on his shoulder and read along.

Kira was in a communications blackout, as they'd agreed before she left. Phone and radio signals were too easy to trace. But she'd promised Savage that he would know what she was up to.

"Trust me, you'll hear," she said before getting on the helicopter.

Sure enough. Texts and fragmentary reports were

shooting across the Congo basin about an avenging jungle demon—a she-devil the locals called Shaba. The demon was killing mercenaries near a copper mine. Ten men and counting.

Savage's mouth curled into a twisted little smile.

"I told you," he said, tapping the screen. "Kira Sunlight is a one-woman war."

Lial reached over and slammed the laptop cover down.

Cal stared at her. "Are you jealous?"

"Are *you*?" Lial responded. She moved her hand down his bare torso and under the sheet. Savage drew a quick breath. The laptop fell onto the floor with a loud clatter.

Lial slid her head off the pillow, then disappeared entirely beneath the satin sheets. A few seconds later, the captain was gasping—in a good way.

Delicious as this arrangement sometimes was for him, Savage understood that it was nothing but a minor distraction for Lial—a way to occupy her mind and body while she lobbied for her next mission. It was understandable that she preferred a captain's bed to a cramped crew berth. And after all, sleeping with the boss was far from the worst thing she had done in her life.

But they both knew that she would much rather be in the steaming jungle instead of Kira.

Or *with* her.

CHAPTER 58

INCREDIBLE. THE WATER was so clear, it seemed like I could see for miles. I was holding my breath, but it was effortless. I couldn't even count how many minutes I'd been under. I'd left my clothes on the beach and I could feel the water against every inch of my body, soothing me as I swam. Everything was peaceful, mystical, magical...

I felt a tug on my ankle. I backpedaled and turned around. Kira shot past me like a dolphin, bubbles streaming from her nose. Her copper-colored hair bobbed and straightened with each stroke. She'd left her clothes on the beach, too. From her outstretched fingers to the tips of her toes, her body was as pale as ivory and taut with muscle, except where it swelled into smooth, gentle curves. She moved with spirit and grace, and when she turned to face me, her smile almost bowled me over, even thirty feet underwater. I couldn't help myself. I took a deep breath.

That's what woke me up.

Shit. Dreaming again.

I rubbed my eyes. I could see from the angle of the sun coming through the slats in my shack that it was still early morning. But I was sweating already and sticking to the canvas on my cot.

I looked around. My battered plastic cooler was sitting about two feet away. I opened the lid and reached in. The ice had melted overnight and my last two bottles of Perrier were floating in a pool of tepid water. I grabbed one, twisted off the cap, and downed the whole liter while lying on my back.

I rolled off the cot and scratched the itchy growth on my face. Ten days now without a shave. I was starting to develop a caveman look. At least that's what I assumed. I hadn't seen a mirror in ten days, either.

I stood up and started my daily ritual. First, I reached into the thatched ceiling and felt for my money bag. Still there, bulging with bills. Then I walked two steps to the back wall and reached behind a rough panel of bamboo.

No!

My goddamn cutlass!

It was gone.

CHAPTER 59

I BANGED MY head on the top of the shack opening as I ran out onto the beach. I looked up and down.

There!

About twenty yards away, a guy was using the cutlass to whack melons in half on a wooden beam, one after the other. He was the size of a mountain, totally bald and glistening with sweat. He was a newcomer. Arrived yesterday. He didn't speak any English, but I'd seen him admiring my weapon. And he was obviously crafty enough to watch where I hid it.

I pounded my way across the sand and grabbed the hilt of the cutlass just as he was about to take another swing.

"Mine!" I shouted, slapping my chest to emphasize the point.

The mountain was in no mood for an argument. He just shrugged. Then he tossed the sliced melons into a basket, put the basket under his arm, and headed back up the beach.

I walked down to the water and washed the melon juice and seeds off the blade. Across the gulf, about two miles away, the city of Dubai was glistening in the sun. Lots of glass and steel, with the highest tower stabbing into the sky like a dagger.

Getting here had not been easy. Or cheap.

My getaway through Europe and across the Black Sea had cost me nearly ten of my hundred grand. No public transportation or rental cars. Too visible. Not that I could have produced ID anyway. My wallet was somewhere in the bottom of a bay on Long Island.

Wads of cash. That's what it took. Truckers, cargo ships, and bush pilots had gotten me this far—almost four thousand miles from Belgium.

I hoped that Leo would be too busy building his army to waste his time chasing down one crazy deserter. But to be safe, I managed to find the one place where a guy my size would fit right in.

There were only about twenty other people on the island. All men. And every single one was a world-class bodybuilder.

The island was a man-made oval of sand, about five acres total. It was one of a few hundred artificial islands a group of rich Arabs dredged up twenty years ago to make a pattern in the shape of the world. Ambitious idea, but I guess the project bombed. Most of the tiny islands were still unoccupied and undeveloped, like a bunch of white scabs in the gulf.

About a year ago, a bunch of bodybuilders decided to squat on this one as a place to work out and prep for Middle East competitions.

Who was going to argue with them?

It was all pretty primitive. Flat sand, barely above water level, with a long row of tiny shacks like mine—maybe fifty square feet each, just about enough room for a cot and a cooler. Along the beach, there were a few chinning bars, a bunch of barbells and benches, and a few tons worth of random weights.

A supply boat showed up every morning with fresh fruit, meat, protein powder, and water. *Lots* of water. The temperature pushed a hundred degrees most days, and except for our sleeping shacks, we had zero shade. There were a couple of porta-potties on one side of the island and a firepit on the other.

And that was it.

All day long, I watched muscle-bound hunks spotting one another on lifts and practicing their poses in the sand. I figured I just looked like one of the weaker contestants. Six-four and in good shape, but not nearly shredded enough for competition. Fortunately, this was the kind of place where nobody asked too many questions. Perfect for me.

For now.

As I wiped the blade dry on my pants, I heard pounding

feet in the sand. I whipped around. About a dozen body-builders sped by, all oiled up and out for their morning run, like some ancient tribe.

In some ways, this place was an anthropologist's dream, ripe for study. Isolated population. Distinct traditions and rituals. Clear hierarchy.

But I didn't feel like an anthropologist anymore. I'm not sure what I was. Adventurer? Soldier of fortune? Science experiment? Escaped convict? I realized that I probably had more in common with my ancestor than with the man I was a year and a half ago.

If anybody saw a Facebook photo of me the way I looked right now, they'd see Doc Savage, Man of Bronze—not Brandt Savage, PhD.

There was only one person in the world who really knew the difference. I looked out over the bluish-green water. She was out there somewhere. She *had* to be.

And I was going to find her. No matter what it took.

CHAPTER 60

FOURTEEN HOURS LATER, I was sitting by a bonfire on the beach. Our nightly routine. Twenty massive bodybuilders—and me.

The temperature had dipped to a tolerable eighty-three degrees. Some of the guys held sticks wrapped with raw meat over the flames, like overgrown Boy Scouts. Here and there, beers were popped. I was on my third.

Off to one side, two guys were belly-down on the sand, arm wrestling. The accents around the fire were from every corner of the world. Most of the conversations were about circuits and definition and isolation, the kind of stuff bodybuilders tend to get excited about. Not me. I mostly just listened.

I saw a flicker of light across the water and heard the churn of an engine.

I sipped my Heineken and watched as a large cabin boat approached, making the crossing from the city.

Right on schedule. There was an onshore breeze, and I could already smell the perfume.

The guys who were eating wolfed down the last of their food. A small group walked down to the beach to meet the boat. The others just stood around, wiping sand off their abs and asses.

The operator drove the boat right onto the sand as he cut the engine. A few of the guys grabbed the prow and tugged it a few feet further up. Now I could hear high-pitched voices and light laughter from inside the cabin.

The cabin door opened, and they appeared. Young women. About fifteen of them. The operator lowered a wooden ramp and the women paraded their way down onto the sand. Some wore miniskirts with halter tops. Some wore clingy dresses. One wore a pink bikini under a sheer, flowing caftan. They were all barefoot and beautiful.

It was the same show every night. Most of the ladies were regulars, but there were always a few new faces, and bodies—some voluptuous, some stick-thin, some athletic. Most of the women were Middle Eastern. A few were Asian. One or two looked European. It was a virtual United Nations of escorts.

I watched the women and the bodybuilders mingling by the boat and pairing off. Some guys pulled their dates toward the bonfire. Others got right down to business, leading them up the dark beach toward the row of sleep shacks. Two couples stripped off their clothes in the surf and waded into the warm water. Lots of splashing and squealing and laughing.

I could see a few of the newcomers giving me the once-over, but the regulars knew to leave me alone. One Asian girl whispered to another as she gestured to me with her thumb. I just smiled. My hearing was excellent. So was my Mandarin. She'd called me a "lump on a log."

The boat operator was sitting on the prow of the boat, his bare brown legs dangling off. Same guy every night. Procurer, pimp, or maybe just transporter. He had a cigarette clamped between his lips. One of the guys handed him a beer. He popped it with one hand and guzzled it in one gulp, foam dripping down his chin. Then he tossed the empty onto the beach and took another puff on his cigarette.

By now, the bonfire was burning down from neglect. Nobody but me left to feed it. I poked a few ashy logs with a stick and watched the sparks rise.

Over the crackle of the fire, I heard a creak from the boat. I looked over as the cabin door opened again. A straggler stepped out, shadowed by the cabin roof. She'd probably nodded off on the way over.

The woman had her back to me as she pulled a tunic off over her head. Underneath she was wearing cutoff shorts and a tank top. For a second, she was illuminated by the fire.

She was tall. Her skin was pale.

And her hair glowed like copper.

CHAPTER 61

I DROPPED MY beer and sprinted toward the boat. My heart was pounding so hard I'd swear I could hear it. I definitely felt it.

"Kira?"

She ducked around the cabin to the port side of the boat, out of sight. I grabbed the gunwale and vaulted myself onto the deck. I ran around the front of the cabin and nearly slipped on the polished wood.

As I turned the corner, I saw one of the bodybuilders lifting the woman off the deck and onto the sand. I took two steps and then a long leap off the side of the boat, landing right behind her. I grabbed her by the arm and pulled her around to face me. Her eyes opened wide and her mouth formed a tight little *o*.

Stunning.

But not Kira.

The bodybuilder planted his hand on my chest and

shoved me back against the hull. I ignored him and looked the young woman in the eyes. "I'm sorry." I pointed to her head. "Your hair. The color. It reminded me of someone." No idea if she could understand me.

The girl's face brightened. "Shaba!" she said, fluffing her spectacular curls.

I shook my head. "No. Not Shaba."

The bodybuilder slid his arm around the girl's waist and started to pull her away.

"Wait!" I said. "Shaba? Is that your name?"

"No," she said with a laugh. "It's Sheila." British accent. Sounded like Kate Winslet.

I looked at the bodybuilder. We'd spoken a few times. A Russian. Broken English. Not a bad guy.

"Give me two minutes with her," I said. "And I'll pay for your whole night."

"Two minutes?" the Russian said. "Can I watch?"

"Be my guest," I said. "All we're going to do is talk."

The Russian and the woman looked at each other. Then she looked at me.

"Right then," she said. "Start talking."

We didn't waste any time. Sheila covered her life story in about twenty seconds. She was born in Amsterdam. Went to boarding school in London. She had just moved to Dubai from Tanzania, where her father ran an import business.

"All the salons there are doing this shade," she said, tugging on one of her curls. "It's because of the girl in the Congo. The one with the copper hair. She's a bloody legend."

"Why? For what?" I asked.

"She kills people," said Sheila, eyes wide. She leaned forward and whispered, "But only people who really deserve it."

"Like vigilante?" the Russian asked.

"Shut up," I said. I grabbed Sheila's arm. "Where did you hear this?"

She waved her hand over her head. "It's in the air down there. Everybody knows."

I took Sheila by the shoulders and planted a kiss on her forehead. Then I pointed at the Russian. "Wait here."

I ran up the beach to my shack. I rummaged through the wall and the ceiling and pulled out my cutlass and my money bag. I ran back down to the boat as fast as I could.

"How much is he paying you?" I asked Sheila. "For tonight."

Sheila bit her lip. "For him, five hundred, US." She looked a little embarrassed. "I charge more in the city."

I reached into my bag and pulled out two thousand in cash. I handed a thousand to the Russian, and another grand to Sheila. "Enjoy your night," I said.

The boat operator was still sitting on the prow of the boat, puffing on a fresh cigarette. I noticed that he'd turned around to face us. Probably heard the whole conversation. Not sure if he understood it.

I climbed back onto the deck and walked straight up to him. "You speak English?"

"I speak money," he said. Guttural Moroccan accent.

"Good," I said. "Then we can communicate."

I pulled out a stack of bills and waved it in his face.

"I'm officially hiring this boat, with you as captain. We're heading south." I jumped off onto the sand and single-handedly pushed the boat back into the surf. "And we're leaving now!"

CHAPTER 62

Democratic Republic of the Congo, 6 a.m.

KIRA WOKE UP sore and miserable in the crook of a sapele tree. She was about forty feet off the ground. Her sling hammock had sagged during the night and her butt was bumping on the branch below.

She slowly eased herself out of her sleeping position, taking care not to knock her bruised rib. All around her, touracos and parrots were chirping and cawing. Looking down, she saw a sleek green lizard making its way across the clearing, tongue flicking, taking its sweet time.

Things were slow in the jungle. And Kira was getting frustrated.

Not a single mercenary had ventured out of the compound at night in the past week. The unit's grimy bar had been shut down. At the end of the day, the men walked straight from guard duty at the mine back to their tents. They traveled in squads of four, diamond formation, rifles ready. They'd even found a few of Kira's more obvious traps and disarmed them.

Even the searches seemed to be losing steam. Every few nights, the miners were sent out again with their torches. But Kira made sure they never saw her. She wasn't about to make that mistake again. She just watched silently from above, like some nocturnal goddess.

Shaba the Silent.

Kira poured a palmful of water from a small pouch and splashed it on her face, rinsing off the salty night sweat. She put the pouch to her lips and took a small sip. As she tucked the pouch away, she heard rumbling in the distance.

She whipped her head around to face the direction of the noise.

Heavy machinery. Falling branches.

Kira pulled out her spotting scope and looked toward the mine. At first, all she could see were waving treetops. Then, through the foliage and rising mist, she saw a line of massive bulldozers. They were moving through the jungle, toppling and crushing everything in their way.

For a second, she thought they might be clearing ground for an expansion of the mine. But they were moving in the wrong direction for that. They were headed straight into the jungle. Straight toward her.

Of course. They were getting smarter now—expanding their perimeter to deny her cover.

As the lead bulldozer crashed through another stand of

trees, Kira could see Gurney himself leaning outside the cab, like he was leading a calvary charge. She focused her scope on the battered path behind his machine.

Shit. He had reinforcements.

A fresh squad of mercenaries was following the bull-dozers on foot. The newcomers were hard to miss. They were all huge, and loaded with equipment. Three white guys. One Black guy. And one guy who could pass for The Rock.

Kira climbed higher into the cover of the leaves and held perfectly still. The machines were getting closer. She could feel the vibration of their treads through the trunk. She looked around for another tree to jump to, but she knew she couldn't make a move right now without being spotted—and probably shot.

She heard Gurney shout from below, "Stop! That's far enough!"

The bulldozers halted in their tracks. The idling engines sounded like menacing growls.

Kira saw the new men—the five giants—walk out in front of the bulldozers. Now she could see that they were wearing tanks on their backs and holding long steel tubes.

Flamethrowers!

"Light it up!" Gurney shouted at the top of his lungs.

The giants pressed their triggers in unison. Bright yellow flames shot out of the ends of the tubes, cre-ating a sheet of fire about twenty yards wide. Even the wet underbrush was no match for the blast. In seconds, the jungle was on fire. The men advanced, apparently unfazed by the heat and the blazing foliage around them. They fired another blast, longer than the first.

Flames were now climbing the base of Kira's tree. She could smell the fuel and the smoke and the singed bark below her. And she could feel the heat rising.

The back of Kira's throat started to burn. She gritted her teeth and stifled a cough. She wrapped up her gear and slung her small pack over her shoulder. The smoke was thicker now, acrid and stinging. Kira doused a headband with water and wrapped it around her mouth. Her eyes stung from the fumes and her vision blurred.

She held her breath. Waited for the smoke to envelop her. Felt for the rope she had planned to use to rappel down. Now it was her fire escape. She grabbed with both hands and pushed off with her feet, swinging from the flaming tree to one fifteen feet away. As she grabbed a new branch with her legs, she felt a stab of pain from her rib. She winced through it and held on.

She was invisible now. A thick haze of smoke hid her from the ground below. When the flamethrowers sputtered out, she could hear the crackle of flames and the sap popping in trees. The leaves and fronds around her waved in crazy patterns as the fire created its own wind.

Kira's rope was useless now, one end still tied to the branch of the burning tree. So she made the next move with her arms alone, swinging back and forth like a pendulum on a branch until her momentum was enough to propel her to another foothold. Then another. And another. Until she was a few yards ahead of the blaze. When she looked back, she could see the jungle being turned into a wasteland.

Her lungs burned. Her side throbbed. Her head ached. She was in a situation that was all too familiar to her.

On the run.

As she gathered her strength for another swing through the canopy, she heard Gurney's voice again, this time crackling through a megaphone.

"Try hiding now, you copper-topped bitch!"

CHAPTER 63

"WE HERE, BOSS! We here!"

The pilot was shaking me by the shoulders to wake me up. His breath alone would have done the job. I was curled up in the hold of a twin-prop cargo plane with a loaded AR-15 by my side and an extra clip in my pocket. Apparently, I'd slept right through the landing.

The cargo! I sat straight up to make sure it hadn't escaped. Strapped against the wall were six huge wooden crates of live, bootlegged boa constrictors. From what I could see through the slats, they had all survived the trip, too. I checked my bag for my cutlass. Still there. So was my money. Just less of it.

For five grand, the captain and his party boat got me from Dubai to the southern border of Oman. From there, I hitched a ride on the cargo flight across the Gulf of Aden and over the Horn of Africa. The pilot was from Kenya. He looked about fifteen. But the trip was free, on the condition that I provide security when we landed. Gun and ammo provided.

The flight was supposed to take seven hours, including two refueling stops. I was asleep the whole time.

As I stood up and checked my rifle, the pilot shoved the cargo hatch open and dropped the ramp. It was hot inside the plane, and even hotter outside. The sun was blazingly bright.

We had landed at Nyanza-Lac Airport on the western edge of Burundi. The airport had been closed for years, but that didn't seem to matter to the pilot—or to the four men sitting in a jeep on the tarmac.

"Who are they?" I asked the pilot.

"They waiting for us" was his answer.

Our greeters were a careless bunch, smoking cigarettes within ten feet of our fuel tank. Their boots were propped against the open sides of the vehicle, and they were loaded with weapons. A gun rack across the back of the jeep held two double-barreled shotguns. Each man had a holstered .45 on his hip and an MP5 submachine gun in his lap.

Apparently, snake trafficking was a dangerous business.

As the pilot started to unfasten the cargo restraints in the hold, I stepped onto the top of the ramp with my rifle cradled in my arms. I threw my shoulders back to look as imposing as possible, but I gave the guys a little nod to indicate I didn't want any trouble. They grinned back.

Good sign. Let's get this over with.

From the doorway of the hold, I could see the eastern shore of the lake about three hundred yards away.

Lake Tanganyika.

One step closer to the Congo, and one step closer to finding Kira—the vengeful Shaba.

If it's really her.

Please, God—let it be her.

CHAPTER 64

I MOVED TO one side as the pilot wrestled the first crate of snakes across the hold and onto the top of the ramp. He was stronger than he looked. The guys in the jeep hopped out and caught the crate as it slid down. They were muttering to one another in a language I couldn't pick out. Maybe Kirundi.

They grabbed the crate by the sides and slid it flat onto the tarmac. One of the guys leaned into the jeep and pulled out a thin metal pole with a hooked end. Another guy grabbed a power screwdriver and unfastened the wooden frame of the crate in front.

"What happens now?" I asked.

"We watch," said the pilot. "We hope."

The guy with the pole stood in front of the open crate and reached in, keeping his feet in a wide stance. The pilot was standing beside me in the doorway. He was practically vibrating with nervous energy.

The guy with the pole had hooked a boa behind its head. He leaned back and dragged it out of the crate. The snake was not cooperating. It kept slipping the hook and coiling back inside. The guy shouted a few words. Two of his buddies hurried over. They bent down and dragged the snake out with their bare hands.

The thing was massive. Thick body, muddy brown with black bands. It must have weighed sixty pounds.

The guy with the hook kept shouting orders. The two men stretched the snake out on the tarmac until it was full length—nine feet at least. A monster. I figured the next thing to appear would be a measuring tape. They probably paid by the inch.

Instead, the fourth guy walked from the jeep with a survival knife. He knelt down and rolled the snake's midsection until it was belly up. Then he jammed the knife into the snake's gut, right up to the hilt.

The snake twisted and coiled into itself. One guy held the head while the other two pulled on the tail, stretching it out again. The guy with the knife went back at it, making the opening a little bit wider. He reached inside with his fingers and pulled out a long plastic packet filled with white powder. Then another. And another.

Jesus. No wonder they needed security.

The boa was thrashing and twisting on the hot tarmac. The guy with the hook pulled out his .45 and blew its head off.

"Maybe that would have been a better place to start,"

I muttered to the pilot. He didn't answer. He was still trembling.

Right. None of my business.

The guy with the hook looked up at us. One of the others carried a packet to the jeep. He sliced it open with a penknife and placed a fingernail's worth of powder on the hood. He took a small glass vial from his pocket, unscrewed the top, and dribbled a single drop onto the powder.

The other three men crowded around him like they were watching a science experiment. The pilot tensed up. I saw him suck in a deep breath and hold it.

After a few seconds, one of the men looked up at the pilot and gave him a jaunty thumbs-up. The pilot started breathing again. His whole body relaxed. He nodded back, and gave a weak little wave.

I looked back into the hold. Christ. Five more crates. The sweat was dripping off my forehead and soaking through my shirt. It was going to be a long morning. Especially for the snakes. The pilot moved back and started unfastening the second crate.

Suddenly a series of cracks echoed across the runway. On reflex, I ducked back from the doorway. When I looked out again, three of the smugglers were lying on the tarmac. One was sprawled across the hood of the jeep. Blood was pooling underneath the bodies.

I heard engines revving in the distance. Two more jeeps appeared from around the back of a closed hanger about a hundred yards away. Each jeep carried two men. Face masks. Guns. No uniforms. Not good.

The pilot crawled up beside me and looked out. I tried to push him back into the plane, but he squirmed away and jumped down onto the runway. He ducked behind the parked jeep for a second, then took off in a sprint in the opposite direction, his skinny legs and arms pumping like crazy.

Another crack. A bullet punched him square in the back and exploded through his chest. In like a dime, out like a cash register. He flopped forward, dead before he hit the ground.

The jeeps were driving in wild, weaving patterns as they headed toward the plane. I took aim and emptied my first clip. I hit the lead jeep. The right headlight shattered and a rear tire blew. The jeep spun out. But the other one kept coming.

I pulled out the empty clip and jammed in my second. I knew that if I didn't get moving, I'd die right there in the plane. I reached back and grabbed the sack with my money and my cutlass. I hopped down and sprayed fire single-handed while I sidestepped toward the smugglers' jeep. With my free hand, I dragged the dead smuggler off the hood and let him flop onto the ground next to his buddies.

The jeep was still running. I jumped over the side door and slid into the driver seat.

I tossed my rifle into the footwell and floored the

pedal. For a few seconds, I was heading straight for the other jeep, like a game of chicken. The driver swerved. I cranked my wheel, made a tight ninety-degree turn, and headed for the lake.

I kept my head down as rounds whizzed past me. My right-side mirror blew off. I checked my rearview. The guys from the disabled jeep were running toward the dead snake. The other jeep was still on my tail. Both men had dropped their masks now. I could see them smiling.

Sick, twisted smiles.

Goddamnit! Kira was right.

These assholes were everywhere.

CHAPTER 65

I'D ALREADY SHOT through both ammo clips. So I just kept my hands on the wheel and jerked the jeep from side to side as I accelerated. The runway had so many potholes that the shooter behind me kept missing. But not by much. Bullets were pinging off the fenders and roll bar. Clearly, these guys weren't here to arrest me for murder. They didn't even want to question me about it.

They wanted me dead.

I bounced off the edge of the tarmac and made a hard turn onto a service road. To the right and left were rows of corrugated metal storage buildings, some with wide-open fronts. Abandoned and empty. I turned left along another row. I looked back. The road was clear.

I cranked the wheel hard and spun into one of the open buildings. I pulled into a corner shadowed by a wooden loft. I cut the engine. Five seconds later, the jeep blew past in a blur.

I waited a few minutes until I heard the sound of the jeep's engine fading. Then it changed direction—back toward the airport. Maybe they were going back to reload. Or maybe the drug-packed snakes were worth more than I was.

I climbed out of the jeep. The storage building had a back exit, a metal fire door that was almost completely rusted shut. I gave it one solid bang with my shoulder and the hinges gave way. I looked back. The rifle was worthless without ammo. And I couldn't imagine I'd find a source for AR-15 clips anywhere close. So I just grabbed my cloth sack and moved out.

The sun was getting low, casting long shadows. I slipped from one slice of shade to the next as I moved down a slope toward the lake. There was a line of shacks and rickety piers by the shore, with nets and buoys piled up alongside. Out in the water in front of me, I could see wooden fishing boats. Dozens of them. Empty. Just sitting there.

I tied my sack around my belt and waded in. There was a quick drop-off from the shoreline. I ducked down and started swimming underwater.

I swam past the keels overhead until I got close to the last one—the furthest boat out. I surfaced slowly, took a deep breath, and started breaststroking the rest of the way.

The boat was about twelve feet long, with a Yamaha outboard mounted on the stern. The hull was in good shape, but riding a little low in the water. I reached up and put both hands over the gunwale, then pulled myself up until my head and shoulders were over the side.

Somebody screamed.

A teenage girl was looking straight at me. She was on her back, legs up, a thick blanket underneath her. A teenage boy was on top of her, his back to me, his hips draped with a towel. The girl grabbed the towel and covered her breasts. The boy whipped around, bare-ass naked. The kids both had light brown skin and beaded dreadlocks. They were very thin and very young.

I motioned for them both to be quiet. They both stared at me with wide eyes. I untied my sack from my belt and pulled out a wad of soggy bills. I tapped the side of the boat. I waved the money. Primitive charades.

The boy blinked once, then looked down at his girl-friend. "Alice," he said with a smooth French accent. "I believe this man wants to buy your father's boat."

CHAPTER 66

Lake Kivu, Rwanda, 1 a.m.

THE MAIN FLOOR of Club Riva looked out on the water—moonlit and beautiful, surrounded by dark green hills. Lial checked the time on her cell as she angled her way through the crowd toward the rear patio.

The music was Berlin techno, and it was incredibly loud. Lial could feel the bass in her bones. It felt good to breathe some outside air, even if it was thick with humidity. She'd only been in the club for thirty minutes, but already her clothes were sticky and saturated with cigarette smoke.

She looked up. Joseph Kabera's small floatplane appeared over the trees in the distance, circled the lake once, then made a slow approach from the west. Lial watched as the plane glided to a feather-soft landing on the water.

The red pontoons churned up white streams of foam until the aircraft came to rest about twenty-five yards from shore. A small dinghy set out from the club's dock. The pilot-side door opened. Lial saw a tall Black man step out onto the pontoon.

It was him. Rwanda's infamous minister of interior security.

Lial knew that Kabera traveled with two bodyguards, but always flew the plane himself. Sure enough, two muscular-looking men clambered out of the rear door. The dinghy swung alongside. The bodyguards steadied it while Kabera stepped in. He wiped a small splash of water off his shoe.

Lial slipped back inside to the crowded bar and caught the bartender's eye. He brought over a bottle of top-shelf vodka and poured her a shot. She downed it, exhaled slowly, then tapped the bar top. Another shot. She slammed the glass down and whipped around, heading for the center of the room.

The dance floor was small for the size of the club, and it was already packed. Lights twinkled in overhead netting and glitter fluttered from the ceiling. Huge Turbosound speakers pumped the music straight down, mainlining it toward the dancers. Lial wore flesh-toned earplugs. Even so, the sound was nearly overpowering. Her estimate: 110 decibels. About the same as a jackhammer.

Lial pushed her dark hair up with her hands and let it fall in a loose tumble over her bare, brown shoulders. She reached down and teased the hem of her very short skirt a few millimeters higher. Then she started moving.

Sometimes it was fun to let go—or pretend to. It was one part she actually enjoyed playing.

In seconds, she was surrounded by other dancers. Striking men. Stunning women. Striking men dressed like stunning women. Black, white, Asian, and every mix in between. It was that kind of club. Lial was careful not to play favorites. She danced with anybody and everybody who moved into her orbit, arms pumping, hips swinging, hair flying. At this rate, she would burn off the booze in an hour.

Plenty of time.

She glanced toward the patio as Kabera slipped in through a rear door with his bodyguards flanking him. Kabera was just thirty-one, and his guards looked barely twenty. The minister was a good-looking man and, by reputation, a real lady-killer. Also, *literally* a killer, with hundreds of extrajudicial murders to his name—men, women, children. Entire families. Sometimes entire villages. All of this Lial knew in detail. She'd studied the reports. She'd seen the photos.

Cal Savage wanted Kabera removed in order to make room for one of his own operatives. It's not that Kabera was too cruel, Savage told Lial. It's just that he was too independent. Savage needed somebody totally loyal to him. A fresh start. It was all part of his methodical chess game.

Lial spun herself toward the edge of the dance floor. She didn't try to catch Kabera's eye. No need. Let him come to her.

CHAPTER 67

Democratic Republic of the Congo, 1 a.m.

IT WAS RAINING hard in the jungle. A pelting tropical downpour. Kira was running as fast as she could through the dripping foliage. Wet leaves and branches slapped against her face and arms with every step. She was now a half mile past the line of fire-charred trees. But it wasn't far enough.

She was running for her life.

Her new pursuers were impossible to shake, even when she could see them coming. And they were easy to see. All five of them. They were the huge men she spotted the day before with Gurney. The ones with the flamethrowers.

This posse was clearly a lot more motivated than the miners. And they were much better trackers. Kira knew good training when she saw it, and these five were pros.

No flaming torches for them. They carried powerful tactical flashlights that cut sharply through the night.

Kira was constantly ducking and diving to avoid being caught in the beams.

She dodged down an animal trail with wild, unpredictable turns. She slipped on a patch of wet moss, fell on her ass, scrambled back to her feet. Her side still hurt with every twist, but there was no time to favor it. She had to plunge on, faster and faster.

She looked for a tree to climb, but the bark was too slick. She only got a few feet off the ground before sliding back down, wasting precious seconds as the five giants closed in.

She turned down another trail—deeper and darker and narrower, with more overhanging branches. Dangerous. There were leopards out here. Kira had heard their sawing roars. And she knew hungry cats would hunt even in the rain.

The sound of the downpour now mixed with another kind of rush. Louder. Off to her left. Running water! Kira burst out of the bush and skidded to a stop on a small mound of mud overlooking a tumbling, foaming river— about thirty feet wide, and moving fast.

She looked back. The flashlight beams were cutting through the foliage behind her, only about twenty yards downstream. She looked at the swollen river. Insane.

She had no choice.

She tightened the strap of her backpack and jumped. She hit the water feetfirst and plunged deep. Deeper than she expected. She saw a dark shape just before it whacked her in the temple. A thick branch, propelled by the current. It dazed her for a second. She scrambled deeper, where the current was slower. She hung there for a moment as silt and debris washed past her. Her eyes began to sting. She flexed her legs and launched herself toward the opposite shore.

Suddenly, another shape was coming toward her, at eye level. Bigger than the branch, and moving in an undulating pattern. Kira squinted through the murk. Her gut tightened.

A river croc!

She had only a second to pull her knife. She wrapped her fingers tight around the grip and pinpointed a spot just behind the reptile's eyes. The thing was almost on her. She could see the bottom teeth protruding over the upper jaw. She raised her knife. She heard a dull pop. The croc's head exploded. The huge body convulsed, then started to tumble with the current, trailing a crimson cloud.

Kira pushed herself toward the surface. She was back close to shore. Lights bounced off the water. She felt a sudden, stinging pain in her scalp. She was being pulled out of the river by her hair.

Her knife was kicked out of her hand. She landed hard on the muddy bank. She grabbed her side in pain as flashlight beams lit her up from head to toe.

Kira shielded her eyes with one hand and looked up. Five massive shapes loomed over her.

The Black guy leaned down out of the glare, so close that she could see his bloodshot eyes and flaring nostrils. He had a shotgun in his hands. It was still smoking.

"Hi there, Goldilocks," he said. "You can thank me later."

CHAPTER 68

MINISTER KABERA WAS sitting at one end of the bar with two women fawning over him. The one with thick blond bangs and a bare midriff had her hand on his shoulder. A petite Asian woman with rough-cropped black hair was tracing patterns on his thigh. He had his arm around the Asian woman's waist, his fingers splayed down over her hip. His bodyguards sat one stool away on either side of him, drinking soda water. Or so they thought.

The second time Lial danced into Kabera's line of sight, he slipped off his stool and made a beeline for her. His bodyguards started to follow, but they were both logy and slow. Kabera waved them back anyway, shooing them like flies.

When he got within a few feet of the dance floor, Lial turned her back on him and plunged back into the crowd, pretending to ignore him. She knew this would only stir the chase response. Men were so damn easy. They could be trained like circus animals. Lial shook her shoulders and allowed Kabera to catch up to her.

It was time to move things along.

Lial had been setting honeytraps since she was sixteen. She considered them cheap and unsavory. But tonight's scam served two purposes. Cal Savage's. And hers.

Right on cue, she felt Kabera's sweaty hand on her shoulder. She turned toward him without breaking her rhythm. He smiled and started to move in sync with her. She smiled back. Not full wattage. Not yet.

Let him earn it.

Kabera wasn't a bad dancer, just a little stiff on the transitions and restricted by his slim-fitting suit. Lial dumbed down her moves slightly to match his. In the crush and heat of the crowd, perspiration glistened on his face and darkened the blue collar of his shirt.

Lial let him get close. Very close. She felt his hands on her waist, his hips bumping hers. He leaned in toward her ear. "Come outside with me!" he shouted. It was the only way to be heard.

"Why?" Lial shouted back, tilting her chin up toward him.

"I want some time with you!"

This time she brushed her damp hair off her cheek and gave him the full treatment. She dipped her eyes, then raised them again. She flashed her perfect teeth in a shy smile. She gave him a little nod and mouthed, "Okay. You win."

Lial could read his reaction. She'd seen it a hundred times.

The minister of internal security thought he'd sunk the hook.

But it was the other way around.

CHAPTER 69

AS KABERA LED Lial out toward the balcony, the two bodyguards started to rouse themselves. Kabera gave them a subtle shake of his head.

The men settled back heavily on their stools as the blond woman and the Asian woman turned their full attention on them. Lial knew the men were in good hands. They were about to have a very interesting night. And they wouldn't remember a minute of it.

The air on the balcony was at least fifteen degrees cooler, and about a hundred decibels quieter. The beat still throbbed in Lial's head as she pulled the plugs out of her ears.

"I should have brought a pair of those," said Kabera, rubbing his head as if he was trying to scrub away the noise.

"I dated a rock drummer once," said Lial. "He's deaf now."

Kabera was right next to her. Lial shifted her weight to one leg, moving her hip closer to his. She leaned forward and rested her arms on the balcony railing. "Beautiful out there," she said.

Kabera slid around behind her. She felt his hands on her shoulders, his lips close to her ear. "It's even prettier from up there," he said. He poked his index finger toward the sky.

"I saw you fly in," said Lial, stroking his arm playfully. "Very smooth."

"I trained in F-16s," said Kabera. He nodded toward the floatplane. It had been towed to the end of the dock just below the club. "That's my little weekend toy."

"Sorry," said Lial, pulling back. "I don't ride in toys."

She felt Kabera's hands slide off her shoulders. He grabbed her right wrist and tugged her toward the stone staircase.

"Stop!" Lial grabbed the stone railing and jerked her hand away. "I've never been in a plane that tiny before!"

"Trust me," said Kabera. "You'll love it."

"No!" Lial shouted. "I'm too scared!"

Two minutes later, she was strapped into the front passenger seat as the props began to spin. Kabera looked over from behind the controls. "Relax," he said over his headset mic. "You'll be fine."

Lial realized that he hadn't even bothered to ask her name. The arrogance was stunning. She adjusted the headset over her ears. Her knees were trembling—voluntarily.

Kabera pushed the throttle forward. The plane started to cruise toward the center of the lake. "Don't act so nervous," he said with a smile.

"I can't help it!" Lial moaned, gripping the seat with both hands.

She was an excellent actor.

CHAPTER 70

KIRA SUNLIGHT WAS chained to a metal chair in a command tent. She'd been there for about an hour, alone. Two of the huge men had carried her back from the riverbank, trussed up like a hunting trophy. They were taking no chances with her. Kira had been working at the lock behind her with her fingernails, but so far, no luck.

Her clothes were soaked, clinging to her body like a wet skin. In spite of the heat, she felt clammy. She'd realized right away that she was in Hemple's old quarters. A small length of twine still dangled from the front pole. She prayed that the snake had been dispatched.

Peering through the tent flap, Kira could make out shapes moving back and forth in the darkness outside.

Suddenly, the flap whipped open.

Captain Rupert Gurney stepped in.

Kira tensed up, but tried not to show it. She had studied Gurney for so long from a distance that it was a jolt to see him this close. He had clean, even features. Thick, wavy hair. A delicate, almost feminine mouth. Two of the giants stood behind him—the guy with the crew cut, and the one who looked like The Rock.

Gurney stopped two feet from Kira's chair. "This is our jungle demon?" he said. "She doesn't look so evil to me."

"Appearances are deceiving," said Kira. "You look like you should be in a boy band."

She saw a smirk crack Crew Cut's face. Gurney leaned down so that his eyes were level with Kira's. He reached over and ran his fingers through her wet hair. He wasn't rough. He was gentle. Even creepier.

"Shaba," he said softly. "Who do you work for? Who hired you?" Kira twisted her head and clenched her teeth. "CIA?" Gurney pressed. "MI6? FSB?"

Kira stared straight at him. "YMCA," she said. "I like to swim."

CHAPTER 71

KABERA WAS FLYING lazy loops over Lake Kivu, a thousand feet up. The club glittered like a gem on the eastern bank. Along the shoreline, Lial could see other patches of light—small settlements and marinas. To the north, she could make out the glow of Goma International Airport, where Kabera stored his plane. A chopper had deposited her there six hours earlier.

Lial stilled her shaking legs, but kept her hands clasped tightly over her knees.

"How do you feel?" asked Kabera. "Getting used to it?"

"Kind of," said Lial. She kept the quaver in her voice. "Where are we going?"

"At the moment, nowhere," said Kabera. "Just enjoying the scenery. But I can take you anywhere you want."

Lial stared out her side window and let a few pregnant seconds tick by. "Are we near Lake Tanganyika?" she asked. "Somebody told me it's really pretty."

Lial saw Kabera's face light up. "It is," he said. "I know a place there. Gorgeous. Right on the water."

"Really?"

Lial made a point of adjusting the small designer knapsack on her lap. It was her subtle cue that she was prepared to spend the night.

She felt the plane make a slow bank. The wing on her side tilted toward the water. Then they straightened out. Lial glanced at the direction indicator on the console. Perfect. It pointed due south.

Kabera slid his right hand off the control yoke. He reached over and let it rest on Lial's left thigh, just below the hem of her skirt. Lial didn't flinch or resist, even when his fingers began a slow creep upward. She bit her lower lip and let it happen.

"Is it fancy?" she asked. "Where we're going?"

"Don't worry," said Kabera. "You'll fit right in."

Lial allowed herself to look a little excited now. She wiggled her butt in the seat, then picked up Kabera's hand and placed it gently back on the controls.

"Focus on flying for now, right?" she said, flashing him a smile.

Kabera smiled back. "Right. Good idea. For now."

Lial reached into her bag and pulled out her lipstick and a small mirror. She reapplied her Stoplight Red. Next, she pulled out an eyeliner pen, concealing the tip in her curled palm. She leaned toward Kabera and pointed past him. "Hey! Is that another plane?"

Kabera whipped his head to the left.

Lial plunged the needle into his neck.

Kabera slumped against the side of the cabin. Lial quickly unclipped herself and reached over to steady the yoke. Then she unstrapped Kabera from his seat. She muscled him out and shoved him into the back. He fell face down into the well below the rear passenger bench, his expensive shoes protruding into the front of the cabin.

The plane was drifting to the left. Lial slid into the pilot's seat and grabbed the yoke. She turned off the transponder and kicked off her high heels, placing her stocking feet on the rudder pedals.

She strapped in and ran her gaze over the control panel. Checked her airspeed, altitude, and fuel level. Nearly full. Which meant a three-hundred-mile range, not counting the reserve. She gripped the control and pulled back slightly. She felt a flutter in her belly as the nose lifted. After gaining another thousand feet of altitude, she leveled out again.

Piece of cake.

It felt exactly like the simulator.

CHAPTER 72

IT HAD BEEN three hours since Gurney and his goons left the tent. Kira hadn't told them anything. She just stared them down. "We'll wait for dawn," Gurney had told his men before stalking out.

Kira's mind had been spinning ever since. What happened at dawn? Torture? Drowning? Beating? Gang rape? Gurney didn't seem like the Geneva Accords type. Neither did his giants.

She could see the sunlight starting to filter through the tent sides.

"Hey!" she called out. *"Hey!"* She was hoping there might be a woman in the unit. Somebody who would bring her a sip of water. Show a little mercy. Her throat felt like it was closing up.

The tent flap opened.

Gurney again. This time all five giants were with him.

"I need water," Kira croaked.

"No you don't," said Gurney. "This won't take long."

He reached into his pocket and pulled out a black hood. Kira pressed her feet against the floor and bucked in the chair, so hard it almost tipped over. Gurney reached out and grabbed her hair. This time he twisted her curls tightly in his fist. "Fight me," he snarled, "and we'll end this right here."

He slid the hood over her head and yanked it down to her shoulders. Kira could hear her own breathing and feel her heart pounding in her chest. She sensed somebody huge behind her. She heard a click and felt the chains go limp. For a split second, she considered making a move. Then she felt her arms being twisted behind her. Rough hands pulled her to her feet.

"Walk, bitch."

Kira felt the hard-packed tent floor under her feet as she shuffled forward. She felt the rough canvas of the tent flap against her cheek as she was shoved through. Now she was outside. She felt the heat of the sun and she could see the light bouncing from under her hood.

"Let's get this over with." Gurney's voice from up ahead.

Kira's training taught her that there was always a way out. But right now, she couldn't find one. She was drained from no sleep. She hadn't eaten in thirty-six hours. She was dehydrated. She didn't know how many weapons were pointed at her. And as strong as she was, she knew she was no match for the guy who was holding her.

She considered letting her full weight drop, faking a faint, but she knew it might dislocate her arm. She thought about trying to bargain, but she had nothing to offer. Then she thought about Doc—imagined him swinging in on a vine to save her, like Tarzan. But she knew that she had only herself. She felt more upward pressure on her arm, like it was about to snap at the elbow. She winced in pain and kept on walking.

"Stop right here." Gurney's voice again.

Kira could feel soft dirt under her feet. The edge of her grave?

She heard the click and feedback squawk from a megaphone, then Gurney's voice again, echoing in the open air. "Listen to me," he said, "*Listen!* For weeks now, we have been searching for a killer in the jungle. The mighty and mysterious Shaba. You have been afraid. Your children have been afraid. Well, you don't need to fear any longer." Kira felt a hand on her head. "Because *this* ... is your Shaba!"

The hood was yanked off. Kira blinked in the glare.

She was standing at the edge of the mine pit. Fifty feet down, hundreds of workers were staring up at her. Women pushed their children behind them, as if they feared she could shoot fire from her eyes. Kira recognized some of the men—the ones who had chased her through the jungle with torches.

"See for yourself!" Gurney pronounced. He turned and grabbed Kira by the neck, pulling her forward. "Shaba is no god. No devil. No monster. She is human. Just like all of you."

Kira felt the pressure on her arms ease off. She turned around. The five giants formed a wall in front of her. The Black man held a shovel. He turned it sideways and thrust it at Kira's midsection.

She grabbed the handle with both hands and thought about swinging it around to smash Gurney's head in. But she knew it would be her last act—only satisfying for the split second before somebody shot her or shoved her over the edge.

Gurney lowered the megaphone. "Welcome to the pit, Shaba."

The giants moved forward, nudging her backward toward the top of the ramp. Kira turned around and put the shovel over her shoulder. She could hear mumbling from the crowd below as she descended toward them. The heat intensified with every step. Reddish dust started to cake her shoes, her clothes, her face.

When she reached the bottom, a group of men crowded around her, grunting and gesturing. One of them reached out and grabbed her arm. Another pulled her from the other side. She felt herself behind yanked back and forth like a doll. A third man grabbed the shovel from her, then tugged up her shirt and ran his rough hand across her belly, as if he was trying to make sure she was mortal.

"Acha! Acha!" A female voice, in Swahili, telling the men to stop.

Kira watched as the young Black woman shoved her way through the crowd. She was slight, but determined. Her arms and forehead were shiny with sweat. She couldn't have been more than eighteen. As she got closer, the men let Kira go and stepped aside.

The young woman held out a bottle of water and put her other hand over her heart.

"*Vanda*," she said. Her name.

Then, "*Hunitishi.*" Meaning, You don't scare me.

CHAPTER 73

I WAS REALLY missing Aaron Vail's speedboat about now. I estimated it had taken me seven hours to travel about three hundred miles down the lake in the creaky wooden fishing skiff, and I was on my second backup fuel tank. I kept close to the shoreline, where the current was milder. But with the trees and bushes so close, I was batting away bugs the size of my fist.

It was almost midnight. I was exhausted. I needed gas. And water.

As I came around the next bend, I saw yellow lights reflecting in the water about fifty yards ahead.

Thank God! I motored straight toward the twinkle.

As I got closer, I saw an aluminum dock projecting out into the lake and a wood-frame building at the top of a steep slope behind it. The building front was draped with yellow bulbs, and there was a neon Kilimanjaro Premium

Lager sign in the window. To me, at that moment, it was like coming across a five-star hotel.

As I pulled up to the dock, a small Black girl hopped down a set of wooden steps from the building. Eight years old, if that.

"I need gas," I said, pointing to my engine, hoping she would understand me and run to fetch her dad.

"Regular or diesel?" she asked. She grabbed the line from my prow and tied it to the pier post with a perfect cleat hitch.

"Regular," I said. "Thanks."

The girl walked to a rusted metal shed set back into the bushes and yanked the door open. She hauled out a plastic ten-gallon tank and pushed it downhill to the dock. It probably outweighed her.

"You thirsty?" she asked, standing up again.

I was coated with grime and sweat. I probably reeked. "How'd you guess?"

She pointed toward the building. "You go up. Have a drink. I'll fill your tank. Pay inside."

I trusted this girl totally.

I grabbed my cloth sack and climbed the steps toward the bar. As I got closer, I could hear laughing from inside, and music. Ed Sheeran. As soon as I stepped onto the porch, I could smell beer and frying food.

I pulled the screen door open. The whole place was the size of a large living room. Wood floor. Two round tables.

Metal fan spinning near the ceiling. And a bar running along the whole left side. A Black man with a gold earring was serving drinks, and he had a full house. Five people.

A shirtless man in cargo shorts occupied the first stool. The rest of the patrons were women. Two were in their twenties, slim and pretty, wearing shorts and T-shirts. The other two were a little older and stouter, in flowery cotton dresses. Their skin colors ranged from chocolate brown to ebony.

And every single one had copper-colored hair.

CHAPTER 74

THE CHATTER STOPPED cold when I entered. I felt like a gunfighter walking into the town saloon. Then the bartender looked up and gave me a wide grin. "Beer?"

"Please," I said. It was more like a relieved groan.

He pulled a bottle from a cooler and popped the cap. I grabbed it and chugged half of it down, then took a seat at one of the small tables. I put my cloth sack on a chair where I could see it. The conversation at the bar ramped up again. Ed Sheeran was still piping out from a speaker on the wall. Nobody seemed that interested in me.

When I glanced out the window, I could see the tiny girl using a foot pump to transfer gas from the plastic tank to mine. I looked over at the bartender and jerked my thumb toward the dock. "Your daughter?"

"My niece," he said. "Neema. Very competent. Working to save up for her own boat."

For some reason, I flashed on the boys back on the

island. Not much bigger than Neema, most of them. I remembered watching them pilot outriggers on choppy seas, mend nets with scissors and fishing line, and catch our dinner with wooden spears. Then I thought about the privileged students in my lecture classes back in Chicago. I seriously doubted that a single one of them knew how to change a tire.

I took another sip of my beer. One of the women walked over and set a plate of fried fish in front of me. "Our treat," she said. "You look hungry."

"You have no idea," I said. "Thank you." I bit into a greasy chunk of battered fish and washed it down with the rest of my beer. Heaven.

"Need anything else?" she asked.

"I do," I said, wiping my mouth with a paper napkin. "I need an off-road vehicle and a high-powered rifle."

Now I had everybody's attention.

"You a safari hunter?" one of the women asked, fingering her copper-tinted dreadlocks.

"Not animals," I said. "I'm looking for somebody—inland."

The bartender shook his head. "Dangerous there."

I nodded. "Which is why I need the gun."

The bartender rested both hands on the bar. He looked me over for a few seconds, like he was appraising me. Then he stepped out to the side and crooked his finger. "Come," he said.

I picked up my bag and followed him down a narrow passageway, past a tiny kitchen with a deep fryer and a refrigerator. He pushed a screen door that opened to a flat clearing behind the building. About ten yards away, a rutted path led off into the bush. Sitting at the edge of the path was a red Land Rover Defender, probably twenty years old, all rusted and banged up. I'd driven Land Rovers on some of my own digs. They were pretty much indestructible.

"It runs?"

"See for yourself," said the bartender. "Key's in the ignition."

I walked over and opened the driver-side door. I slid in and turned the key. The engine fired right up. A puff of oily exhaust blasted out from the rear. But after that, things settled down. All the displays were working. Fuel tank read full. I bent down to check the floorboards for holes. When I sat up again, the bartender was holding a rifle. It looked like it belonged in a military museum.

"Mauser K98," he said. "The best."

I'd gotten plenty of weapons training from Kira, but mostly in small arms. This thing looked like it could take down a rhino.

"Ammo, too," said the bartender. He opened a metal box filled with shiny brass cartridges.

I appreciated the one-stop shopping. And I couldn't afford to be picky. "How much?" I asked. "For the truck, the gun, and all the ammo?"

The bartender turned it over in his mind for a few seconds. "Fifty million," he said.

It took me a second to register that he was talking about Congolese francs.

"How much US?" I asked. I had no idea of the exchange rate. I hoped that he was somewhere close to being honest. I saw him doing the math in his head.

"Twenty thousand," he said. "Low miles on the truck."

I glanced at the odometer. It read 96,000. He was right. Not bad for a Land Rover. And besides, I didn't see any other options on the lot.

"Fifteen thousand," I said. I needed to feel like I was getting a deal.

"Eighteen thousand," said the bartender.

"Only if the gun works," I said.

"Check it out," he said. He pulled a single cartridge out of the box and pressed it into the rifle's open chamber. It made a satisfying click. He put the rifle over his shoulder and headed for the wooden steps that led down toward the dock. "Come," he said. I followed.

Neema was leaning against a pier post when she saw us heading down. She perked up.

"Neema!" her uncle called out. "Target!"

I saw the girl scramble off the dock into the underbrush. A few seconds later, she emerged with a rusted tin plate.

The bartender shoved the rifle bolt forward and down. He handed the gun to me. "If you're going where you say, I hope you know how to shoot."

I looked down at Neema. She was holding the plate

like a Frisbee. I put the stock of the gun against my cheek and pointed the barrel out over the water. I slid my finger onto the trigger. I gave Neema a little nod. She flexed her skinny legs and flipped the plate out over the lake, about thirty feet into the air. I followed the silhouette against the sky through the front sight. At the instant the plate started to fall, I pulled the trigger. The plate spun like crazy and dropped into the water about twenty yards out. Direct hit.

Neema gave me an appreciative look.

I turned to the bartender and shook his hand. "Deal," I said. "Gun. Ammo. Truck." I ruffled through my sack and pulled out twenty thousand dollars, then peeled off two grand and stuffed it back. The bartender's eyes opened wide. He held the bills up and riffled them like a card deck. Then he gave me that wide grin again.

Neema pointed to my boat. "Filled up," she said. "Ready to go."

"Good," I said. "She's all yours."

CHAPTER 75

LIAL SCANNED THE surface of the lake, checked the direction of the ripples, and banked the floatplane for an upwind landing. She leveled off at three hundred feet and then throttled down slowly, slowly—until she felt the jolt of the pontoons on the water. Not as smooth as the minister's landing, she thought to herself, but good enough.

She maneuvered the plane to the edge of the lake, where dark jungle foliage met the water, and cut the engine. She unstrapped herself from her seat, then grabbed her knapsack and slung it over her shoulder. She opened the door and started tugging the limp Joseph Kabera out of the rear of the compartment, legs first. She dragged him onto the left pontoon and felt for a pulse. Nothing. Not that it would have mattered. She pulled a folding knife from her bag and stabbed Kabera hard through both lungs and his gut and rolled him into the water. His wounds bubbled as he started to sink slowly into the murk. The crocs would arrive soon enough. They would leave no trace.

Lial tossed her knapsack into the undergrowth on shore, then lowered herself off the pontoon into the warm, shoulder-deep water. Bracing her feet against a sunken log, she pushed hard on the right pontoon until the plane started to move out into the current. She watched it spin slowly on the water and drift off. By morning, it would be miles away.

Lial waded to shore, grabbed a thick vine, and pulled herself up onto the bank. It was covered with coarse wet grass and leathery fronds. A few yards in, she found a small, mossy clearing. She stripped off her wet party clothes, right down to the skin. She reached into her bag and grabbed a T-shirt, sports bra, underwear, and jeans. She slipped them on, then pulled out a pair of athletic shoes and a loaded Glock. She pulled her long dark hair into a ponytail and secured it with an elastic. She grabbed a cluster of wet leaves and scrubbed off what was left of her makeup. Then she checked the safety on her gun and stuck it under her rear waistband, feeling the cool metal against her back.

Deep breath. In and out. That's better.

She was starting to feel like herself again.

CHAPTER 76

I WAS PAST the Mitumba Mountains, bouncing across the savanna. It was getting to be dusk. I knew I was in dangerous territory, for too many reasons to count. But I'd come this far, and I wasn't about to slow down now. I'd drive all night if I had to. From what I'd learned from my friends at the bar, the Shaba legend had started in the Kolwezi region, a few hundred miles to the southwest. That was my destination.

I knew that even if I was headed in the right direction, finding one woman in the African wilderness would be nearly impossible. I just hoped that the reports would get more detailed the closer I got. That might increase my odds. All that really mattered right now was to find out if the demon they called Shaba was really Kira—and if she was still alive.

The savanna was flat and covered with hip-high grass. Here and there the landscape was broken by bushy-topped trees with skinny trunks. Over the past few hours, I'd seen herds of giraffes, antelopes, and zebras. I knew for sure there were lions and hyenas lurking out of sight. As long as I kept moving, I trusted that the engine noise would keep them at a safe distance.

I had my sack with the cutlass and what was left of my nest egg in the footwell of the truck. The Mauser was clipped into a gun mount on the dashboard. The extra ammo was rattling in the glove compartment. I had about twelve gallons left in my fuel tank and a twenty-gallon reserve strapped to the rear fender, along with a ten-gallon container of water.

I was moving along an old hunting trail—basically two deep ruts with grass in the middle. There were long stretches where I could chug along at forty miles an hour. Other spots were so sketchy that I could barely crawl. I was in one of those spots now.

The trail was so pitted and rough that the truck was rocking back and forth. The transmission was complaining. I'd been in low gear for the past five minutes.

All of a sudden, I heard weird screeching ahead. I looked to my right and saw a pack of vultures peeking above the grass about fifteen yards off the trail. I don't know what made me stop. Maybe it was my old scientific curiosity—the research professor in me coming out. I kept the engine running, set the brake, and grabbed my rifle from the mount. As soon as I stopped moving, the smell hit me. Thick, musky, putrid.

The birds looked up as I walked toward them, but they didn't budge. They had purple-pink jowls and massive black bills. One of them reared up and stretched out its full wingspan—about eight feet from tip to tip. Trying to intimidate me.

When I pushed through the final stand of grass, I gagged, then almost vomited. The vultures were standing on top of an elephant carcass. It was a large female, a recent kill. There was a hole from a large-caliber bullet in her forehead, with dried blood caked below. Both tusks had been sawn off close to the jaw. Her trunk lay like a huge gray worm on the ground. The grass near the carcass was pressed down and roughed up. I could see boot prints in the dirt underneath.

The screeching of the birds got louder as I got closer.

Then I heard something else.

Human voices.

They were coming from my truck.

CHAPTER 77

I CHECKED MY rifle and made sure there was a round in the chamber. I crouched low and crept as quietly as I could back toward the Land Rover.

When I was ten feet away, I pulled up short. Two scrawny Black teenagers were standing on the far side of the vehicle. They had machetes stuck through their belts and automatic rifles by their sides. One had two lengths of ivory over his shoulders. The other guy was holding my cutlass.

I stepped out of the grass with my gun up. I thought my guests would turn and run, but they didn't. The guy with the ivory held out one of the tusks. "Trade!" he called out.

I shook my head. "No trade." I said it three times. But I wasn't getting through. The guy with the ivory held one of the tusks at its thickest point and tossed over the truck toward me, making his offer. The tusk spun in the air and landed in the grass at my feet. It was about five feet long, bloody on the thick end and pointed at the tip.

The other guy was busy rummaging through my bag. He pulled out a wad of bills and held it up. His eyes widened. His buddy dropped the second piece of ivory. The two of them started pulling on the bag, bickering in Swahili. I only knew a few words, and they were talking too fast for me to catch the drift.

I was out of patience anyway.

I cocked the gun. At the sound of the bolt, they both shut up. I waved the barrel back and forth between them. I didn't want to shoot anybody in cold blood, but I didn't come all this way to be robbed by two skinny poachers.

"Nenda!" I shouted. "Go!"

I saw them both blink. Then I felt something hard against my temple. A hand reached around and yanked the rifle away. A white hand.

"No trades." His voice was in my ear. French accent. "We'll take it all. The sword, the cash, and the truck." He barked some orders in Swahili to the other two. "And the Mauser." He tossed my rifle toward the Land Rover, way out of my reach.

I knew the pressure against my skull was from a pistol barrel. I could feel the guy's bulk behind me. He wasn't tall, but he was thick. I wondered how fast the other two were with their rifles. Then I remembered one of Kira's lessons. Act weak, finish strong.

I sank to my knees. "Please!" I moaned. "You can't leave me alone out here!" I felt the gun barrel slide off my head.

"Don't worry," said the guy behind me. He leaned around, far enough for me to see his ruddy face in my peripheral vision. "You're on the savanna, and it's about to be dark. You'll have company soon enough."

I dropped my head and felt for the tusk in the grass. I grabbed it with both hands. Then I whipped around with every ounce of strength I had. I heard a sound like an axe splitting a watermelon. When I looked up, the tusk was rammed through the guy's mouth and poking out the back of his skull. I grabbed his pistol as it dropped.

The Black guys started to pull their rifles off their shoulders. Way too slow. I stepped forward and made a couple quick downward jerks with the pistol. They got the idea. Both of them dropped their rifles on the ground, then their machete scabbards, then their hunting knives. My cutlass and the open bag of money were lying on the hood of the Land Rover.

I used my basic Swahili again. *"Nenda!"* This time, they took the hint. They both turned around and started running, knees high, until they disappeared into the tall grass. The humane part of me hoped that they'd get back to their camp or their truck before dark. But when I thought about what they'd done to that poor elephant, I didn't hope quite as hard.

I tucked the pistol into my pocket and tossed the

Mauser back into the truck. I grabbed both automatic rifles and slung a machete scabbard over one shoulder. I tried to imagine what my students back in Chicago would think if they saw me right now. They'd probably assume I was a big-game hunter or a homicidal maniac—or maybe a live-action role player from some video game.

The truth is, I looked exactly like Doc Savage. The OG. And I was afraid that I was starting to turn into him. I'd just killed a man with an elephant tusk.

But if that's what it took to get Kira back, I'd do it again.

CHAPTER 78

THE SUN WAS directly overhead. Kira was on her hands and knees at the bottom of the mine, using her shovel to scrape loose dirt off yet another pile of rocks. It was hot, sweaty, endless work. And at the moment, she didn't see a way out.

While her complexion could take a lot of sun, it was not meant for this kind of intensity for days on end, especially when the sun was directly overhead, shining down into a pit that concentrated the heat like an oven. Her pale skin was blistered, and her hands were raw from the constant digging. Each worker was allowed four bottles of water a day, barely enough to replace what they sweated away. Kira had already gone through most of her ration.

"This one, not that one." The young woman named Vanda worked right next to her, helping her sort the valuable rocks from the junk. She had a good eye. Other workers, especially the children, stayed clear. Vanda said they still thought Kira possessed evil powers.

When they first met, Kira spoke to Vanda in Swahili. Then, word by word, she started teaching her English. In the beginning, the vocabulary was limited, like their world. "Rock." "Water." "Copper." "Tired."

And, of course, "baby."

Once Vanda had enough English in her brain, she talked about her baby all the time, usually with tears streaming down her face. She also talked about how dangerous the mine was, how many other people had died there.

"This place means death," she said. "I will die here, too."

Kira wiped the sweat from her eyes. "No," she said. "You won't."

Suddenly Vanda's spade was blasted out of her hand. The handle shattered and flew away from the blade. A bullhorn crackled from above. *"No talk. Just work."*

Kira jumped up to check Vanda's wrist. It was grazed by the bullet, but not broken. Kira poured what was left of her water bottle over the wound. Vanda pulled away. She crawled to a wooden crate and pulled out another tool.

Kira pulled the broken handle of Vanda's spade under her sleeve. She let Vanda see it, but nobody else. Then she hunched over and picked up two junk rocks. With small, quick movements, she started pounding and filing the three-inch metal prong.

The pit was a prison. And she was honing a shiv.

CHAPTER 79

LATE THAT NIGHT, the five giants from Belgium sat slumped on their cots in their sweltering barracks tent. It was too damn hot to sleep. A generator-powered fan blew air from one side of the tent to the other, but it wasn't enough to dry the sweat from their bodies, even with their shirts off. And it didn't deter the massive insects, which managed to dodge the currents to land on their backs and necks.

Blodgett wiped the damp dirt off his crew cut. "God, it stinks in here."

"My ball sack is drippin'," said Fenwick. His rough Scottish brogue somehow made the image even more visceral.

Marley reached into a Styrofoam cooler and pulled out a beer. He uncapped it with his teeth and drained it without stopping. White foam dribbled down over his dark skin. He tossed the empty out through the tent flap and wiped his chin. "When's payday?" he asked.

"End of the month," said Harper. "Ten days."

"Not soon enough," said Tagaloa.

"Whaddya think Gurney's makin'?" asked Fenwick. "For standin' around talkin' through his toy bullhorn?"

"You mean the guy we're being paid to protect?" said Harper. He leaned over and spit onto the floor. "Poncy boarding-school prick."

Tagaloa leaned back on his elbows and stretched his long brown legs out. "You know who was a *real* prick?" he said. "Leo's ancestor. Old King Leopold. I looked him up. He ran the whole Congo like it was his own private plantation for twenty-odd years. And you know what happened when the workers didn't produce? He had their goddamn hands chopped off."

"Hey!" Fenwick contorted his fingers to imitate Leo's twisted claw. "Whaddya think? Leo's hand. Maybe it's some kind of karmic payback."

Harper stretched out to his full six-ten length on the cot. His blond ponytail dangled off the end. "You guys ever think we're working for the wrong side here?"

Marley stood up, his bald head brushing the ceiling of the tent. He let out a loud and aromatic beer belch. "Since when did you grow a conscience?"

Harper swatted at something buzzing around his ear. "Dunno," he said. "Maybe it's the bugs."

CHAPTER 80

The Arabian Sea, 10 p.m.

ALONE IN HIS quarters aboard the *Prizrak*, Cal Savage was in a fury. He pressed the Rewind button and watched the report from a Rwanda TV station for the third time.

"*...and so far, authorities have no answer regarding the disappearance of Security Minister Joseph Kabera. His empty floatplane was found at the southern edge of Lake Tanganyika, but there was no trace of the official. His security guards are reportedly being questioned in Goma. More when we know it...*"

Still no trace of Kabera! And where the hell was Lial? Savage hadn't heard from her since her chopper set down at the airport. It wasn't unusual for her to go dark during an operation, but what happened out there? Was Kabera a confirmed kill or not? Did somebody else kill them both? It wasn't a plane crash, that's for sure. From the TV images, the floatplane looked pristine.

An intercom buzzed. "Captain. I have them here."

"Have who?"

"The two poachers."

Savage stood up. He needed something to go right tonight. Maybe this was it.

"Bring them."

He turned off the video as the cabin door opened. One of the ship's Kenyan security guards had his hands on a pair of skinny Black men. They looked like they had just been pulled out of the bush. From what Savage had been told already, the young men had no ivory for him tonight, but they did have information.

"Tell the captain," said the guard, shoving the men forward. They both looked confused. "*Nitatafsiri,*" said the guard, pointing at his own lips. "I translate."

Both men started to babble at once in rapid-fire Swahili. Savage waved his hand impatiently as if trying to clear the air. "Stop! What are they saying?"

The Kenyan guard stepped forward. "They're talking about a giant white man with a red truck—on the trail toward Kolwezi. Southern Congo." The guard let the young men babble on for a few more sentences, then picked up the translation again. "They say he killed their tracker, then stole their weapons and left them on the savanna to die."

Savage felt his stomach drop. He stared at the young men, first one, then the other. "Tell them they got lucky," said Savage. "And tell them next time, they'd better bring ivory. Lots of it. That's what I hired them for."

The guard put Savage's words into Swahili, then pulled

the two men around and shoved them back out through the cabin door. Savage called out to the guard. "And tell them I'll find them a new tracker!"

The captain sat down heavily in his padded chair. Damnit. It was Doc Savage for sure. He was alive. Somehow, he had figured out where Kira Sunlight was operating, and now he was on his way to find her.

Cal Savage was not about to let that happen. Separately, those two might be manageable, even useful. Together, they were a potent force. The combination was just too dangerous—for him, and for his plans. As long as they were both breathing, they were a significant threat.

Lial would be his natural choice for the job. She never turned down wet work. But she was currently missing in action. Maybe dead herself.

Hold on . . .

In a flash, the captain realized exactly who he needed. He grabbed the sat phone and placed a call to the mainland. He thought it over for a moment while the call went through. The solution might be overkill for just two targets.

But if anybody needed overkilling, it was Doc Savage and Kira Sunlight.

CHAPTER 81

IN A RUGGED outpost on the southern coast of Somalia, Cal Savage's protégé Abai picked up the call. The former *Prizrak* crew member listened intently as the captain outlined the mission.

With the ugliness concerning the warlord's clan behind him, Abai was firmly in command of the local militia—a band of fifty, all under twenty-five, with scores of battles under their belts. Most of them had been soldiers since before they hit puberty.

The instant the call ended, Abai walked out of his tent and surveyed his troops, scattered around the compound in small groups, cooking over propane burners and playing video games on their phones. The men—mostly boys—were already hopped up on khat, which they chewed constantly. They were always ready for action, the wilder the better.

The tiny bay at the edge of the command post was filled with military-grade rigid inflatables and Poluchat-class PT boats, recently liberated from the Somali navy. Crates lined up on the sand held automatic rifles, ammo, and RPGs.

Abai signaled to two tall brothers, Bilan and Abshir, two of his toughest fighters. The brothers knew that Abai was the man who had hung their older sibling from the rigging of a superyacht. But he had earned their loyalty by letting their father live. Also, he paid well.

Abai barked his orders in Swahili. Bilan and Abshir turned and got the rest of the boys moving. Within a few minutes, the air was filled with the roar of marine engines. The troops piled into the boats, guns and ammo belts hanging from their skinny frames. No uniforms, just an assortment of cargo shorts and T-shirts, most of them emblazoned with the logos of heavy-metal bands. Some wore long, flowing red bandanas around their foreheads. They looked like pirates, which most of them were.

As the flotilla mobilized, there were yips and shouts and random gunshots into the air. The troops were excited. Being out on the water was better than sweating in camp, and any kind of action was better than doing nothing.

Abai waded into the surf and climbed aboard one of the PT boats. He walked up to Bilan, who was behind the wheel, and ordered the boat out into the Indian Ocean.

He turned and watched the rest of the flotilla spread out in formation behind him.

He directed his small flagship south toward the coastline of Tanzania, the country that stood between him and the Congo—and the two people he'd been assigned to terminate.

CHAPTER 82

I WAS BEGINNING to have second thoughts about abandoning the Land Rover.

I'd sold it to the manager of a gas station near Kianza for forty-four million francs. In two days, I'd only put a few hundred miles on the truck, but they were hard miles. By the end, the transmission was getting balky. I was happy to get most of my investment back.

I figured that in this part of the world, a huge, heavily armed white man in a red truck might set off alarms. If Kira was really in a fight with mercenaries, the last thing I needed was for them to see me coming. So I bought a backpack, loaded it with camping tools and beef jerky, strapped my guns on my shoulders, and headed out into the jungle alone. On foot.

As daylight faded, I was regretting my move.

I'd spent time in jungles before—once on a research expedition down the Amazon as a grad student, and once on an archaeological dig in Costa Rica. But back then I was part of a team, working from established base camps. We had tents and cooks and fresh food trucked in.

I had none of that now. I had only myself.

The foliage was so thick I could hardly see the sky. It was like being in a huge terrarium. I was hacking my way through the underbrush with a machete, whacking branches and vines as thick as my wrist. Every strike sent up flakes of bark and a flurry of bugs. Most of them seemed to find their way into my ears and eyes.

I was marking my progress in yards, not miles. And before I knew it, it was dusk. I'd hoped to reach some kind of a village or outpost for shelter. At this point, even the kind of lean-to Kira and I built on the island would look pretty damned good. But I knew I couldn't sleep on the ground. I'd be eaten alive by bugs, or something bigger.

I thought about climbing a tree, but I didn't see any branches that would hold me and all my gear.

I took another swipe at the vines in front of me. Then I stopped. When I blinked the sweat out of my eyes, I thought I saw a rectangular shape poking out of the jungle about twenty yards ahead. Not natural. I thought my mind was just making it up.

I hacked my way a few yards closer. Nope. It was real. And man-made. As I pushed more branches aside, I could see a frame of rough timbers, grayed and rotted. It was the opening to what looked like a dark cave. There was a pile of rocks alongside and a post that held a metal sign dangling from a single rusted hook.

I could only translate one word on the sign, but it was enough.

Lucky me. I'd discovered a gold mine.

CHAPTER 83

I INCHED MY way through the opening, pistol raised. It had been a long time since anybody pulled a nugget out of this place. It was pitch-black inside and it smelled like cat piss. I couldn't hear or see anything. I looked at the ground to see if there were any bones or feathers that would tell me it was a predator's den. But at that point, I don't think a pack of jackals would have scared me off. I was dead tired, and I needed to sleep.

I put down my weapons and wrestled a few loose timbers across the entrance, blocking it halfway up. That was to deter four-legged intruders. I stuffed rocks and dirt into the openings to keep out anything that crawled or slithered.

As I rested my backpack against the wall, I wondered how deep the mine went, and if anybody had ever gotten rich here. But I was in no mood to explore. I sat down and settled my head against my pack. I had a pistol in one hand and a machete in the other. I think I was a little delirious from the heat. As I drifted off, my mind started spinning with crazy thoughts and images—mostly about my ancestor.

I wondered how many of the Doc Savage adventures I'd read about had been true and how many had been fever dreams. Voodoo thugs, giant spiders, headless zombies— I knew I could conjure up any of those creatures right now, and they would feel absolutely real. I took a few deep breaths of the sour cave air, and I was out.

*   *   *

I don't know how long I slept. But the instant I drifted back to consciousness, I sensed that I wasn't alone. There was rustling overhead.

I grabbed my flashlight out of my pack and aimed it up. When I switched on the beam, a chill shot through me. I dropped the light and scrambled to my feet. The roof of the mine was quivering and alive. It was packed from front to back—with bats! While I was sleeping, they had flown home to roost.

I grabbed my backpack and weapons and vaulted over the barricade. I could hear scratching and squeaking behind me and I swore I could feel tiny claws in my hair. I hunched over and slapped my head with both hands. But all I felt was my own sweat.

For a second, I wondered if I could have slept right through a bat bite. What if the rabies virus was already coursing through me? I checked my arms and felt my neck. No pinpricks or blood dots. At least none that I could feel or see. But I shuddered just the same. I'd been spending the night with a few thousand pointy-fanged killers.

I needed to get away from the mine opening, as far and fast as possible. It was still dark, but I could gauge my position. I turned west, facing a dark curtain of green. I raised my machete. Before I could swing, I heard a chop.

Then another.

Somebody else was cutting through the jungle. More than one person. Maybe twenty yards away.

I heard more blades swiping, then the wet stomp of shoes and the rattle of metal equipment. I saw the flicker of headlamps. I ducked down and saw shapes moving through the underbrush. Men and boys with heavy weapons.

It looked like a small army.

CHAPTER 84

ABAI WAS LEADING from the rear, waiting for the point men to clear a path with their blades before he ordered the whole column forward. He knew that his men were wishing they were back on the water right now. Because this was a punishing trek. Hot, humid, and buggy. Even in the middle of the night, the temperature was still in the nineties.

Two days back, the flotilla had landed near Dar es Salaam on the Tanzanian coast. From there, a fleet of trucks and jeeps had transported the militia across the savanna and through the upper bulge of Zambia. But here, in the thick of the jungle, motorized vehicles were useless.

Besides, Abai didn't want to announce his arrival. The grueling hump through the jungle would pay off in the element of surprise. He had the destination from Captain Savage—a small copper mine near Kolwezi, in the

Lualaba Province. Mission: eliminate the two primary targets. As a bonus, take back the mine.

Bilan was standing alongside the commander, rifle across his shoulders, waiting for the path to be cleared. "Forty men," said the warlord's son. "For two people?"

"The force fits the mission," said Abai curtly.

Abai couldn't wait to turn his troops loose. The boys were itching for a fight, and the captain had warned him that his targets would not go down easily.

CHAPTER 85

KIRA WAS TUGGING on her chains in her nightly quest to find a comfortable position. She was in Hemple's tent, with the day's sweat still crusted on her body. Her back and joints ached from bending and kneeling for fourteen hours straight.

And she was alone.

Vanda and the other workers were quartered in their squalid tent city just below the compound. But Gurney made sure that Kira got special treatment. Every night after she climbed up the ramp from the pit, her wrists were zip-tied and she was led back to the compound at gunpoint. She was apparently considered the ultimate flight risk.

The truth was, Kira thought she might be safer here than she would be in the tent village with her coworkers. Many of them still considered her a demon, and she knew they wouldn't think twice about stabbing her in her sleep.

But here, sleep was hard to come by.

The tent was never totally dark. A small lamp hung from the ceiling, casting an eerie yellowish glow all night long. And it drew bugs. Kira was constantly shaking her head to get them out of her hair and clenching her lips to keep them out of her mouth.

She sat on the hard-packed dirt floor, with the chains wrapped tightly around the post behind her. For the first few nights, she had tried to work the post loose, but she soon realized that it was set in concrete. It wasn't going anywhere. The lock was out of reach above her, and none of the contortions she tried brought it any closer.

Kira's mind was restless and resourceful. It was how she'd been trained. But at some point every night, her machinations about escape were overcome by her desperate need for rest. She had reached that point now.

She inched back against the post, which was the only support for her head. She had figured out that if she slouched at just the right angle, she could nod off for a few minutes at a time, pooling enough precious energy to survive another day. Those were the times she found herself thinking about Doc, dreaming she was with him, swimming in warm, clear water...

Kira felt herself drifting into that cloudy nether state. Then, suddenly, she felt a gloved hand clamp tightly over her mouth.

Her eyes popped open. Her heart was racing. She whipped her head around, but the post blocked her view. A second later, she felt the chains loosen around her torso.

"Stay quiet." A woman's voice.

The glove slipped off her mouth. Kira could move now. She rolled onto her knees and stood up in a crouch, hands up, ready for anything.

In the glow, she could see the intruder. T-shirt, jeans, dark ponytail. Kira knew the face in an instant. It was Lial. She had a gun pointed at Kira's forehead.

Kira had a spit-second choice to make. Assess or attack.

"If you want to live," said Lial, "follow me."

CHAPTER 86

KIRA NODDED. LIAL lowered the gun. She backed toward the rear of the tent and dropped to the ground, sliding out the way she had apparently come in, through a small slit in the canvas.

Kira dropped and followed her through, headfirst. She found herself face-to-face with a lifeless guard on the ground, his throat neatly sliced and still oozing. Lial led the way along the rear of the tent row. She moved noiselessly from shadow to shadow, perfectly anticipating the paces and turns of the guards in front.

Within a minute, they were at the edge of the compound. There was a small gap in a coil of concertina wire. Lial used her gloves to widen the opening. Kira slipped through. Lial followed.

They crouched just outside the concertina wire and looked at the expanse they would need to cross. Where there used to be thick foliage, there was now just a bulldozed stretch of reddish dirt, rutted by rain. Construction equipment sat in the middle, and there was a row of industrial dumpsters on one side. Uprooted trees and crushed branches had been pushed into a pile at the edge of the clearing. Kira made a dash for the pile and vaulted over it, cutting herself on a cluster of dried thorns. Her adrenaline was pumping so hard she hardly even felt it.

On the other side she started sprinting, surprised at how much strength she had left in her legs. She could hear Lial matching her step for step, across the edge of the dirt clearing and through the maze of blackened stalks left by the flamethrowers.

Kira could feel her lungs burning. Her pulse thundered in her ears. But she didn't stop. Not until she burst out of the fire zone and into the wet shelter of the jungle. She turned, breathing hard, and looked back toward the compound. Lial was at her shoulder.

"No dogs, right?" said Lial. "No drones?"

Kira shook her head. "But good trackers. Relentless."

"The watch switches in ten minutes," said Lial. "That's when they'll find the guard."

"Right," said Kira. "And then they'll come. Full force."

Lial adjusted her backpack. "You lead."

Kira spotted one of her old animal trails and started pushing through the overgrowth. She could feel Lial behind her, far enough back so that the branches wouldn't whip into her face, but never letting Kira get too far ahead.

Kira's mind was working, recalling every bit of data about Lial that she could. From their brief encounter on Cal Savage's yacht, she knew three things. Lial was skilled. She was ambitious. And Savage trusted her with important missions.

Was this one of them, Kira wondered? Had Lial freed her just to murder her in the jungle, or bring her back alive to Savage's yacht? What was in that backpack of hers? Zip ties? Sedatives? Was this an exfiltration, or a recapture?

Kira glanced back. Lial's pistol was tucked into her waistband. Even if she was fast, and Kira assumed she was, it would take her at least a half second to draw and fire. She also had a knife somewhere. The dead guard was evidence of that.

They were approaching a fork in the trail. Kira had traveled both routes many times. The path to the right was straight, but muddy. The path to the left was winding, but solid.

On instinct, she turned right, then made another decision. A big one. Potentially fatal. As she moved along the trail, she grabbed a dead branch lodged in a tangle of vines. She took another step, then whipped around holding the crude club in her fist.

Lial already had her pistol out. Kira spun on the ball of her foot and kicked it out of her hand. The gun went flying into the underbrush. Lial stepped forward, inside the swing range of Kira's club. In a flash, Kira felt her legs being swept out from under her. She hit the ground with a stunning jolt. In an instant, there was a knee in her gut and a knife at her throat.

"Why would you do that?" Lial asked.

Kira had a number of moves to make. But she sensed that Lial knew them all. Instead, she tried to read her eyes. What the hell were her intentions?

"If you came to kill me, just make it fast," said Kira. "I'm not going back."

"Back where?"

"Back to Cal Savage! Back to that goddamn ship of doom! I'd rather die here."

Kira felt the pressure on her solar plexus ease up. She saw the blade flick away from her jugular.

"Understood," Lial said. "Same."

CHAPTER 87

LIAL STOOD UP and plunged into the underbrush in the direction her pistol flew. A few seconds later she popped out with it. She checked the chamber and stuck it back into her jeans.

"I don't get this," said Kira, back on her feet. "I thought you were Cal Savage's right hand."

"Don't call me that," said Lial, eyes flashing. "I work the game, same as you." She took a step closer. "We went to the same school."

Kira took in a sharp breath. "Kamchatka? You were there? When? I didn't..."

"We never met," said Lial. "Different cohorts. I was only twelve when you left. Everything went crazy after that. Guards were executed. Teachers were tortured. They wanted to figure out how you got out, who helped you."

For a second, Kira flashed back to that night. The pounding terror of leaving the only home she had ever known. The searing pain of the acid melting the bars on the dormitory window. The long drop to the ground. Then...the harrowing months and lonely years that followed.

"Nobody helped me," said Kira. "I had only myself." Her heart was thudding, and not just from the fight. She felt a sudden need to fill in the picture on Lial, this mystery woman with an Algerian name and an unplaceable face. "Do you know where...?"

"Where I was born?" Lial had anticipated the question. "No idea."

Not a surprise. That's how the school operated. Students were recruited as infants, kidnapped without a trace. All were children of unusual promise, lost to their families forever, then trained and launched into the world as political operatives, rogue scientists, and assassins. Now Kira understood where Lial got her skills. They'd had the same instructors.

"Where did they send you?" asked Kira. "Where have you been?"

"Poland first. Then Cambodia. Haiti. Afghanistan..."

"Cal sent you to find me?"

Lial shook her head. "I was on another mission, but I had your location. Cal has no idea where I am. With any luck, he thinks I'm dead. I'm done with being his bait and his executioner. I don't want any part of his grand scheme. I came for you because I want to be free, like you. You're the only example I have."

Kira wiped the sweat off her forehead with the back of her hand. "You think I'm some role model? You think I'm free?" She almost laughed. "I tried. I really did. I tried to leave the dark stuff behind. But it kept finding me. It's taken everything and everyone I ever loved. Now look at me. Look at where I am. Until they caught me, I was picking off pigheaded mercenaries for a living. Maybe killing is what we were meant to do, you and me. Maybe there's nothing else for us."

Suddenly, a loud Klaxon sounded from the compound.

"Shit!" Lial ducked down into the foliage.

In the next instant, Kira saw flashlight beams converging at the edge of the bulldozed no-man's-land. More lights than she'd ever seen before.

Kira could feel Lial staring at her, as if she was trying to bore inside her head. It was an intensity she hadn't felt in a long time. "You know the jungle?" Lial asked. "All these trails?"

Kira nodded. This was her territory. She knew every inch of it.

Lial cocked her pistol, then handed Kira her knife. Kira wrapped her hand tight around the grip.

A nod sealed the alliance. They both understood the code. It had been pounded into them since they were little girls.

As of this moment, they were going to survive together. Or die that way.

CHAPTER 88

VANDA SAT BOLT upright at the edge of her cot, wakened by the Klaxon and shouts from the compound on the bluff above. She was packed into a small, sweltering tent with five other women, shoulder to shoulder. She was the youngest. The others were sleeping and snoring through the commotion, exhausted from the long day's work.

Vanda slipped off her cot and stepped out through the front of the tent. The cooking fires were still smoking. Through the haze, she could see the beams from the search party's flashlights above. More shouts. Pounding boots. Rattling weapons.

"Two columns!" "Move out!" "Find her, damnit!"

Her?

It had to be Kira! She was the only female up there—the

only worker dangerous enough to be locked in chains every night.

Vanda felt a piercing fear. She knew instantly what all the lights and the shouting meant. Somehow, some way, her only friend had escaped. And if they caught her again, they'd kill her for sure.

CHAPTER 89

KIRA LED LIAL down the left-hand path, the one with the crazy turns. It wasn't easy to navigate in the dark. Surface roots and drooping vines appeared out of nowhere, knocking them off balance as they ran. When Kira looked back, she saw light beams slicing through the jungle behind them. It looked like every man in the unit was out on the search.

Kira rounded a bend and pulled Lial behind a thick tree. They were both breathing hard. "We need to split up," said Kira. "Divide their attention. It's our best chance."

Lial nodded, looking into the tangle of trees and vines around them. She pointed left. "I'll head that way. You stay on the trail." Lial grabbed Kira's arm. "Don't worry. I won't lose you."

Kira looked toward the approaching lights. "They're almost at my trapline."

"What kind of traps?"

Kira's face flickered with a tight smile. "Every kind we learned in school."

There was a loud snap in the distance, followed by a sharp cry of pain. "One down," Kira whispered. Lial nodded, then ducked under a vine and disappeared into the darkness.

Kira gave Lial some lead time, then cupped her hands and made a howling sound, part animal, part human. She saw a cluster of lights shift in her direction. She headed off down the trail. From behind her, she heard another scream, then another, as the pursuers hit her trip wires. Kira couldn't even remember how many traps she'd set. Not enough. The lights kept coming.

She heard the rush of the river to her right, but she wasn't about to risk another night crossing. Instead, she took another branch off the main trail, moving in an arc toward where she estimated Lial would end up. By then, she hoped the mercenaries would be spread out and scared. Maybe they'd even give up. What was she worth to them anyway? At this point, she was just another slave in the mine.

The trail narrowed and dipped into a small ravine. Kira slowed down to traverse it, placing one foot in front of the other. Suddenly, she sensed movement to her rear. She froze in place, still as a stone. Flashlight beams flickered overhead. One of the teams had moved ahead of the rest! Kira could hear footsteps on the sodden jungle floor. She flattened herself against the bank of the ravine, held her breath, and waited for the patrol to go past her.

After the footsteps receded into the distance, she followed the ravine until the trail rose again. The instant her right foot touched level ground, she heard a loud crack. Her right leg collapsed. She dropped straight down. Her hip stopped her fall with a bone-jarring jolt. When she tried to pull herself out, pain shot through her left leg. She pushed aside a pile of dead brush and looked down to see a cluster of wooden spikes jabbing into her thigh.

It was a pit trap.

And not one of hers.

Kira heard foliage rustling to her right. She twisted her upper body to face the sound. "Lial?" she called out in a hoarse whisper. "I need help!"

The foliage parted.

Rupert Gurney stepped through.

His thick hair was matted and he was sweating through his green uniform. He held his rifle at his hip. It was pointed at Kira's head.

"You think you're the only one who can set a trap, Shaba?" Gurney's eyes were bloodshot and he sounded a bit deranged, maybe drunk. "I hope our design meets your standards."

Kira twisted and strained, but the more she struggled, the deeper the spikes dug into her flesh. She was in agonizing pain, but damned if she was going to show it.

"Why not just set a few land mines and be done with me?" she said through gritted teeth.

"Blow you to bits?" Gurney sneered. "Then how would

we know for sure it was you? Unless you left some hair behind." He took a step closer. His jaw tightened. "Look. Shaba. Whoever you are. I don't know where you came from. I don't know how the hell you got away. All I know is that it's time for your little legend to be over. Time for me to bring home the trophy."

He aimed the gun and fired.

The shot clipped Kira's shirt and barely nicked her right shoulder. Gurney dropped the gun and stood for a second with his knees partly bent. Kira froze as he fell to the ground face-first. A three-inch metal prong was sticking out of his brain stem. A shrouded figure stood behind him.

"Vanda!"

The skinny young Black woman bent over Gurney's body and twisted the shiv. "For my son," she whispered in his ear.

Vanda crawled over to Kira. Together, they managed to work the spikes loose from the springs and drop them into the pit. When Kira crawled out, dark red patches were seeping through the punctures in her pants.

Vanda reached up and grabbed a handful of wet leaves from a bush. She knelt down and pointed at Kira's wounds. "Wash!"

Kira grabbed Vanda by the shoulders. "Vanda, you have to go back! Same way you came. Back to your tent. No talk. Say nothing. Understand?" Kira put a finger over her lips. "Nothing!"

Vanda nodded. She understood. As she backed up on her hands and knees, her foot bumped into Gurney's body. She started shaking. Tears streamed down her face.

Kira wrapped her in a tight hug. "My friend," she whispered. "My good, true friend." Then she let go. Vanda stood up and slipped into the underbrush. In a second, she was gone.

Kira slid her shirt off her shoulder and checked the red stripe left by the bullet. A mild graze. Nothing to worry about. But her thigh was another matter. It was burning from the puncture wounds. Kira sat with her back against a tree and sliced her pant leg open with Lial's knife. She assessed the damage. Her quads and hamstrings were intact, but if the spikes had been dipped in poison, all the wet leaves in the world wouldn't help.

Suddenly, a powerful light blasted through the darkness in the distance. It was a spotlight, descending from the sky. Kira could hear the throb of an engine and the whipping of rotor blades.

The sound was coming from the compound. A helicopter was landing.

Reinforcements?

Kira grimaced and squeezed her eyes shut. Could this night get any worse?

CHAPTER 90

BLODGETT HADN'T BEEN expecting company, but he was ready to blast whoever it was to kingdom come.

He and the other four giants kept their rifles trained on the chopper as it descended. Gurney had ordered all five to stay behind and guard the compound. And now it looked like they might have to earn their money.

The giants knelt down and shielded their faces as the chopper landed in the clearing, blowing up a huge cloud of debris and red dust. When the engine shut down, all five men stood up and moved forward, rifles aimed toward the cabin.

The door opened. It looked like there was only one soul on board—the pilot. He jumped out, hands raised, stooping under the prop wash.

"I'll be damned!" said Blodgett, lowering his gun barrel. "It's Leo!"

"I hope to hell he brought money," growled Marley.

Leo walked over from the landing zone, red-faced and irate. He got right to the point. "What the hell is going on down here?" He looked past the giants. "And where's Gurney?"

Harper nodded toward the jungle. "Out there. Chasing demons."

"One of the workers escaped," Tagaloa explained. "A constant troublemaker."

"Christ!" Leo turned and started walking toward the mine. "A nettlesome worker? Does that explain why shipments have slowed?" Blodgett looked at his buddies. Was this what Leo's visit was about? Did he really come all the way from Belgium for a production check?

Leo reached the platform that overlooked the mine pit. He walked out onto it, then looked back at the giants in a rage. "Where is everybody? Why is nobody working?"

The five men looked at one another. Then Fenwick spoke up in his thick brogue. "It's one in the morning, Chief. Kinda hard to sort rocks with a flashlight."

Leo was clearly in no mood for excuses. He waved his clawed hand in the air. "Then find generators! Bring in work lights! This mine should be producing around the clock! If you hulks can't do it, I'll find people who can." He turned back toward the empty pit and placed both hands on the rail. Like a king on his balcony. "*Everybody is disposable!*" he shouted.

Smack!

A bullet hit him square in the forehead.

CHAPTER 91

THE SHOT CAME from the jungle.

Kira blinked as the man from the helicopter tumbled headfirst into the mine. Her curiosity had overwhelmed her instinct for self-preservation. She had worked her way back to the edge of the pit, crouching behind a felled tree trunk, close enough to overhear what the stranger had been saying. She saw the way the five giants kowtowed to him—right up until the second his skull exploded.

A few seconds later, the entire tree line erupted with gunfire, splintering the wooden platform and kicking up dirt on the rim of the mine. Kira saw the giants take cover behind anything they could find. They leveled their rifles and started to return fire. The air crackled and popped with single shots and long automatic bursts. Muzzle flashes lit up the compound.

Kira pressed herself flat onto the ground, lifting her head just enough to peek around the tree trunk.

Suddenly, a figure flopped down beside her with a heavy thump. Kira rolled onto her side and brought up her knife. A hand grabbed her wrist. "Stop! It's me."

Lial's face was shiny with sweat and streaked with dirt. She released Kira's hand and nodded toward the jungle. "Cal's men—a Somali militia," she said between breaths. "About fifty of them."

"Why are they here? What were they saying?"

"They have a very specific mission," said Lial. "They came to kill you."

That was a bit of a gut punch, but in a strange way, Kira felt flattered. "Me? Why send a whole army?"

Lial inched forward on her belly and peeked over the dead tree. "Because they think Doc Savage is here with you."

Kira felt a surge of adrenaline. She grabbed Lial's arm. "Doc? So he's still alive?"

"Apparently Cal thinks so." Lial glanced down and saw Kira's blood-soaked thigh. "What happened there?"

"Stupid. The assholes set a trap, and I walked right into it."

Another volley of fire blasted from the jungle, pinning the giants down. Lial reached into her backpack and fished out a plastic syringe. She pulled the needle cap off with her teeth and spit it away. She nodded toward Kira's hip. "Pants."

Kira tucked her thumb under her waistband and lowered it enough to expose the top of her right buttock. Lial jabbed the needle in. "Gentamicin," she said. "Kills almost anything." She tossed the syringe away. "How's the pain?"

Kira's leg was throbbing and burning from hip to toe. "It's fine." She knew Lial would have said the same thing.

The firing from the jungle was getting more intense. Kira saw the first line of invaders emerge from the trees, taking positions on the opposite side of the mine. The five giants were laying down a field of fire, but they were clearly outgunned.

Kira realized now that this was her fight. She was done running. But to engage, she needed weapons and ammunition and support. Lial seemed to know what she was thinking. She pulled out her Glock, slid in a fresh clip, and rose to her knees. She pointed toward the right flank of Cal's force. "I'll go make a nuisance of myself. Do what you need to do." She made a dash for the undergrowth.

Kira moved around the edge of the trunk and started crawling toward the compound. Every move put her punctured thigh in contact with the rough ground. Agony. She gritted her way through it and kept going. Kira had been shot at more times than she could remember. But this was different. This was a battle zone. It was terrifying. It was deafening. The air was buzzing with death.

As she moved through the field of fire, puffs of red dirt exploded around her. She heard bangs from Lial's pistol in the jungle. Muzzle flashes started blasting in that direction. The distraction was working. It was giving the five defenders time to find better cover and reload.

Kira inched closer, circling behind them. The giants reminded her of Doc. At least in size. They were fierce fighters. And for the moment, they were holding off the men who came to kill her.

That made them her new best friends.

CHAPTER 92

BLODGETT AND HIS mates made a strategic retreat to a position behind a row of three huge metal dumpsters. Now they were firing from between the containers and over them, as rounds hit the metal panels like blows from a sledgehammer.

Blodgett emptied a full clip, then rolled onto his back and pulled another from his pocket. As he jammed it home, he saw movement behind him. They were being flanked! "Check your six!" he shouted.

The others whipped around as Kira stepped out of the shadows, hands up. "I'm unarmed! Don't shoot!"

Blodgett put his sight square on her heart anyway. "What the fuck?" he muttered.

Another volley hit the dumpsters. The giants turned to return fire. Kira dropped to the ground and crawled forward until she was wedged between Blodgett and Marley behind the middle dumpster.

"Did you boys miss me?" she asked. She reached over and pulled a .45 from Marley's holster. She stretched out in a prone firing position and started placing shots from between two dumpsters. On the other side of the mine, one intruder fell. Then another. And another.

Fenwick looked over. "Jesus! Shaba doesn't miss!"

Kira was out of ammo. She made a gimme motion with one hand. Fenwick tossed her another clip.

"Who the hell are we shooting at?" asked Tagaloa between rounds.

"Somali militia," said Kira. "They're looking for me."

"You're popular tonight," said Harper as he reloaded. "Gurney's looking for you, too—personally." A bullet kicked up dirt beside him.

"Gurney's dead," said Kira, getting off another shot. "And the rest of your buddies were probably ambushed by these guys. I wouldn't count on them for reinforcements. It's just us."

Blodgett lifted his head to peek over one of the dumpsters. A bullet pinged off the metal rim. He ducked back down. "They're advancing!" he called out.

Kira emptied another clip, driving a few intruders back under cover. "Don't stop!" Kira shouted. "Keep the pressure on!"

Blodgett looked over at the young woman beside him. She had caused him a shitload of trouble over the past few weeks. And now this. "Tell me something. Why the hell should we fight to save your ass?"

"Because she's earned it!" A booming male voice from behind.

Blodgett whipped around.

He saw a huge man silhouetted against the night sky, two rifles braced on his hips and a cutlass through his belt.

Kira dropped her pistol and screamed. *"Doc!"*

CHAPTER 93

I FELT LIKE my heart was about to explode through my chest. Bullets slammed against the dumpsters as Kira launched herself into my arms. It was really her!

At that moment, nothing else mattered. Not pain. Not exhaustion. Not even gunfire. "My God!" Kira shouted into my ear. "Where the hell have you been?"

I lowered her to the ground and wrapped myself around her. "I've been looking for a demon with copper-colored hair," I said. "Seen one?"

The others had stopped shooting. They were just staring.

"Aladdin?" said Fenwick, squinting. "Is that you?"

"I'll be damned," said Tagaloa.

Kira looked up at me. "Wait. You know these guys?"

"We went to the same school," I said.

Kira looked bewildered. "University of Chicago?"

I shook my head. "Foreign study."

Suddenly an RPG round hit the dumpster at the far end, lifting it two feet off the ground. Tagaloa and Harper were blown back across the dirt, weapons flying. They both shook off the impact and crawled back to their positions.

Then everything was quiet from the other side.

I huddled with Kira next to my old comrades. "What's happening?" asked Fenwick.

"Maybe they gave up," said Harper.

"They're getting into position for a final assault," said Kira. She plucked another clip from Fenwick's pocket and reloaded the .45.

"Anybody got some extra nine-mil ammo?" A female voice.

I swung my gun around. I saw a petite woman with a ponytail holding up a Glock. Kira jumped up to grab her and pulled her down with the rest of us. The woman looked over and stared at me. She squinted in the darkness. "Wait. You're Doc Savage!"

"Right," I said. "And who the hell are you?"

"This is Lial," said Kira. "She saved my life. She used to work for Cal Savage."

Cal Savage? The only Cal Savage I'd ever heard of was my ancestor's twin brother. He'd been dead for decades. "Who the hell are you talking about?"

Kira realized that I had some catching up to do. I thought I was the only Savage left in the world.

"Listen to me," she said. "I'm talking about Cal Savage the *Fourth*—your third cousin."

"I didn't know I *had* a cousin!"

"That's because he's been living in the shadows his whole life. And now he's your worst nightmare. The *world's* worst nightmare. He's the one who sent the assassins to kill us in Chicago. He's the one who had the boys on the island murdered. He's the one who kidnapped me." She pointed her pistol toward the invaders on the other side of the dumpsters. "And he's the one who sent the army out there. They came for us. You and me."

"And after you're both out of the way," said Lial, "he plans to take over the world, one failed country at a time."

Marley was looking at me with a furrowed forehead. I could see that he was trying to follow the thread, but he was a few steps behind. "Doc Savage?" he said. "Like from those old books?"

There was a loud sizzle and a pop overhead. A flare ignited, casting an eerie red glow over the entire compound. Blodgett looked out between two dumpsters and stuck his rifle through the gap. "Lock and load, boys and girls—here they come!"

CHAPTER 94

NO TIME TO think. Everything was reflex now. I took a position next to Kira and started firing with one of the poachers' AR-15s. I could see fighters approaching from about fifty yards away, darting and weaving as they came, rifles blasting. Rounds were hitting all around us.

Marley took a bullet to the shoulder and spun backward until he landed flat on his back. "Fuck this!" he shouted toward the sky. He threw down his rifle and rolled onto his knees. Then he started running in a low crouch toward a row of tents about twenty yards away. I never pegged Marley for a deserter, but then, I'd never seen him in a real firefight.

The attackers kept coming. I emptied one clip and loaded another. I aimed and pulled the trigger. The gun jammed! I reached for my other rifle, the antique Mauser. A shot ricocheted off the dumpster and tore a fresh hole in my shirt.

I saw Lial pick up Marley's rifle and start shooting. But within a few seconds, she was out of ammo.

I looked down the row and saw that Harper and Fenwick were out, too. That left me, Kira, Blodgett, and Tagaloa. Not enough firepower. The incoming rounds were pinning us down. It wouldn't be long before they overran us. I pulled out my cutlass in case it came to that.

Then, over the gunfire, I heard a wild shout from the other side of the dumpster. Suddenly, the whole battlefield lit up with flames. I crawled out between the dumpsters and saw Marley standing spread-legged with a flamethrower, driving the attackers back. Some of them dropped and squirmed on the ground, coated in fire. There was grimy smoke everywhere. It was hell on earth.

I kept firing, picking my shots. Then I saw Kira and Lial alongside me. "Get back, damnit!" I shouted. Lial was using a gun she must have gotten from one of the other guys, and Kira still had the .45. They were crouched side by side, covering our flanks while I focused on the field straight ahead. Marley's fuel tank was empty now and his fire was out. I saw a skinny attacker with a red bandana burst out of nowhere. Marley knocked him out cold with the handle of the flamethrower. With my last bullets, I took down two more coming straight at me.

And then it was over.

Kira and Lial held their fire.

The field in front of us was clear, except for a bunch of bodies, some of them still burning.

Marley dropped his flamethrower and knelt down in the dirt. The rest of our team emerged from the other side of the dumpsters. "Holy shit," said Tagaloa.

I dropped my rifle and went over to check Marley's shoulder. His entire right sleeve was soaked with blood. I ripped the shirt open and applied pressure to the wound. Marley grimaced with pain. It was messy, but there was no major damage. "You'll survive," I told him.

"Damn right," he said. "I haven't got paid yet."

I saw his eyes shift. I turned around. A figure staggered out of the haze. He had a pistol pointed at Kira. I heard Lial shout, "Abai! No!" She jumped between them as the man fired. I saw Lial spin backward as Kira fired back. The man dropped onto the ground.

I ran over. Kira was bent over Lial. I saw a dark-red hole in her shirt and a stream of blood oozing from her mouth. She looked up at Kira and spoke between gasps. "That's the last time...I'm saving you tonight." Kira pulled Lial to her chest and held her. We both saw the exit wound. Kira looked at me and shook her head. There was no chance.

Lial was still talking. "Bring me...his comms." She nodded toward the dead man on the ground. I grabbed the sat phone off his belt and handed it to her. I watched her hands tremble as she pressed a three-digit code. The speaker crackled and a male voice came through. He sounded anxious and excited. "Abai! What's the report?"

Lial held the phone close to her mouth. Her voice was

weak, but clear. "Cal, it's Lial. I'm here . . . with Abai. The mine . . . is secure."

The phone cracked again, the voice rising. "Lial? You're there? What about Sunlight and Savage?"

Lial looked up at Kira, then over at me. "We found them," she said. "It's over. They went down together."

She cut off the transmission and let the phone drop. Kira lowered her gently back down onto the ground. "I'm sorry," said Kira. "It should have been me."

"It's okay," said Lial. "It feels good . . . to be free."

Her head drooped back. She was gone.

CHAPTER 95

NONE OF US got any sleep that night.

At first light, I was standing at the edge of the mine when the workers started moving up in small clusters from the tent village. Even from a distance, I could see that they were terrified. Women stayed behind the men. Children huddled behind their mothers. They'd obviously heard the shots and explosions from the night before, and they had no idea what was waiting for them up here. But apparently, they were even more terrified of not reporting to work.

The edge of the compound was lined with bodies, covered in canvas tarps. There were still dark bloodstains on the ground and bullet marks everywhere. The platform overlooking the mine was practically in splinters.

Kira stood beside me with a bullhorn in her hand. Blodgett, Marley, Harper, Fenwick, and Tagaloa stood behind us, arms folded. No weapons, for once in their lives.

Kira put the bullhorn to her mouth and pressed the Talk button. Her words echoed across the compound. *"Njoo hapa!"* she said, "Please, come here!" Then, *"Usio-gope!* Don't be afraid!"

I noticed the pretty young Black woman at the head of the crowd. Tall and regal. She couldn't have been more than eighteen. I knew it had to be Vanda. Kira had told me all about her. The crowd followed her right over to where we were standing.

Kira put the bullhorn down as the workers formed a semicircle in front of us. Men, women, kids. Maybe two hundred in all. I could see that some of them avoided looking at Kira, and I understood why. They were still worried that she was a demon.

Kira put her hands on Vanda's shoulders and turned her around to face the other workers. "You all know Vanda," Kira called out. "She will translate." Vanda let out a nervous breath, then nodded firmly.

"The mine is closed for the day," said Kira. "But you will all still be paid."

As Vanda called out the translation, Marley and Tagaloa dragged a huge chest out in front of us. The chest had been liberated overnight from the command tent. It was overflowing with money.

"Tell everybody to line up," said Kira.

"Kuunda mstari!" Vanda called out, making a column shape with her skinny arms.

The semicircle collapsed into a single-file line. I could

hear the workers mumbling. But nobody left. Frightened or not, they were all desperate to collect their fifty-cent wage.

Kira beckoned the workers forward. She reached down into the chest. Into each worker's hand, she placed a thousand dollars in cash—about five years' income. I saw mouths gape in disbelief. A ripple of excitement started to run down the line. When it reached the workers in back, they leaned out and craned their necks, looking forward with wide eyes.

As each family of workers collected their money, some of them started hopping and dancing in the dirt, waving the bills in the air or stuffing them inside their shirts. I heard shouts of *"Asante, asante!"* Thank you, thank you! Then, *"Asante, Shaba!"*

When all the other workers had been paid, Kira turned to Vanda. She handed her a thousand dollars—then another thousand. *"Kwa mwanao,"* said Kira softly. "For your son."

Vanda wrapped her long arms around Kira's shoulders. Tears were streaming down her dark cheeks. Then an incredible smile broke through.

I'm not sure why Kira assigned the next part of the speech to me, but I was more than happy to give it.

I asked Vanda to quiet the workers.

She wiped her eyes and clapped her hands together. *"Nyamaza!"* she called out. *"Nyamaza!"*

The shouts and celebration instantly settled down. The

workers clustered around us again. Vanda nodded to me, ready to translate. She had no idea what I was about to say.

I cleared my throat and pointed toward the pit. "Tell the workers that this mine now belongs to them."

Vanda blinked. She hesitated. I nodded. Then she called out the words, clear and strong. This time there was only stunned silence.

I had more.

"All the profits from the mine will go directly to the workers," I said. "And from now on, the person in charge here . . . will be Vanda."

Vanda looked at me, then at Kira. Her mouth hung open. Kira grabbed Vanda's arm and squeezed it. "You're the boss now," she whispered. "Speak up. Tell them!"

She did.

The crowd started chanting her name. *"Vanda! Vanda!"*

"Hours will be shorter," I called out. "Your children will go to school every day, not to work." I turned to the five giants behind me. "And if anyone bothers you, these men will handle it. They are not your supervisors. They are your protectors."

Vanda translated it all. Gleeful shouts burst from the crowd. Women rushed Vanda and smothered her with hugs. Men gave her enthusiastic pats on the head.

I watched as one of the smallest kids approached Marley. He lifted his eyes as if he were sizing up a mountain. Marley grunted, then reached down with one hand and swung the kid up until he was straddling his thick neck.

The kid stuck his arms straight up into the air as if he'd just scored a goal. The crowd cheered.

I looked over at Kira. She was smiling at me. I felt a sudden rush of pure joy. I thought I'd never see that smile again. I grabbed her around the waist and pulled her close. Then I leaned down and kissed her, long and deep. Right there in front of everybody.

The cheers got even louder.

CHAPTER 96

WE SPENT THE rest of that day burying the dead. With the help of some of the workers, we planted Abai and his minions in long rows near the rim of the mine, as a warning to any future intruders. Kira insisted on a separate plot for Lial, under a spreading limba tree at the other end of the compound, near where Vanda had buried her baby.

The next morning, we were standing next to Leo's helicopter to say our goodbyes. Harper had checked out the engine, hydraulics, and the fuselage. A few bullet holes, but no serious damage. The tank had enough fuel to get us to Mbala Airport in Zambia. We could fill up there.

We were leaving the five giants with enough cash to cover their salaries for a year, time enough to hire and train some local guards for when they moved on. They were mercenaries at heart, but they were also men of honor. I looked each of them in the eye as we shook hands. Marley. Fenwick. Harper. Blodgett. Tagaloa. I knew I could trust them. So did Kira.

Vanda brought us a sack filled with bananas and berries for the trip. I gave her a hug, then stepped back as Kira wrapped her up in her arms and whispered into her ear. Something in Swahili. Just between the two of them.

"Sure you don't want some extra muscle, Aladdin?" asked Fenwick.

"No, thanks," I said. "We need to do this alone."

"It's a family matter," added Kira. She gave each of the giants a quick hug then stepped back. "I want you all to remember who you work for now." They all nodded like obedient schoolboys. Marley turned and gave Vanda a proper salute. Vanda patted her heart with the palm of her hand.

It was time to go.

Blodgett handed me a nylon duffel wrapped in plastic. It was packed with weapons and ammo. "Happy hunting," he said.

Kira had already strapped herself into the pilot's seat. I heard the engine whine. The rotor started to turn. I tossed the duffel into the back with my own bag. I ducked under the rotor and climbed into the passenger seat from the other side. I fastened my shoulder harness as Kira flicked switches on the control panel. We both put on our headphones. She wiggled the stick and we lifted off, spraying dust and trash as we ascended. When we cleared the trees, Kira banked hard and headed east.

"Ever flown one of these before?" I asked.

Kira gave me her cocky little smile. "How hard could it be?"

CHAPTER 97

WE REFUELED IN Mbala, and again in Dar es Salaam. We waited at the airfield there for nightfall. Now we were out over open water, heading north toward the Arabian Sea. Kira stayed low, barely brushing the waves. We could see the lights from oil tankers and cargo ships glowing the distance.

"What am I looking for?" I asked, scanning the horizon.

"An invisible yacht," said Kira.

I glanced over to look at her in the glow of the cockpit lights. One of the young mine workers had donated a tank top and a pair of gym shorts to replace Kira's bloody clothes. I could see the puncture wounds on her thigh below the hem. The bruises looked red and angry on her pale skin.

"How's the leg?" I asked.

Kira shrugged. Since the day I first met her, she'd never talked about injuries. Never complained about pain. She just sucked it up. "If it was poison," she said, "I'd already be dead."

I felt a lurch as she dropped the airspeed. In a few seconds, we were hovering over the water like a huge dragonfly. Kira pointed through the cabin bubble into the distance. "There."

The moon was casting bright reflections on the water. For a few seconds, I couldn't see anything else. I shifted in my seat and leaned forward. I squinted. Wait. Yes! I could make it out now—a faint unnatural outline blending with the sea and sky, about a half mile away. The camouflage was nearly foolproof, especially at night.

"That's the *Prizrak*," said Kira. "Cal Savage's ghost."

I felt a bitter taste rising in my throat. I thought about the assassins who tried to kill us in Chicago and the murdered boys on the beach. I now realized that it was Cal Savage who had sent Aaron Vail to find me. I thought about being dragged and nearly drowned behind that speedboat. I thought about what Cal Savage had done to Kira, kidnapping her, then sending her off to one of the deadliest places on the planet. All to serve his maniacal plans. Who knows how many deaths he'd been responsible for along the way?

"Are you ready?" Kira asked.

I nodded. Eighteen hours ago, I didn't even know Cal Savage existed. Now, relative or not, I wanted to wipe him off the face of the earth. The world would be better for it.

"Is there a helipad?" I asked.

Kira shook her head. "They'd shoot us down before we even got close."

She was right. It's hard to sneak up on somebody in a helicopter, even in the dark. But we were now hovering over the sea, with no land in sight. What did she have in mind?

"Grab the duffel," she said.

I reached behind my seat and pulled out the plastic-wrapped bag. I felt the chopper descending even closer to the water.

"Open your door," Kira ordered.

Was she kidding? I yanked the handle and let the door fly open. The chopper tilted hard to the right.

"Jump!" shouted Kira. We were banked so far over, I had to look up to see her. She jabbed her finger toward the open door. "*Now!*"

"What about you?" I shouted.

"I'll be right behind you!" she shouted back.

I pulled off my headphones and held the bag to my chest with one hand. I grabbed the sack with my money and cutlass in the other. I unstrapped and took a deep breath. I slid out of the seat feetfirst and dropped about twenty feet straight into the water and down into the darkness. As I kicked my way back up, I worked my shoes loose and let them drop. Too much deadweight.

As soon as I resurfaced, I saw the chopper hovering off to my left, about twenty yards away. The engine was laboring, and waves were slapping the skids. Kira was ditching! Suddenly, the nose tilted forward and the rotor hit the water, throwing up a huge wall of spray. When it cleared, the fuselage was bent and the cabin was flooded and sinking.

"Kira!!"

The cockpit was almost totally under now. The cabin lights were sparking and blinking out. I started kicking toward the wreck. Then I felt something grab my leg. I whipped around.

Kira surfaced right behind me and spit out a stream of seawater. "Let's go, Doc," she said. "Beautiful night for a swim."

CHAPTER 98

MY ARMS AND legs were burning. Lungs, too.

We'd covered most of the distance underwater, about twenty yards at a time. It took us about thirty minutes to get close. The current was against us, and the weapons bag was a drag around my shoulders.

We surfaced about ten yards from the yacht. Even up close, it was hard to tell where the water ended and the ship began. The engines were quiet and the anchor lines were out. The *Prizrak* was rolling gently on the waves.

We swam close enough to touch the hull. It rose up in a gentle curve about twenty feet to the main deck. No way up. Not without grappling hooks. Kira ducked underwater again and headed toward the stern. I took a deep breath, made a surface dive, and followed her bubble trail.

We came up again next to a low platform at the rear of the ship. The surface was pebbled rubber. I saw a pair of

Jet Skis covered in black canvas near the rear of the platform. There was a small light facing down from the upper deck, and the bundled Jet Skis cast a thick shadow over the starboard side. I pulled the duffel strap off my shoulder and eased the bag onto the platform, then climbed aboard.

Kira had a knife in her teeth. She sliced the plastic cover and unzipped the bag. I reached in. There was a little seepage from the swim, but the guns and ammo clips were mostly dry.

I pulled out an M4 rifle, one of Blodgett's spares, tipped with a silencer. Kira pulled out Marley's .45, his parting gift to her. I pulled my antique cutlass out of its sack and stuck it through my belt. I put the sack with my money into the duffel and pushed it under the Jet Skis.

I figured I'd come back for it later—if I came back at all.

We both slithered up onto the platform and just lay there in the shadow, catching our breath. I could feel the rise and fall of the ship underneath me. The back half of a fiberglass lifeboat projected out over us about twenty feet up. I could hear music from somewhere inside the ship. Sounded like Foo Fighters.

Kira inched over to me and whispered in my ear. "He's got cameras everywhere," she said. "We need to move fast. Cal's cabin is on the main deck, amidships, right below the bridge."

I nodded, then grabbed her by the arm. "Stay with me," I whispered. "And be careful."

"When am I not?" she whispered back.

She rolled to her left and started climbing the short staircase to the deck. I flicked my safety off and followed right behind her. Water from our wet clothes dripped onto the treads.

Kira took the first steps onto the main deck, leaving shiny wet prints on the teak. She pressed her back against the outer wall of the rear cabin. I slid in beside her.

We inched forward together, watching for movement, looking for cameras, listening for alarms.

Suddenly, I heard footsteps on metal. I grabbed Kira and pulled her behind me. A man with a rifle popped out of a stairwell about ten feet ahead of us. *Thip, thip!* I put two bullets through his chest. He tumbled backward, out of sight.

I led the way forward. We made it another few yards along the cabin wall.

There was a loud bang. Then the whole damn ship lit up.

Caught!

CHAPTER 99

A SPOTLIGHT BEAM pinned us against the cabin wall. Two shots splintered the decking between our feet. My adrenaline went into overdrive. Kira rolled right and got off three shots with her pistol. The spotlight exploded in a fizz of flame and smoke. I saw two figures drop over the rail.

"How many?" I asked. "How many in the crew?"

"Ten, maybe twelve. Lial said they're all killers."

I heard movement right above us on the main deck. I stepped away from the wall and aimed up. Took three quick shots. Dropped three shooters. Kira was already moving toward the main cabin.

"Twelve o'clock!" I whispered. Footsteps were coming from around the curve of the partition directly ahead of us. The next second, I heard footsteps behind me. We both dropped to our knees, back-to-back, I heard Kira's gun blast three times and heard three loud thuds. I saw four shadows crossing the stern. I shot two on the move. The other two stuck their barrels out from behind the partition and fired blind. The bullets tore through the decking and blasted a gap in a wooden railing. When the shooters stuck their heads out to check for results, I popped them both.

I felt Kira's shoulders pressing against mine as she reloaded.

We waited, guns raised. My heart was pounding.

Nothing but silence.

Kira stood up and waved me toward the main cabin. She tried the door. Locked. She stood back and fired a round through the latch. The door flew open. I stepped through first, gun raised. I saw a rumpled bed, a control console, and another open door. When Kira came in behind me, I held her back. Were we walking into an ambush?

We heard footsteps on the upper deck, heading for the stern. Kira pushed right past me. "It's him!"

I followed her through the cabin to the port side. A metal staircase led to the top deck. Kira started up. I grabbed her around the waist and scrambled past her. No way I was letting her go first.

I stepped onto the top deck. It was lit up by a dozen lights, aiming from every direction. Through the glare I spotted a slender guy in shorts and a T-shirt trying to work the controls for the lifeboat launch. Another crew member? I felt Kira come up behind me. She aimed

over my shoulder and fired once. Her shot split the lifeboat cable. The boat slid backward on metal rails and
dropped over the stern. We heard the splash when it hit
the water. The man turned with his hands up. "Don't
shoot!"

Kira moved past me, her gun aimed at his head.
"Nowhere to go now, Cal," she said.

I blinked in the glare. Holy shit. This was no crew
member. This was the captain. I was looking at Cal
Savage.

I moved closer, searching his features for some family
resemblance. Then I realized that he looked exactly like
I used to—pale, skinny, and scared. He stared back and
forth between me and Kira, not believing his eyes.

"I know," I said. "We're dead."

Cal looked past us toward the stairs. "Lial! Where's
Lial?"

"Free of you," said Kira.

I saw a change come over Cal's face. Something clicked.
A mental adjustment. He took a step toward us.

"Then it's just us now," he said. "The three of us." He
slowly lowered his hands. I could see his mind working,
spinning, calculating. "The world has no idea what that
means—what the three of us can do together. Doc Savage. Cal Savage. Kira Sunlight." He spread his arms out.
"This yacht? It's a trinket compared to what we can have.
What *you* can have. Everything is in play. I've done the
hard work. All we have to do now is . . ."

Kira fired a shot into the air.

"Cal," she said. "Stop talking. Lial told me everything."

"So we *do* have a future together," I said. "At The Hague. When we watch you being tried for crimes against humanity."

I saw Cal's expression shift again—to defiance. "In that case," he said, looking straight at me, "this is our last family reunion."

He pulled up his shirt. Thick strap. Blinking light.

"Bomb!" Kira screamed.

A white blast. My hearing cut out.

I was flying. Then falling.

Then nothing.

CHAPTER 100

THE NEXT LIGHT I saw was the sun.

It was blazing hot, burning down on me as I floated in greenish-blue water. My arm was wrapped around some kind of plastic bolster, and my whole body was in pain. I tried to shake my head clear. The water was coated with a slick of oil. It was on my skin and down my throat. My stomach heaved. I lifted my head and screamed out, *"Kira!"*

Silence.

I churned my legs to whip myself around in a circle. I was bleeding from my head and my arm. Shards of fiberglass and small bits of wood floated by. I was surrounded by the *Prizrak*—in pieces. I felt something bang against my leg. I reached down. My cutlass! My clothes were in shreds but somehow the blade was still stuck through my belt.

The glare on the water was blinding, but I had to get

moving. I had to start searching. I picked a direction and started kicking, shouting out between strokes. *"Kira!... Kira!"*

No response.

I was gasping and choking. My throat was burning. My mind was reeling. I couldn't absorb the reality of my situation. I couldn't accept that I'd lost her again. But it was true. And her death was on my hands.

It was my plan to attack the ship on our own. We could have asked for help. We could have brought the giants. What the hell made me think we were so invincible? Pride? Arrogance? My damned Doc Savage genes?

I pushed through a patch of blackened plastic debris. I ducked under again and tried to rub the oil off my face.

When I resurfaced, I was in a whole new mass of flotsam. The bolster was losing its buoyancy. I looked for a beam, a life jacket, anything that would help keep me afloat. Or should I just admit defeat and give up? Start thrashing and let the sharks come for me? Without Kira, what the hell did it matter?

I spotted something squarish and beige in the distance. Maybe part of a wooden chair, mostly underwater. As I stared, the current started to turn it away from me. Behind it, I caught a flash of color.

Bright. Like copper.

Kira!

I took a gulp of air and made a surface dive. I left the bolster behind and started kicking and stroking underwater with everything I had. No more pain. Every sensation faded except for the feeling of the water pulsing past me. My eyes were wide open now. I didn't even feel the sting of the saltwater. I refused to lose sight of the figure ahead of me. It was getting clearer through the green ripples. Pale skin. Blue shorts. Long, dangling legs.

It was her! It *had* to be her! Please, God, let her be alive . . .

I surfaced about three feet away and grabbed her. Her eyes were closed. Her lips were crusted. Her shoulders were sunburned to a bright red. There was a gash on her forehead. One arm was wrapped around the legs of the wooden bar chair. The other dangled loosely in the water. I shook it. *"Kira! It's me! Wake up!"*

She was limp. Lifeless.

Then, suddenly, her head twitched and her legs started moving. I felt a surge of hope. I shook her again. Her eyes half opened, then immediately clamped shut again from the glare. But she saw me and heard me. I knew it! She grabbed my arm and squeezed it. Her cracked lips curled into a slight smile.

"Sorry," she mumbled. "This seat is taken."

I wrapped myself around her. I kissed her neck, her hair, her sunburned shoulders, every part of her that I could reach. "I love you, Kira Sunlight," I said.

I realized that I'd never actually said it before. Not in so many words.

"What a coincidence," she rasped. "I love you, too."

She lifted her head out of the water and wrapped one arm around my neck. We were alive and we were together, but we were still in big trouble—bleeding, exhausted, and in the middle of the Arabian Sea.

"Uh-oh," Kira said softly. "Look." She was squinting into the distance. I followed her line of sight. Then I saw it.

A low shape was headed straight for us, kicking up a small wake.

Kira barely had enough energy to speak. "If those are pirates," she mumbled, "I'll be really pissed off."

CHAPTER 101

THE BOAT WAS coming at us through the glare of the sun. I pulled the cutlass out of my belt as it got closer. My heart was thudding. Whoever it was, I was ready to fight with everything I had left.

I heard a man shouting.

I raised my hand to shield my eyes as the boat pulled up alongside. It was all wood, about forty feet long, with an open deck in front and a cabin at the stern. I could see nets dangling over the side and poles with tackle poking up from the rails.

A wave of relief washed over me.

Not pirates. Fishermen.

A slender brown-skinned man was leaning over the gunwale, both hands reaching out.

I grabbed Kira under the arms and towed her over. The man grabbed her right wrist. Then a woman in a headscarf appeared and grabbed her left. Together, they hauled her up the side of the boat and onto the deck.

I reached for the rail with one hand. Pain shot through my shoulder as I muscled myself partway up. The man and woman grabbed me by the belt and pulled me in the rest of the way. I flopped down on the deck next to Kira, spewing saltwater.

Suddenly, the man and woman backed off. I realized that I was still holding the cutlass. I stuck it back through my belt and held up both hands. *"Rafiki,"* I gasped. "Friend."

"Friend," the woman repeated. She bent down to help Kira to her feet. The man did the same for me. They half carried us into the boat's low-roofed cabin and laid us down on thin foam mattresses. Then the woman took over. I felt my wet clothes being tugged off. Then I felt a cool cloth on my head and the sting of antiseptic on my arm. I looked over. Kira got the same treatment. The woman covered our bare bodies with a blanket and backed out of the cabin with our clothes. "Friend," she repeated.

I tucked my cutlass close to my side, then felt for Kira's hand under the covers. I closed my eyes. My brain was spinning. Maybe I had a concussion or sunstroke. Maybe I was delirious. None of this felt real. But if it was a dream, it was a good one.

And if I was dead, maybe this was heaven.

CHAPTER 102

I MUST HAVE slept for twenty-four hours. When I blinked awake, the sun was almost in the same place it was when we arrived. I could smell smoke and heard the sizzle of something cooking. Kira was already awake. She poked my arm. "Look," she whispered. "Somebody's here."

I lifted my head off the mattress. Two young kids were peering into the cabin. A boy and a girl, maybe seven or eight years old. Skinny. Barefoot. In shorts and T-shirts. The boy whispered to the girl. She whispered back, then doubled over, laughing.

The woman from yesterday appeared in the doorway and nudged the kids aside.

"What's so funny?" I asked. "What are they saying?"

The woman grinned, showing a bright smile with a gap in the middle. "They say you're a very big fish."

She tossed our clothes onto the blanket. They were clean and dry and warm from the sun. And the holes had all been mended. We got dressed under the covers and then crawled out onto the deck.

The man was busy at the stern baiting hooks. Kira turned to the woman. "You speak English?"

She shrugged. "Mostly Arabic and Somali. But enough English to get by."

The man set his fishing pole in a socket and walked over, sure-footed on the tilting deck. The woman grabbed his sinewy arm. "I am Ayann. This is Dahir, my husband." She pointed at the kids. "Our son, Hani. Our daughter, Halima." They were both standing at the stern with their skinny legs apart, holding long heavy-duty fishing poles.

I rubbed my head. Was I crazy? "The kids," I said. "Where were they yesterday—when you found us?"

"They were hiding in the hold," said Ayann, "until we knew it was safe."

"Want food?" asked Dahir.

"Yes!" said Kira. "Anything."

There was a small propane stove in the middle of the deck with a smoking pan on top. Dahir lifted the lid and reached in with a fork. Ayann pulled two metal plates from a bin. Dahir speared two fillets of fish out of the pan and served them up. Ayann reached into a battered cooler and pulled out two icy bottles of mineral water.

Kira and I sat back against the cabin and wolfed down the fish. It was charred and flaky and delicious. I polished off my water bottle in one long gulp. Ayann handed me another. "Your names?"

I hesitated. Should we make something up? Did we need new identities? Could these people be trusted?

No hesitation from my partner. "I'm Kira," she said. I guess she was tired of hiding.

"Okay then. I'm Doc."

Dahir was wiping the grease from the cooking pan. He stopped and looked over. "You are a doctor?"

I shook my head. "Not the useful kind."

"It's a nickname," said Kira. "Family tradition."

"*Samaka! Samaka!*" Halima was shouting. Her pole was bent into a steep curve. Kira and I jumped up as the tiny girl leaned back and reeled in a huge silver-green fish. She trapped it with her bare foot as it flopped onto the deck, then pulled out the hook and tossed her catch into a hatch. She reached into a small bucket squirming with live sardines. Within ten seconds, she rebaited the hook and threw her line out again.

"She's very quick," I said.

Dahir grinned as he checked his own line. "Most days, she catches more than me."

Ayann told us that the family came from a small village near Burgabo. For most of the year, they lived and worked on the boat, chasing schools of bonito and Spanish mackerel up and down the coast. It was too dangerous to live inland. For years, rogue militias had been kidnapping children and trafficking them, or turning them into soldiers.

"That was your boat?" Ayann asked. "The one that sank?"

Kira glanced at me. "No, not ours," she said. "We were just . . . passengers."

The family had seen the explosions, said Ayann. They lit up the sky. First one bang, then an even bigger one.

"Did you see any other survivors?" Kira asked. "Any bodies?"

Ayann shook her head. "Only you two."

I looked at Kira. Cal had wired himself with the first charge, then timed the main charge to follow. He wanted to be sure there was nothing left. We'd been very, very lucky. If Kira and I hadn't been blown off the top deck, we would have gone down with the ship.

Then my mind spun to another outcome.

What if I'd survived without Kira? What if I'd found her dead, instead of alive? For me, life wouldn't have been worth living.

*   *   *

That night, Kira and I watched the stars come out together. We'd given the family back their cabin, which was their bedroom. We were lying on the roof as the boat bobbed gently, anchored somewhere in the middle of the sea.

"I'm sorry for all this," Kira said. "For everything I've put you through."

"It's not your fault," I said.

"It *is* my fault," she said. "If you'd never met me, you'd still be Professor Brandt Savage, PhD. You'd be back in

Chicago teaching anthropology. I should have just left you there—safe and content."

"I might have been safe," I said. "But I wasn't content. I just didn't realize it."

"Are you saying you're really happier like this—as Doc Savage?"

I rolled onto my side and propped myself up on my elbow. Kira turned toward me. I brushed her copper hair back from her beautiful face. "I'm saying I wasn't happy until you found me, and I'm willing to accept whatever comes with it. I don't intend to lose you again."

She put her arm around my shoulders and pulled herself onto me. She kissed me. I kissed her back. I could feel the warmth of her skin, the rhythm of her breathing, the pounding of her heart.

I realized that I had no money. No home. No family. But in that moment I realized that there was only one thing I needed.

That would require a single question from me—and the right answer from Kira.

I hoped the answer would be yes.

CHAPTER 103

IT WAS PROBABLY the world's shortest engagement. Twelve hours, to be exact. The ceremony itself was simple, but joyous.

I pried a diamond from the hilt of the cutlass and enclosed it in a circle of fishing wire to make a ring. Ayann found a simple white tunic in the hold for Kira's wedding dress. Hani was our ring bearer, and Halima made a radiant flower girl.

Kira and I stood hand in hand at the prow of the small boat while Dahir blessed our vows in three different languages. It was the first wedding he'd ever performed as a captain, and he wanted to do it right.

His final pronouncement was in perfect English: "You may kiss your bride."

So I did.

When I pulled away, tears were streaming down Kira's cheeks. That was new.

"I've never seen you cry before," I said.

She wiped her eyes with the back of her hand. "Maybe you're my only weakness."

Dahir steered the boat toward a tiny peninsula jutting out from the mainland. I pulled out my cutlass and pressed the grip into his hand. He looked stunned.

"This is for you," I said. "For marrying us—for saving us." I ran my fingers over the gems on the hilt. "These will buy you a whole fleet of fishing boats, or a whole new life. Do what's best for your family—and always keep your children safe."

Dahir took the cutlass and held it tight against his chest. His mouth moved, but he couldn't speak.

"It's all right," I said, patting his shoulder. "No words necessary."

The keel scraped the sandy bottom as we glided toward the empty beach. We hugged Ayann and the kids goodbye, then hopped off and waded to shore. The peninsula was beautiful, dotted with banana trees. Fat, juicy crabs scurried across the rocks, and schools of fish wiggled through the shallows. It would do, for a while.

We waved as the boat pulled away. Then it was just the two of us. I pulled Kira close.

We had nothing.

And we had everything.

EPILOGUE

Three years later...

IT HAD TAKEN me most of the past two years to build the boat. I had some help from the locals, and from my wife, of course. But mostly I followed the plans in my head, and my own instincts.

She was a forty-foot schooner, twin masted, mahogany throughout. Dacron or Kevlar would have been smarter choices for the sails, but I went with original sailcloth from an island craftsman. For me, there was just something about the way it whipped in the wind.

The boat was resting in a deep lagoon near our hut. The sun was warm, and the water was transparent turquoise. Kira and I were sitting in a small skiff as she dipped a fine-tipped brush into a jar of gilt paint.

I'd left this final touch to her. She had a more artistic flair. And besides, the name was her choice. I sat back as she applied the last delicate stroke to the lettering.

Orion II

"How does it look?" she asked.

"Seaworthy," I said.

The air filled with a high-pitched trilling sound. I looked up.

Leena!

Our two-year-old daughter was forty feet up, swinging on a line, with one arm waving free. She was a nimble climber with absolutely no fear of heights. We had trouble keeping her out of trees. And today she had apparently decided to scale the mainmast.

Kira shielded her eyes with one hand. "Leena! Come down!"

Leena's face lit up. She had her mother's smile, and her independent spirit. Whatever we told her to do, she found her own way to do it.

Instead of just shimmying down, Leena placed her bare feet on the top crosstree and launched herself into the air, legs and arms straight, head tucked between her elbows. Spectacular dive. From the height of a four-story building.

She speared through the surface with barely a ripple and started kicking underwater toward the far side of the lagoon. I watched her copper-colored hair bobbing and flowing with each stroke. It was as if she'd been born for the water.

"Like an Olympian," I said to Kira proudly.

She wrapped her arms around my shoulders.

"No," she said. "Like a Savage."

JAMES PATTERSON
THE WORLD'S #1 BESTSELLING WRITER

ABOUT THE AUTHORS

James Patterson is the most popular storyteller of our time. He is the creator of unforgettable characters and series, including Alex Cross, the Women's Murder Club, Jane Smith, and Maximum Ride, and of breathtaking true stories about the Kennedys, John Lennon, and Tiger Woods, as well as our military heroes, police officers, and ER nurses. Patterson has coauthored #1 bestselling novels with Bill Clinton and Dolly Parton, and collaborated most recently with Michael Crichton on the blockbuster *Eruption.* He has told the story of his own life in *James Patterson by James Patterson* and received an Edgar Award, ten Emmy Awards, the Literarian Award from the National Book Foundation, and the National Humanities Medal.

Brian Sitts is an award-winning advertising creative director and television writer. He has collaborated with James Patterson on books for adults and children. He and his wife, Jody, live in Peekskill, New York.

JAMES
PATTERSON
RECOMMENDS

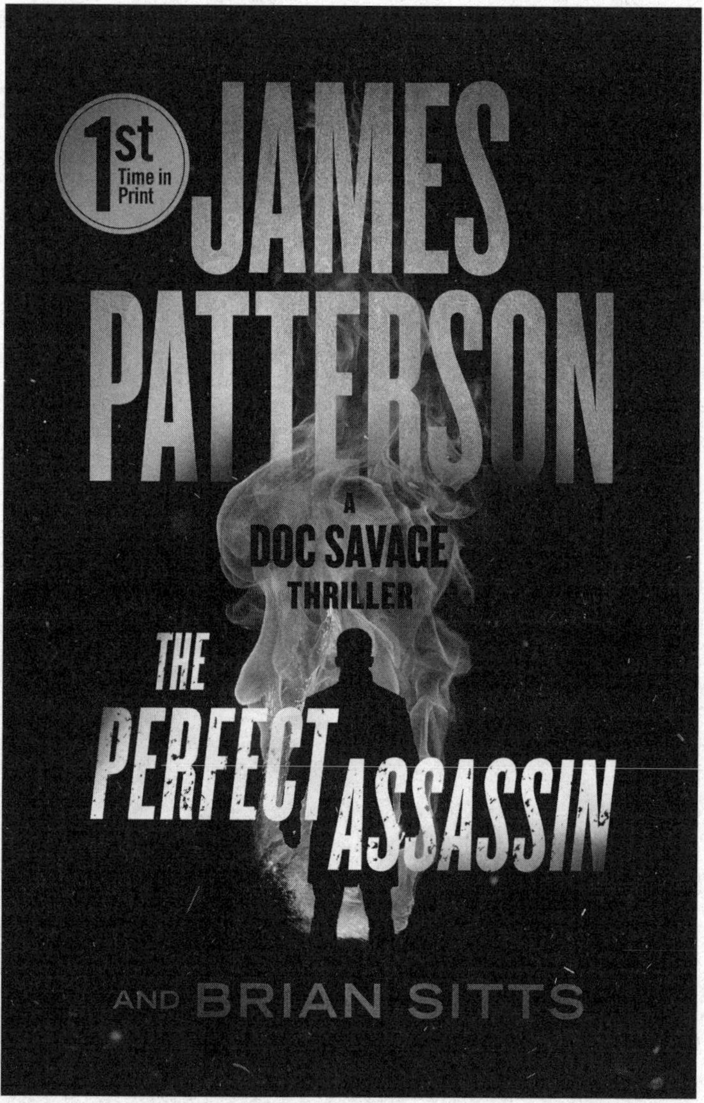
1st
Time in Print
JAMES PATTERSON
A DOC SAVAGE THRILLER
THE PERFECT ASSASSIN
AND BRIAN SITTS

THE PERFECT ASSASSIN

Dr. Brandt Savage is on sabbatical from the University of Chicago. Instead of doing solo fieldwork in anthropology, the gawky, bespectacled PhD finds himself enrolled in a school where he is the sole pupil. His professor, "Meed," is demanding. She's also his captor.

Savage emerges from their intensive training sessions physically and mentally transformed, but with no idea why he's been chosen, and how he'll use his fearsome abilities. Then his first mission with Meed takes them back to her own training ground, where Savage learns how deeply entwined their two lives have been. To prevent a new class of killers from escaping this harsh place where their ancestors first fought to make a better world, they must pledge anew: Do right to all, and wrong to no one.

JAMES PATTERSON

AND BRIAN SITTS

CRIME HAS
A NEW ENEMY.

THE
SHADOW

A THRILLER

THE SHADOW

Only two people know that 1930s society man Lamont Cranston has a secret identity as the Shadow, a crusader for justice—well, make that three if you include me, and it is my great honor to reimagine his story. But the other two are his greatest love, Margo Lane, and his fiercest enemy, Shiwan Khan. When Khan ambushes the couple, they must risk everything for the slimmest chance of survival...in the future.

A century and a half later, Lamont awakens in a world both unknown and disturbingly familiar. Most disturbing, Khan's power continues to be felt over the city and its people. No one in this new world understands the dangers of stopping him better than Lamont Cranston. And only the Shadow knows that he's the one person who might succeed before more innocent lives are lost.

JAMES PATTERSON
J.D. BARKER

ONE KISS
AND YOU'RE DEAD

1ST TIME
IN PRINT

DEATH OF THE
BLACK WIDOW

DEATH OF THE BLACK WIDOW

A twenty-year-old woman murders her kidnapper with a competence so impeccable that Detroit PD officer Walter O'Brien is taken aback. It's pretty rare for my detectives to be this shocked. But what Officer O'Brien doesn't know is that this young woman has a knack for ending the lives of her lovers—and getting away with it.

Time after time, she navigates her way out of police custody. Soon Walter becomes fixated on uncovering the truth. And when he discovers that he's not alone in his search, one thing is certain: this deadly string of secrets didn't begin in his home city…but he's going to make sure it ends there.

JAMES PATTERSON

1ST
TIME IN
PRINT

THE MIDWIFE MURDERS

AND RICHARD DiLALLO

THE MIDWIFE MURDERS

I can't imagine a worse crime than one done against a child. But when two kidnappings and a vicious stabbing happen on senior midwife Lucy's watch in a university hospital in Manhattan, her focus abruptly changes. Something has to be done, and Lucy is fearless enough to try.

Rumors begin to swirl, with blame falling on everyone from the Russian mafia to an underground adoption network. Fierce single mom Lucy teams up with a skeptical NYPD detective, but I've given her a case where the truth is far more twisted than Lucy could ever have imagined.

From the Creator of the #1 Bestselling Women's Murder Club

JAMES PATTERSON

2 SISTERS

DETECTIVE AGENCY

FIRST
TIME IN
PRINT

& CANDICE FOX

2 SISTERS DETECTIVE AGENCY

Discovering secrets about your own family has a way of changing your life...for better or for worse. Attorney Rhonda Bird learns that her estranged father had stopped being an accountant and opened up a private detective agency—and that she has a teenage half sister named Baby.

When Baby brings in a client to the detective agency, the two sisters become entangled in a dangerous case involving a group of young adults who break laws for fun, their psychopath ringleader, and an ex-assassin who decides to hunt them down for revenge.

For a complete list of books by

JAMES PATTERSON

VISIT
JamesPatterson.com

Follow James Patterson on Facebook
@JamesPatterson

Follow James Patterson on X
@JP_Books

Follow James Patterson on Instagram
@jamespattersonbooks